I0576294

TREY ROBERTS
AND THE
ANCIENT RELICS

~

Book 1

By
Lee Magnus

Cover by Jose Erwin Mallare

Tanarkin House

Tanarkin House
An imprint of Michael Matthew Publishing
First Tanarkin House paperback edition November
2019
The Library of Congress Catalog 2019951494
ISBN 978-1-7340748-0-2 (Ebook)
ISBN 978-1-7340748-1-9 (Paperback)

To my amazing boys who constantly inspire me

Contents

The Science Teacher

Nick Hampton walked a sandy street. The noon day sun blistered the back of his neck, but he barely noticed. He wandered aimlessly, searching in vain for an unknown object in a nameless town accented by a vast desert to the south and a large lake to the east. He was neither anxious about the destination or casual in his lack of control.

A stoic glare from an elementary school aged girl prodded a shiver in his spine. She appeared from nowhere wearing a headdress of neat golden tassels decorated in vivid pink and plumb wrappings. Without removing her glower, she raised a listless finger toward a donkey and several young men wearing keffiyehs loitering outside of what looked like a shop made of clay – the design of most structures in the village. A sign hung above the door depicting a shield with wavy horizontal lines bordering a green jewel riveted in the chief point.

The girl was no longer at his side when he turned back. He looked again to where she pointed, finding himself in the shop facing a furrowed man with grey hair and a long, more grey than black beard. The shop keeper's hauntingly leery eyes stared motionlessly through Nick's soul.

Nick observed a key attached to a ring on the shopkeeper's wrinkly right thumb which rested on the counter. He glanced around the room and thought the walls were odd; fully decorated with knives of many shapes, colors and sizes.

A woman appeared in the doorway behind the old man. A large wooden box with a golden keyhole prominent on top rested like an altar in the center of the room behind her. A crystal geode shone brightly several feet above the box. It grew brighter until the radiance forced Nick's attention away.

Nick's awareness was drawn toward a barking dog standing on a chair with front paws pressed against the window. He didn't remember it upon first glance around the room. The dog was dark red with white paws and a white tail. A handsome dog, one you would keep indoors but off the furniture – a dog you would be proud to walk around the neighborhood.

The bark became louder and more explosive as it turned toward the hapless dreamer. Its face became gnarled and bloody. Sapping drool flung about its mouth and dripped to the floor. The malicious canine leapt from the chair toward Nick as it grew six times in size…"NO! NO! NOOOOoooooo!"

Nick awoke in a cold sweat, panting – relieved to be awake.

"Ugggg. I hope I never see that guy in real life," he mumbled to himself.

He reflected on the dream a few moments then noted the details in a pocket journal.

A crisp morning nipped at his ears when he emerged from the restless night. Frost-covered blades of grass below a lonely hammock chilled bare feet as he reached for a pair of worn leather hiking boots. He attempted to shake off the overnight cold which had seeped into his bones but was left with little satisfaction in the act. Snow-covered ridges occupied the distant view like everlasting thoughts of companionship – always out of reach. A dense fog escaped his mouth as he released an after-yawn exhale. He pulled a hoodie over the tattered shirt he wore the previous day (and several days before for that matter), which exposed a rounded bicep with bulging veins splattered with his own blood mixed with that of another less fortunate beast. He favored his left leg as well as the bandaged arm as he booted up.

The nagging thought remained – *Why am I here?*

A small fire popped as it heated a tin cup of water he would soon use to extract the bitter essence from tea leaves he picked earlier that week.

The forest teemed with laughter as he gathered his kit. The caw of a bird, the chirp of a bug - they all seemed to be mocking him and his ludicrous journey.

Minutes later, soothing warmth of the tea would bring forth a continued desire to complete the task and the necessary confidence that he would survive to find the hidden item an old mystic said would be here.

The Science Teacher

He let the fire burn out as he tried to absorb every last bit of heat. He then covered the ashes and continued to plod an overgrown trail like a conscious zombie – each step was awkward and painful. The base of a makeshift cane dotted the cold ground with rough indentions. A repetitive knocking sound drew his attention. With his eyes, he traced a tall spruce to reveal a black bird with white spots, possibly searching for breakfast. He then regained focus on his mission and grimaced upon taking another laborious step.

He reviewed the hand-drawn map unaware of the challenges resting ahead. He turned west, deeper into the oriental jungle, mindful of the recent encounter – the reason for his gaiting limp. Wading through impenetrable brush and bending back wooden limbs, he arrived at a large flat rock face near the base of a small mountain. His heart paced up. His eyes brightened. He almost smiled.

Could this be the end? he ruminated hopefully. "The end of the beginning," he replied out loud.

Wiping away layers of grimy muck revealed archaic symbols that haven't been viewed with a human eye in eons. He compared the inscription to the map confirming he was in the right place – the validation offered a glimmer of optimism. He trudged around the east side over a boulder and overgrowth to find hidden behind a dense bush, a small skinny fissure just wide enough to crawl through.

He shined his light into the hole to reveal nothing but darkness.

He tossed in a small bag of various items (for he wouldn't fit with it attached) then followed it into the tiny opening – hoping he was the only living thing beyond the entrance. He left his remaining possessions next to the bush.

Good thing I passed on the doughnut at the airport, he laughed as he barely squeezed through. He scraped a rock with his hip, causing him to curse at the added pain.

The hollow expanded once he breached the entrance. He wiped away dust and grime to notice he could reach to either side and had about a foot to spare over his head. Damp grey-green moss clung to crumbling rock walls. He searched with the flashlight to find nothing out of the ordinary other than the fact he was in a small cave in the middle of a northern Chinese forest.

He steadily trudged through undulating tunnels. He wiped away webs and dripping roots as he looked diligently for the marking stone. The uneven ceiling produced several crags of which he squatted to avoid. He inhaled, more frequently as he progressed through the passageway, the fragrance of decayed plants (and he thought possibly the remains of an animal of some sort).

After a stretch of uneventful walking he whispered to himself excitedly, "There it is!" He settled the light on a stone protruding from the wall in the distance ahead. "The marking stone *is* real."

In a relieved state of excitement, he eagerly waltzed several careless steps forward. Suddenly the ground gave way plunging him into a deceptively covered pit. The flashlight fell to his side. Several large objects scurried through the luminescence casting creepy shadows onto the walls. He lifted himself up painfully and looked up into the darkness. He clutched the light – then gasped.

"Spiders! Oh my god massive spiders!" he screeched like a little girl.

He jumped and shivered wildly. Trying to ensure none were on him, he rapidly brushed his hands all over his body. Breathing became a hasty pant. He waived the light around the deep pit quickly from side to side kicking several writhing multi-legged bodies to the edge of the trap – each landed with a dull thump. Huge black arachnids with long hairy legs travelled the floor and wall of the circular pit. Some were as big as a basketball.

Gathering himself trying not to freak out, he took a second to think. He used a retractable stick from his pack to clear a path and brush away the aggressive ones that got too close. He drove several tent stakes into the hard dirt wall to create a ledge about 4 feet from the ground. After putting away the stick, he jumped to the ledge with his good leg then painfully propelled himself with the other high enough to grasp the edge of the hole with both hands. Furry legs crawled next to him, over his hands and up his back. He paused in fear, clinching his eyes shut, as one crawled sluggishly over his shoulder then across his face to exit the dank prison. Doing all he could to maintain composure, he slowly lifted himself out as the monstrous creatures scurried to the surface seemingly happy to be free.

Shaking off the creepy feeling, safely out of the snare, Nick pushed against the protruding stone. The wall cracked open exposing a narrow passage.

After a few steps into the passage he carefully navigated a trip wire. He rubbed a finger over tiny holes of death lining the walls intended to greet anyone else less vigilant. He grimaced at his lack of caution that led to the spider trap. That same carelessness would have him forever pinned to the wall in this tunnel.

Turning left down a corridor he stopped abruptly next to an overly protruding root emerging from the ceiling. Further inspection indicated the root was all that kept a large section of the tunnel from total collapse.

Carefully navigating under the root trap he found his way to the end of the passage to find a wall – a dead end.

"This can't be," he said to himself. "All the other signs were there." His face shriveled into a painful grimace.

He slid a hand across the scratchy rock wall. Just before he turned to leave in utter defeat, his hand dipped into a camouflaged depression. He wiped away webs and dirt to reveal a small opening. A large maroon colored six-legged bug swiftly crawled onto his arm with pincers flailing. He casually brushed it away before inserting a sturdy telescopic baton into the dark hole. Something inside forcefully collapsed, jarring the baton from his hands. He rubbed his hands on his pants unsuccessfully alleviating the pain. He then leaned with all his weight onto the protruding baton and pried the fallen object up while simultaneously reaching in and around the baton with the other hand. His feet dangled off the floor as he shook and wobbled on the baton. He quickly retracted his hand only once as his balance slipped, again slamming the protective object inside the hole onto the baton.

He again leveraged his weight onto the

makeshift lever then said joyfully, "There it is!" as he strained to feel a small box recessed in the back of the perforation in the wall.

After significant effort navigating the object around the baton and the trap trigger, he pulled out a small ceramic box. Carefully opening the foregone repository revealed a thin copper-colored metal rod bent in the shape of a triangle. He gazed upon it as if it were the key to untold riches or perhaps the holy grail. However, he knew not what it was or why he was sent to retrieve it. He closed the box, secured it in his pack then exited the tunnel, careful to avoid the traps and spider pit. He thought about the upcoming journey back to America. *School starts in two weeks and I haven't yet prepared for my students.*

Backtracking four days through the forest past a cave that made him shiver and grasp his arm, he finally arrived at a 4x4 truck he rented the week before. He drove all day and night to a tiny village where he took the first train to Beijing from where he departed to Dulles International Airport.

A King's Curse

"Happy Monday morning!" said Nick Hampton greeting Trey Roberts at the door of the Lownes Middle School science lab.

"What's up, Mr. H!" he said tapping a hanging human skeleton, watching it dance a choppy jig. His bright hazel eyes skimmed the room as if looking for something out of place.

The lab smelled of ammonia and burnt soap. A poster of the periodic table hung over a shelf stacked with nondescript books. His shoes squeaked on the freshly mopped floor. Trey wondered if an earlier experiment had gone wrong prompting the recent clean up but instantly let the thought slip from his mind.

"What's that?" Trey inquired as he pointed toward a waist high metal structure near the corner of the lab.

"Wha...Oh that," Nick said running his hand through thick wavy brown hair. I'm, uh, testing the conductivity of this rare copper laden igneous stone," he said quickly covering up the display.

"It sure looked like an elaborate set up for a simple test."

"It's well, um, I suppose. So, what brings you by so early this morning?"

Trey recognized his science teacher's evasion of his questions regarding the display but didn't hesitate to continue the conversation. "I thought I'd tap your mind on gravitational waves before I go to home room. I read up on them last night. Scientists recently detected light and gravitational waves from a neutron star merger. To think, Einstein had it right all along."

"It is cool, Trey. Did you know it took physicists over 400 years to discover light is both particle and a wave?"

Trey sat on a desk across from Nick who was standing next to a smart wall.

"Of course. Everyone knows it started with Newton and Huygens," Trey replied.

Nick crossed his arms and said, "You'd be surprised at how little people know about science, Trey, especially 8th graders who are more concerned about which video game they're supposed to be playing. Not everyone thinks physics is cool. I'm sure old man gravity has a few more details to share over the next several decades."

"I can't wait!" Trey beamed.

"How's your mom?"

"She's good. She's been really busy with the museum."

"That's right. She has a big show coming up. When is it, the fourteenth?"

"I think so."

"Tell her to let me know if I can help in any way."

"Sure thing. Oh yeah, she wanted me to thank you again for taking me to the robotics challenge last week."

"It was my pleasure, Trey," he smiled

"She said she's making a pie to thank you."

"She doesn't have to do that. Is it pecan?" he said with begging puppy dog look.

"Ha Ha! I don't know. I'll tell her."

"Mmmmm. I can't wait," Nick replied rubbing his stomach and closing his eyes.

"I have to get to History class. Catch you later Mr. H!"

"See you in class, Trey!" he said ruffling Trey's thick curly hair that tapered down into a clean fade.

Nick glanced back to the covered display, giving it a worrisome regard.

Trey looked back at Nick with a smile just before he disappeared into a throng of children in the hall.

"Hey T!" hollered Marcus Bouer from across the hall. He held a familiar smug smile.

Trey shifted his burdensome backpack then walked to the short, skinny boy with neatly combed black hair.

The pair commenced a series of hand gestures; a fist bump, followed by a two-sided slap, a chest high grasp that converted into a handshake. They resumed the conversation after a short thumb war battle.

"Dude! You always win!" Trey smiled.

Marcus said in a scruffy voice with a wide grin while holding up and wiggling both thumbs near his face, "Kid! You can't beat the monster thumbs."

Trey laughed and lightly batted down Marcus' hands then asked, "So what's up?"

"How about catchin' a movie after your match this weekend?" he replied as he adjusted oval wire-framed glasses.

"Yeah that'd be great! Sunday afternoon is better. We usually all meet for dinner after the matches."

"That'll work for me."

"Something funny I hope?"

"Of course," Marcus said.

"I have to grab something from my locker. I'll catch you later!"

"Ok, see ya, Kid!" Marcus said walking on without him.

History class bustled of robust conversations around summer activities, sports events and gossip of who loves who. The walls were decorated in sayings such as,

*"You can't change the past, but you can **learn from it**"*

and

*"Those who cannot remember the past are condemned to **repeat it**."*

Trey waved at someone in the back of the room

then brought his attention to the front desk headed by a hefty mid-sixties woman with greying brown hair pulled in a tight bun. She greeted him with only a sullen glance above half-lensed glasses.

He gave her a polite nod. He smiled and said nervously, "I hope you had a great weekend Mrs. Hawkins."

Her face softened into a faint smile. She replied, "I did Trey. Thank you for asking."

He felt good about the smile he brought to Mrs. Hawkins. She always seemed unhappy. The students in history class were good enough. *Maybe it's something at home*, he thought to himself as he passed her desk.

He turned down his row holding onto the previous thought then unexpectedly tripped on something in the aisle, stumbled into several desks, then knocked Marcus to the floor before he sprawled across a desk. He righted himself facing a surprised girl. The class became instantly silent while everyone processed the embarrassing moment. Then, in unison, it roared with laughter.

He was unmoved by the directed amusement at his expense because he was too consumed with the beautiful person staring back at him. Teenage lust overpowered motor functions, fireworks exploded in his stomach. *Oh my god. It's Sarah Thompson. She's looking right at me.* His heart galloped, his mind whirled. Mesmerized by big brown eyes, he didn't move for what seemed like a whole semester. Her raised brows highlighted radiant wavy blonde hair. Roses and lavender filled his senses. Her perfect slightly parted lips were shaded in a light pink. Her head turned ever so slightly to the left. With a soft smile she said in a voice that could melt mountains, "Hey Trey Roberts. Nice of you to drop by," after which she giggled the sweetest most lovely giggle in all humanity.

The world as he knew it stopped. The roaring mass echoed distantly in his mind. His next moves were in slow motion compared to reality.

Without removing his eyes from hers or saying a word, he gave her a wavering smile then slowly pushed himself off her desk. He turned to help Marcus with wide eyes and a petrified face.

"Kid!" Marcus said under his breath. "You ok?"

Awareness seeped back. Anger boiled to the surface of his skin which was easily mistaken for embarrassment. He cut a vicious eye at an oversized oaf who offered a wicked smirk in return as he pulled a large foot back under his desk.

"Yeah. I'm fine," he replied curtly, pulling his glare from the instigator.

"Class! Please settle down! Mr. Smith, will you please keep your feet to yourself?" Mrs. Hawkins said in a yodel-like, vacillating voice.

"Yes, Ma'am," Donald said in an overly agreeable manner.

"Mr. Roberts, please find your seat."

Trey nodded then took the third seat behind Sarah in the adjacent row.

"Ok class, last week we discussed the Korean War...."

As she droned on, Trey couldn't help but steal another look in Sarah's direction. He slowly drifted off for a moment, daydreaming of a warm spring day, wind rustling her hair, walking hand in hand...

"Mr. Roberts?" Mrs. Hawkins requested under raised eyebrows.

"Premier Kim Il-Sung, Mrs. Hawkins," he said in step, slowly drawing his attention away from Sarah's exquisite loveliness.

"That is correct. Kim Il-Sung was the leader of North Korea during the war," she replied moving on with the lesson.

After class, Donald gave Trey a crooked grin that went unnoticed as Sarah waved a chest high bye when she passed. In a thick daze, he left the room and the building with Marcus who led them to P.E. Marcus rambled on about something, but Trey hardly heard a sound.

While Trey was highly athletic, his short stature compared to other eighth grade boys along with a general indifference to basketball usually influenced his choice of activity during P.E. Marcus' disinterest in sports always made him a great walking partner.

"Why do you let him pick on you like that?" asked Marcus as they lapped around the track. "You could easily take him. I know he's got at least fifty pounds on you, but I still think you'd have no problem."

An ultra-skinny boy passed them, maintaining a steady pace.

"I mean," Marcus said pointing at the passing boy, "If you were Thomas, he would smash you. But you have skills. What good are they if you don't use them?"

"If I were Thomas, I'd just keep running for

another thirty seconds and Donald would give up," Trey said snickering. "I don't know why I don't stand up to him. I guess I sort of feel bad for him."

"Why?" Marcus said with a sour face. "Why would you feel sorry for that guy? He's awful."

"I know. He moved in with his grandmother who lived on my street about three years ago. She died like a year later. I didn't know him before that. My mom said they couldn't afford the house, so they moved into government housing. He seemed like a nice kid. But he hung around his older brother a lot who was always in trouble, so I didn't get a chance to know him that well. Donald, you see, was held back a year. The school offered a tutor, but his mom was gone all the time and he wasn't motivated enough to make the sessions on his own. Donald basically raised himself, and not too well up to this point. He hangs with Bobby and Carl, two of the dumbest kids in school. The trio couldn't prove the Pythagorean theorem to save their life. It wasn't until last year that he took notice of me. It was like all of a sudden, he hated me. I don't know what I did."

"Yeah, that's tough, but he has to take responsibility for his actions at some point. What about his dad?"

"He says he never met him."

"So, enough about that dufus. Tell me about it," Marcus said excitedly as he faced Trey.

"Tell you about what?" Trey replied confused as to what Marcus was referring, but sort of had a good idea by how he was acting and what had happened in history class.

"So, what was it like?"

"What was what like?" Trey replied defensively

- now knowing exactly to what Marcus was referring.

Marcus lightly hit Trey in the chest with the back of his hand then said, "Kid please! Sarah! You've been talking about her for the past two years."

"No, I haven't."

"Yes. You have. I'm your best friend. I know you. I've been telling you to talk to her and you just keep ignoring me."

Trey looked down and away. He felt his ears turn red admitting his feelings for a girl but with Marcus, it didn't seem so bad. "Yeah. I know. I should've talked to her by now. But she's way too pretty for me. She'd shoot me down before I even opened my mouth."

"You're crazy, Kid. With those dreamy hazel eyes?" he said grinning in a way that conveyed the compliment but didn't reveal an exorbitant amount of sincerity. "No way. Plus, she didn't shoot you down today did she?"

"That was different. That was an accident. She didn't have a choice to acknowledge me."

"But she talked to you - and smiled."

"That doesn't mean anything. What was she supposed to do, just ignore the fact that I nearly knocked her out of her desk? Just because I've never spoken to her doesn't mean she can't be nice. I mean, we've only had two classes together, ever, and she's super popular. I bet she's nice to everyone."

"You seriously have a confidence issue. You should just talk to her, and now you have a reason. Tell her you're sorry for smashing into her desk. She'll probably think you're funny if you bring that up. You should definitely use this to your advantage."

"Yeah. She'll laugh at me and walk away.

Probably go tell all her ultra-popular friends so they can *all* laugh at me."

"You need to lighten up, Kid. Why do you care what anyone else thinks? Don't worry about what she or anyone else will say and just do it. Talking to girls is the same as talking to anybody. Just go say hey and if you can, find something to compliment her on."

"Yeah. I'm not gonna do that. It'll be ok. Just let it go."

"I can't let it go. This may be your only opportunity. You have to take it."

"No. I think I'll just let it go. Besides, she probably doesn't like –"

Marcus' expression instantly changed. "What," Marcus said abruptly with serious eyes. "She probably doesn't like what – smart guys like you?"

"You know what I mean."

"Seriously? You think she wouldn't like you because you come from a mixed family? She's not like that and frankly you should be ashamed you even thought it."

"You wouldn't understand." Trey hung his head and distanced himself from his long-time friend.

"The hell I wouldn't," Marcus retorted angrily and closed the space between them. "I've known you nearly all my life. I've seen you take crap from racist clowns before. Trust me. It hurts me just as much as you."

"I doubt that, but I know you've been there for me." Trey chuckled.

Marcus' eyes narrowed. "What. What are you laughing about?"

"Nothing," Trey said with a smile.

"Hey. I had that eighth grader on the

playground back in sixth grade," Marcus pleaded. "I couldn't let him talk to you like that."

"No dude! That was great. You jumped on top of that big kid without even thinking about it. Your banshee scream frightened everyone." Trey glanced at his friend to assess his level of excitement then said, "You were lucky Mrs. Patterson got there quickly."

"Yeah. You're probably right. I had a black eye for two weeks after that."

Trey shuffled his feet as he said, "I'm probably just overreacting with Sarah. She's just...I don't know."

"More like making excuses to not do what's best for you."

"You think so?"

"Have I been wrong before?"

"Plenty of times."

"Then this time I'm right based on odds," Marcus said with a shining grin.

"Whatever you say."

"Does that mean you'll talk to her?"

"I don't know. Maybe."

"Well, that's better than no."

A whistle blew, indicating time to change back into school clothes.

Trey!" said Coach Rafiq, Trey's soccer coach, from across the track.

"I'll catch up with you after school," Trey said to Marcus.

"Later, Kid!"

Trey sprinted to Coach Rafiq, a medium sized dark-skinned athletic man with muscular legs who spoke with a rich Spanish accent.

"What's up, Coach?" he said with his hands on

his hips catching his breath.

Rafiq spoke slowly in order to enunciate properly as if he were new to the language. "At practice today, we'll go over this weekend's match and run our normal drills but tomorrow I'd like you to help me with the 4-2-3-1 formation. We've had trouble controlling the ball in the middle of the pitch. I'd like us to have it down by the match this weekend."

"Yeah, Coach. That's a great idea. If we can learn that one as a team, it'll bring Philippe up with the wingers which should give us plenty of passing options. Plus, it works well as a transition from our typical four-three-three."

"Great, Trey. You are doing very well this season," he replied, placing a hand on Trey's shoulder. "You played a heck of a game against a formidable team last weekend. Keep it up and making the high school varsity team will be no problem."

"Thanks Coach."

"Speaking of the high school team, Coach Ward would like you to join their practice next week. They practice the same time but on field four."

"Really? The high school team? Why?"

"I feel they will challenge you in a way the middle schoolers can't. You understand?"

"Yeah, I think. Thanks for setting it up, coach. I'll be there next week."

"I'll see you later at practice."

"Ok. See you then, Coach!"

Trey walked toward the gym ruminating on the conversation with Coach Rafiq. *The high school team? I can hang with these inexperienced middle school kids, but high school is a different game entirely. I'm not sure I'm ready for that much of a challenge,* he kicked a rock across the trimmed grass, *not even just on the practice squad. Maybe I'll talk to him about it today after practice. I just don't know.*

Even knowing his favorite class was next didn't keep him from sulking the entire way there – thoughts lost in the fear of a non-existent event, one that hasn't yet occurred.

"Hey Trey! Ready to walk Max's Planck today?" asked Nick as Trey, for the second time today, emerged through the doorway of the science lab.

"Dude. That was weak. Even for a middle-aged science teacher." He chuckled at his own comment and softly slapped Nick's shoulder which lightened his mood after dwelling on the day's earlier events. He continued, "Don't I wish you could teach us about quantum theory."

"Yeah," said Nick crossing his arms, "That's a bit too advanced for the rest of the eighth graders, except for maybe Sarah." Nick regarded Trey for a moment and smiled a warm fatherly smile before saying, "I heard you had an encounter with her today."

"How do you know about that?" Trey replied, startled. He felt heat rush to his face and defensiveness enter his thoughts.

"I overheard a couple students in the hall say a big kid tripped you into her desk."

Trey's guard gave way to the excitement of reliving the moment.

"It was lit, Mr. H! She smiled then said, hey Trey Roberts! She actually said my name! It was the most wonderful six seconds of my life."

Nick brandished a large smile. "You know you

should really thank him."

"Who, Donald? I'm not sure I'll go that far, but I suppose you're right. I bet it'd eat him up to know how I feel about it now."

"By the way, I'm only thirty-five. Don't call me middle-aged just yet," Nick said with a raised eyebrow.

Trey smiled then said, "I see we have a sub the next few days. Where're you off to now? You just returned from China over the summer and earlier this year you left us for a rainforest in Costa Rica. Are you going through a midlife crisis?"

"No, Trey. I'm not going through a midlife crisis," he said rolling his eyes.

"But don't you guys buy ridiculous sports cars and chase hot women rather than traveling the world looking for lost artifacts? Besides, that's what archeologists do right? You know, like the guy with the fedora and whip?" he said emulating snapping a whip. "Science guys are supposed to occupy sterile labs and read complicated texts. What's the deal, huh?"

"I said I'm not middle-aged and I'm not going through a crisis. For your information, I'm travelling to a desert oasis in western Egypt and possibly one in Eastern Libya, I leave tonight."

"Still chasing lost treasure, huh?"

"I suppose you can call it that," he said as he leaned against his desk.

"But you almost died in Costa Rica trying to summit a mountain just to talk to some creepy old man and in China you were mauled by a bear. You're lucky to be alive."

"Che was a cool dude," he said, raising his eyes to the ceiling as he reminisced. "We spent six days in meditation on top of that mountain. I suppose the bear was a close call, but the pit of bird spiders really freaked me out, eekssh."

"Bird spiders? You didn't tell me about those."

"Yeah, bird spiders are numerous in China, bigger than your head and very deadly." He held his hands together in a way that looked like a big spider. He then wiggled his fingers toward Trey's face who reflexively jerked away as if Nick's hands were a real spider. "I was moving through a tunnel on the map Che drew then all of a sudden, the floor gave way. I found myself in a pit surrounded by massive spiders."

"That's crazy Mr. H! But it sounds really exciting. I hope I can join you sometime – without the spiders, of course."

"Me too Trey. There's the bell." Nick stood and turned to the students saying, "Everyone find your seat. Let's get class started."

Trey loved science class. Not because he would learn anything (his knowledge of science exceeded that of most people) but because he loved science and Mr. Hampton too. Mr. Hampton had been a source of wisdom, guidance and support during Trey's most trying personal moments since they first met when Trey won the science fair as a fourth grader with a realistic replica of a Tokamak.

Today, Trey wasn't engaged – Nick took notice.

After school, Trey walked himself home while Marcus stayed at school for band practice. That night, after a grueling soccer practice and a warm meal prepared by his mom in their small three bedroom home in an ordinary suburb west of Washington D.C., Trey laid awake in his bed; thinking of Sarah's gorgeous face, the way she gracefully floated from classroom to hall to locker to lunch as if nothing foul could ever touch her, her voice of which even Jackie Evancho would be jealous, her hair gently flowing behind her as if a warm summer breeze preceded her every move. He dreamily drifted away in a pillow of teenage love crushing away at his heart.

The next day, Trey avoided the park as usual on his walk to school. Marcus waited on him at the entrance of his neighborhood.

"Hey Marcus."

"Sup, T?"

They performed their handshake routine before continuing the walk to school.

"Did you finish that English essay yet?" Trey asked.

"No. Not yet. We have till Friday. I'll do it Thursday night. You?"

"Nothing like waiting till the last minute, huh? I did it over the weekend. Soccer practice gets in the way of a lot of stuff during the week for me."

"I suppose it does." Marcus kicked a rock then watched it bounce off the sidewalk before he abruptly changed his friendly demeanor.

"What's eating at you?"

"What? Oh. Nothing."

"Spit it out, dude. I know when something's bothering you."

Marcus looked at his friend with a confused smile. He walked a couple more steps before saying as he stared ahead, "We've been friends for a long time, right?"

"Yeah. Ever since that day with Malik Thorngood in second grade. Why?" he replied concernedly while looking a Marcus.

"Oh my god! I haven't thought about him in years!" he said quickly turning to face Trey. "You flicked a big nasty slimy-green booger on his face in front of everybody. What was it that they called him?"

"Boogerface," Trey said turning his head down.

"Yeah! Boogerface! HaHa! That's it!" He slapped his knee and slightly calmed. We weren't very creative back then, huh? I don't think he'll ever live that one down. I swear, Kid, that was the funniest thing I think I've ever seen!" he said laughing like someone was tickling his ribs.

"I still feel bad about it," Trey said solemnly.

"Of course you do." Marcus said as he patted Trey on the back. "Don't sweat it. What were we seven back then? Besides, you really helped me out. He was being a big jerk to me, and you stepped up."

"Yeah, I really stepped up. In all my infinite wisdom, the only thing I could think of to do was pull a nasty boog out of my nose and flick it at him." His face cringed as he made a violent flicking action with his thumb and forefinger.

They walked a few steps regarding the moment when Trey said nonchalantly, "But I guess you're right, he did deserve it."

They looked at each other and busted out laughing.

When the laughter subsided, Marcus put his hands in his pockets and wore a more serious expression then said, "I don't think my parents are getting along. They've been fighting a lot lately. I heard them say something about divorce. I'm kinda scared about that possibility and I thought...you know..."

Trey regarded Marcus, "What? That, I might be

able to help because my parents are divorced?"

Marcus returned an I'm sorry I mentioned it expression.

"I can't help your parents, Marcus." He looked at the cracked sidewalk as they continued to walk.

"No. That's not what I mean. What's it like?"

"You mean what's it like to have divorced parents?" he replied with an expression like he caught a whiff of something smelly.

"Yeah. I guess. Maybe, what was it like when they got divorced?"

"Oh. I don't really remember," he said returning his gaze to the concrete path. "It's been a few years and I've barely heard from my dad since. I remember mom crying a lot, though. She seemed to be really scared and jumpy the year before Dad left. She always made up some lame excuse, but I knew it had something to do with him. I thought for a long time that it was my fault."

"There's no way it was your fault. That happened what three or four years ago?"

"It could have been my fault. I never did any of the stuff he wanted me to do. He always wanted me to play baseball – said he didn't understand soccer."

"Stop telling yourself that crap. It's not true."

"No really. I was difficult back then. I got bad grades and fought a lot with him. We hardly ever saw eye to eye. He was always trying to teach me something. It got really annoying. All he would do is say the same stuff over and over."

"You got bad grades?" Marcus said unbelievingly.

Trey pulled his shoulders closer and said, "Yeah. I was a terrible student. I wouldn't do any of my homework. I'm surprised I didn't get held back in 5th grade."

"But you won the science fair in fourth grade. You're the smartest person I know."

"I've always liked science. That has nothing to do with school. It was the only thing Dad and I had in common."

"That doesn't sound like you at all. How come I didn't know about your grades?"

"Like I would tell anyone any of that."

"I get it. I probably wouldn't have told you either. I'm sorry to ask."

"Don't be. I'm okay now with grades."

"No. I'm sorry I asked about your parents. I mean, your dad leaving and all must have been hard."

Trey typically dealt with sadness with anger and it showed in his face as it reddened, and his voice became harsh. "It was. I don't know why he left me and mom. I hate him for that, and I hate him for putting Mom through all the misery." Trey closed his eyes took a deep breath. He then looked into the sky, wiped a hint of wetness from his cheek and calmed down a little before continuing, "I'm doing much better now. Mom and I get along great. She gives me lots of freedom...probably too much, but I know being a single mom is hard. I'm sorry I'm not much help. Your dad is pretty cool. I'm sure he'll stick around."

"Yeah, I hope so. I didn't know any of that. Why didn't you ever tell me before?"

"I don't know. We were so much younger then and it just didn't come up before now."

"How about not being so closed up about this type of stuff in the future, okay?" Marcus said softly.

"Sure, but only if you do the same," Trey

replied with a genuine smile.

"I'm cool with that, Kid. I'm not hiding anything," Marcus smirked then said as he unexpectedly stopped Trey on the corner facing the school, "Crap. Look. There's Donald and his imbecile friends at the front steps. Let's go around."

They were vigilantly walking with their heads down when they heard, "Hey, Flay Dumberts!" Donald clumsily jumped over the railing from the third step nearly falling down upon an awkward landing.

Recovering quickly, he said, "Had any great *trips* lately?" He slapped Bobby's bony back as he sniffed a goofy snigger. Bobby and Carl released grimacing laughs in response to Donald's prompting.

"Yeah, uh, Flay. Had any good falls lately?" Carl said idiotically.

"Shut up, Stupid!" Donald snouted at Carl.

Marcus spouted in response, "That's a good one, Donald. You come up with that all by yourself or did you learn it in your second year in sixth grade?"

Trey's surprise in Marcus' retort was plastered to his face. Marcus is not athletic nor was he typically brave. He's just a skinny kid with a loose mouth that often times gets him into trouble – just like it did today.

"You better watch your mouth, Nerd, or you'll be eating my fist!" Donald spat as he slammed his fist into his other open hand.

Marcus couldn't help himself. He responded in the voice of a cliché ivy school professor, "But my chubby little friend, your tiny brain couldn't possibly perceive the complex nature of the phrases of which I speak. It must sound like utter gibberish considering your *meager* intellect and *slavish* nature."

Dumbfounded, Trey couldn't suppress a reflexive snort at the comment.

Donald's face became so red cars would have stopped at the sight. He was a bull wearing jeans and a black polo a size too small. His beady eyes pierced the space between he and Marcus.

"Hey, uh," Trey said to Marcus in a soft voice as he nudged his friend's shoulder. "I think we should run now."

Donald's thick but not obese frame rapidly closed on them. Trey and Marcus darted toward the east side of the building.

With Donald's thundering roar behind them, they hurdled the fence to the playground. Marcus' shirt snagged and nearly toppled him to the grass slowing them down enough for Donald's band to gain significant ground.

"They're too fast! How are they catching us?" Marcus cried.

"They don't have any books!" Trey responded as he glanced behind.

"Of course, they don't have books! Why would they have a bag full of books in middle school? We must be the dumb ones!" Marcus shouted sarcastically.

They rustled through swing sets hoping to aid their evasion then crossed the basketball court.

Trey heard huffing and a hint of wheezing from close behind. Carl and Bobby trailed off, but Donald was on their heels.

They dashed through the door of the east wing then skidded to a halt in front of a tall, lanky Principal Papperton. Donald nearly smashed into them as he recklessly propelled through the double doors. His face twisted into a confused red orb upon recognition of the change in events.

"Out for a run before school, boys?" Principal Papperton inquisitively questioned the winded boys as he peered down upon them.

"Run?" Trey asked panting.

"Yeah! Run! You know how we like our exercise...and Trey, you know, has that big game this weekend. Just trying to make sure he's ready," Marcus said between heaving breaths with an unconvincing smile.

Donald said nothing during the encounter. He slumped in a huffing mass as the adrenaline left his veins.

"Right," Principal Papperton said not believing the unlikely ruse. "This door is to only be used during school hours. You must enter through the front."

"Yes, Sir," said Trey.

"Yes, Sir," said Marcus. "We won't forget again."

"You three get to class," he said regarding them sternly before exiting the building.

Donald regained his breath then turned to Marcus. He violently shoved him into the wall and said, "Your mouth has earned you an appointment with the *pain* teacher." He instantly let go of him looking to ensure Mrs. Crabtree didn't see his aggression as she entered the hallway. He turned to Trey and said with an evil sneer, "I'll see you in history!"

Donald strutted off as if he'd been crowned biggest jerk at Lownes Middle School.

Trey and Marcus shared a wide-eyed, raised-eyebrowed look confirming their shared feelings on the experience.

"Dude!" Trey said to Marcus in a serious but thankful voice. "You nearly got us into a fight at school."

"I know. I'm sorry."

"Why'd you say that? You knew he'd get angry."

"I don't know. It sort of just came out. You know I don't have full control over my mouth," he said in a mischievous grin.

"You're gonna have to figure that one out before it gets us into big trouble."

"Working on it. Gotta run," he said turning away from Trey. "I have to take a leak before history!'

"Later, Marcus," Trey replied distantly as he watched his friend dart through two girls who seemed to be caught off guard. Marcus turned and gave them a playful smile as he continued backwards a few steps then disappeared around a corner.

The rest of the day was uneventful: Trey walked the back of History class to his desk, careful to avoid contact with Donald; Sarah waved and smiled at him upon taking her seat; he turned his English essay in early receiving an approving nod from Mrs. Tolleson and the mostly bald substitute science teacher required them to read and answer questions for the in-class assignment of which Trey quickly filled in the correct answers and was granted permission to spend the remainder of class in the library. After perusing a book on the science of air flight, the bell rang ending school for the day.

Tuesday afternoon was pleasantly warm. The sky frolicked with wispy white clouds. Three small birds played in the grass several yards away hopping and flitting over each other in careless delight. Rows of cars lined the school drive across the yard, waiting to pick up sons and daughters.

"Man, Ms. Johnson would not get off your back today," said Trey

"I know, she thinks I would have an A if I'd give more effort," said Marcus as they walked out of the main building.

"Then give more effort."

"School isn't as easy for me as it is for you, Trey."

"Watch out dorks!" said Donald as he pushed Trey into Marcus. They both nearly tumbled down the steps leading out of the building.

Several teachers nearby took notice of the commotion.

Donald, aware of the onlookers, walked by chuckling. "What are you looking at!" he yelled at a random kid who witnessed the insolent act.

The birds scattered when he trampled through them.

"He really doesn't like you does he Trey," said Sarah walking up from behind completing the triangle.

"Oh, hey Sarah," Trey said coolly as he glanced quickly at Marcus standing just behind her. Marcus was nearly jumping up and down in excitement. Trey tried to not show too much eagerness or panic when he turned back to Sarah. "He's just angry with life and I guess he chooses to take it out on me." He paused then as an afterthought said, "I like your dangly earrings. They look like golden crescent moons." He glanced again at Marcus who was enthusiastically holding up his thumbs in approval.

"Thank you." She offered him a warm closed lip smile before continuing with her previous concern. "I'm sorry he's so mean to you. Someone should say something," she said with a frown.

"No! Trey should kick his butt!" said Marcus vehemently as he reentered the conversation.

"I'm not gonna fight him, Marcus. He'll eventually find something more productive to do with his time."

"And what if he doesn't?" asked Sarah behind big, beautiful eyes.

"I don't know. I'm not doing anything about it today, so let's just move on. Ok?"

"I would kick his butt if I were you. He deserves it," said Marcus. "Just throw a couple quick chops to his head. Maybe that'll knock some sense into him," he continued as he sliced his hands through an imaginary object. Sarah giggled at Marcus' antics.

"It wouldn't solve anything. Plus, he'd probably just find someone else to pick on," said Trey, still taking the conversation seriously.

"Fine. Someone should do something before I have to unleash a hurting on him," Marcus said as he put more force behind his air karate demonstration. He added a goofy round-house kick and a 'Kiiiya!' to finish it off.

They all shared a laugh at the performance.

"You're really into physics?" asked Sarah gracelessly changing the subject as well as turning directly to Trey. "My locker is outside Mr. Hampton's class and I, um," she looked down before raising her eyes to meet his, "I overheard you two talking today."

He shrugged his shoulders and looked at the

ground before addressing her. "Yeah, I guess. I like to think about how things move through space and time."

"That's cool," she said looking up at him. My father took me to a Michio Kaku lecture on our trip to New York last year," she said.

"No Way! You saw Kaku in person!" Trey lost all semblance of his previous discomfort.

"Not just saw him, I met him after the lecture!" Her eyes beamed.

"Oh my god, you've got to be kidding me! You have to tell me all about it."

"I guess I'll see y'all later," Marcus said with his hands out at his side as Trey and Sarah walked away together.

Trey gave Marcus a wave without looking back.

"Bye Marcus," Sarah turned and said.

"I can't believe it. He ditched me for a silly girl. Some best friend he is," Marcus said jokingly to himself as he watched them walk off. "I'll just walk myself to chess club," he continued confidently.

Trey found it difficult holding his side of the conversation. He forgot what they were talking about each time he looked her way.

"I usually go through the park to get home," said Sarah. "It's faster."

"How about we stick to the street, today?" said Trey shyly.

"Is it because of Donald? He's such a jerk."

She's beautiful even when she frowns. He thought.

"The park?" he replied returning from his personal thoughts. "I know. It's best if we don't run into him. Especially today."

"I get it. I heard about them chasing you two

this morning. Gracie in homeroom saw you through the window and yelled, Donald's gonna kick Trey's butt!"

"Really? People saw that?" Trey said disheartened.

"Sure did. I'm glad he didn't catch you."

"He nearly did. Had it not been for Mr. Papperton making his morning rounds."

"What was Marcus talking about? Do you think you could really win a fight with him?"

"No one wins fights, Sarah."

"I guess you're right," she said as she bumped him in the shoulder with hers. She ran her hand through her hair and poured her eyes into his.

Trey's heart skipped. He stumbled on the next step.

She shared a playful laugh.

He bumped her in return when he caught his balance.

He desperately wanted to be close to her, hold her, kiss her. Emotions erupting from every pore, but he contained the starry feelings.

He brushed his hand against hers.

She smiled at him.

He pulled away tucking his hands into his pockets - afraid of her improbable rejection.

They continued walking a few steps in silence.

Trey slumped in his gait while eyeing the park for trouble as they walked along the sidewalk. Noticing his concern, she continued, "I heard his dad left when he was really young."

"Who's? Donald's? I wasn't..."

"It's ok," she said softly.

"Maybe so," he replied. "Some say he died. My mom said she heard he worked for the government. She mentioned he travelled a lot and was super protective of what he was up to. Never talked about work to anyone. One day he left and never returned, no body, no call, nothing."

"Really? When was that?"

"I don't know. Donald said he never met him, so I guess over thirteen years ago. Well fourteen for Donald."

"That must be terrible to not know your own father. Mine is great. I don't know what I'd do without him. He is the kindest man I know. My parents have a relationship like no other. He and my mom are so in love. It's really gross most of the time. They kiss a lot, like they're still dating. My dad would do anything for me and most of the time he does."

"He sounds like a great guy. I'm not so sure it's always a good thing. I sometimes wish I never met mine. I could then make up all sorts of great people he could've been other than the loser who left me and mom."

"I'm sorry. I didn't know." She flushed with embarrassment.

"It's ok. I'm learning to deal with it. Back to a happier topic," he said with a forced smile. "Mom said Donald's mom went crazy after he left, died, whatever. She thought he left for another woman – maybe even had another family."

"Shoot. I'd be mad too if I were her and that's what I believed happened," Sarah said.

"You live in this neighborhood?" he asked as they turned into Whispering Woods.

"Yeah, almost six years."

"I live in Tall Pines just up the street."

"No kidding! We should hang out more," she said. She lowered her head then looked up at him while tucking her hair behind her ear.

He watched, as if in slow motion, as her hand gracefully caressed a supple cheek as it fell from her ear to rest on her forearm.

"Yes, we should," Trey said with a grin too big to conceal.

"Would you like to walk me to school tomorrow?" she asked with a flutter of the eyes.

"Yeah! Tomorrow. Sure." he stuttered, attempting to contain his eagerness.

She smiled and said, "See you tomorrow morning." Then she turned gracefully on one foot and walked away. She waved as she shot him a smile over her shoulder.

He stood in the middle of the road with a goofy grin until the horn of a car jarred him from the trance. He trotted out of the road, waving apologetically, and then walked the quarter mile to his house not remembering taking one step.

"Hi Mom!" Trey announced as he entered the small kitchen that hadn't been updated in a decade.

"Hey Sweet T, how was school?"

Trey's mom was tucked inside a slender navy pant suit. She styled her tight cropped hair with the front brushed to the side. It occasionally drifted over her right eye.

"Good," Trey replied to her greeting. "The front door doesn't close well."

"I know. Mr. Taylor, the landlord, said he'd be by later to take a look at it and the hot water heater.

How'd you do on your," she gave him a sideways look, "wait a minute, why are you smiling?"

"What, who me?"

"Yes, you," she replied bluntly.

"Can't I be happy on occasion for no reason at all?"

"No. There's always a reason. Is it a girl?" she asked eagerly.

"No, Mom. No," he replied unconvincingly. I just had a good day today....but nothing really special happened. I just enjoyed this nice day."

"Ok," she said looking at him questionably. "But let's just note that you're acting very strange," she said with large eyes and raised eyebrows. "I made you a sandwich, it's on the counter."

"Thanks," he replied happily.

"I leave in fifteen minutes for the museum. Aunt Kathy will stop by after soccer practice to bring back a dish she borrowed last week. She'll stay with you for an hour or so."

"Mom, I'm thirteen, I don't need a babysitter."

"I know, it's not for you. Your cousin James is in college now, she doesn't have a job and really needs to feel useful, so I told her she could make sure you were okay tonight while I'm gone."

"Arggg! Ok. Fine. Is she bringing food?"

"Yes. She said she made a lasagna in the pan she's bringing back."

He smiled and said, "Make me cheesy French bread toast and I'll forgive you."

"It's already in the oven," she smirked.

"You're the best! Thanks, and good luck with the exhibition."

"Thank you, Trey, I've been working on it for a

long time. It's really exciting my work is finally getting notoriety."

"I'm proud of you mom! I can't wait for the opening."

"Me too," she said.

"One more thing about Aunt Kathy, why do we call her *aunt* anyway? Isn't she really a cousin?"

"I suppose you're right but let's just keep it like it is okay?"

"Sure."

"Mom?" Trey said reluctantly.

She looked at him curiously in response.

He paused not sure if he wanted to say what he intended to say.

"What is it. Trey? You can talk to me," she said reassuringly.

He looked away and said, "It's nothing."

"Go on, Sweet T. Tell me what's going on."

"It's just that...there's this boy at school. He's not very nice to me."

"Are you getting bullied? Tell me who it is, and I'll go have a word with his mama!" She said aggressively.

"No, Mom. No. It's not like that. He's just not nice and I don't know what to do about it. I'm not scared he'll hurt me or anything, but I do want it to stop. I'm just not sure what to do."

"Oh, baby,' she said warmly. "I think you should talk to him. Try to find out why he's targeting you. Often there is something beneath the surface and if you can get to that you'll have an opportunity to not only solve you're bully problem but also help him tremendously."

"Talk to him? I don't think I can do that."

"Trey," she said powerfully, "It won't be easy, but I know you can do hard things. You understand?"

"I think so," he said actually unsure if she had helped at all but happy she had so much faith in his ability to approach Donald to try to figure out why he is so mean.

She hugged him, a little longer than usual, and then walked off down the hall.

She returned to the kitchen several minutes later and just before she left him at the house alone, she said seriously looking up with dark brown eyes, "Remember Trey, you can do hard things." She nodded then walked out without knowing she might not ever see her only son again.

Trey sat at his meager desk attempting to work on homework for the day but kept thinking of his walk with Sarah. He relived every moment, wincing at the regrettable ones. He wondered if she would have held his hand had he reached for it, if he messed it up somehow with the awkward moment. A knock on the door broke his contemplation.

He walked to the door to find Marcus, "Hi Marcus."

"You ready for practice?" Marcus said, dressed in a tucked-in white long sleeve button up collared shirt and bow tie. He was also holding a black rectangular case.

"Yeah, let me grab my boots and I'll be right out." Trey took a second look at Marcus' attire then asked, "Why are you so fancy?"

Marcus sighed, "We have a band rehearsal for the play this weekend. Mrs. Lofton wants it to be just like it will be during the live show, dress and all."

"Oh. Okay. You have a solo in it, right? Are you nervous?"

"You know me, I don't get nervous about anything."

"I'll have to agree with you there. I don't recall an instance since I've known you...or maybe you're just good at faking it," Trey joked and jabbed him lightly in the stomach.

"Hey, Kid. I'll fake you upside the head with this case if you don't watch it," he replied playfully.

Walking down the busy sidewalk Marcus said as he swung the violin case side to side, "So, tell me. How did it go with Sarah?" He smiled a cheesy grin then said quickly, "Did ya kiss her?"

"No," he retorted defensively. "I just walked her to her neighborhood. Did you know she lives in Whispering Woods?"

"Really? You didn't kiss her? Tell me you at least got to first base."

"First base *is* kissing you big dummy," Trey said with a chuckle.

"Oh. I thought that was...well...never mind. What a stupid metaphor. Baseball's a silly game anyway. A bunch of guys just sit around waiting on another guy to hit a ball. What's the fun in that?"

"Exactly. That's what I used to tell Dad. He said baseball was the greatest sport ever invented."

"Yeah. Okay," Marcus said leery of continuing a conversation about Trey's dad. "So, you said Whispering Woods? Travis Rashi lives there. I go to his house every other week to play chess. I've never seen her there, but I don't suppose I would since we never go outside."

"Good thing you have Travis. I can't go ten minutes with you. You really have that game figured out."

"We have a competition coming up in New York City. I'm super excited about it."

"I know you'll do well. No one plays chess like you. I wish I could have that skill on the pitch. Your strategy would be invaluable."

"Thanks, Kid," Marcus smiled.

"Have fun at band," said Trey as Marcus turned toward the school and raised a single hand. He rapidly shot his index finger twice in the air in a so long salute.

Trey was left to continue his thoughts about Sarah on his way to the soccer complex. He noticed three scrubby men who looked to be in their fifties staring at him intently from across the street. He thought it strange and had an uneasy feeling but just ducked his head and picked up his pace. They made no move to follow.

Trey arrived at the soccer fields a few minutes ahead of time, shook off the odd feeling he carried from his walk, then joined his teammates. Coach Rafiq addressed the boys and then the team broke onto the pitch under grey clouds of which replaced the previously blue sky. Trey noticed a tall, dark-haired woman leaning against a silver sports car taking what seemed to be too much interest in a middle school soccer practice – taking too much interest in him. He tried not to think she was looking specifically at him or that she may be related somehow to the other three guys. He stopped and sent her an unsteady glance. He looked away for a moment and then back to see if she was still looking but found her driving away.

"Strange," he said to himself and didn't pay it another thought for the rest of practice.

After practice, drying sweat chilled his body as he walked home in the cool, dusky evening. No sign of the threesome from earlier. He entered the dark, empty house – immediately started a shower with a fluctuating temperature. Afterward, frustrated by the unsatisfying shower and alone in his room, he began thinking of the strange woman again when a sudden knock at the door startled him. *Did someone just enter the house?* He stood up quickly, alarmed.

"Trey? Are you here?" came a shrill voice from the kitchen.

Trey relaxed as he entered the kitchen. "Hi, Aunt Kathy."

Kathy was a thin woman in her fifties with bushy, chemical-colored blonde hair and pale skin. She carried a large orange purse decorated in a white flower print.

"Hey Trey," Kathy said as she planted a big kiss on his right cheek. "I'm so glad we get to spend some time together. I brought a lasagna."

"It smells yummy," said Trey as oregano and melted cheese caught his attention.

"It's nearly six, let's grab some plates and have dinner, shall we?" she asked.

Trey set the table, then grabbed a spatula for the feast.

They sat and Trey continued, "So, how's James? Is he getting settled into to college life?"

"You know James, he just sort of goes with the flow. We were up there last week helping with a few things. I'm not sure that boy will ever learn to do his own laundry."

"It must be nice having him so close."

Kathy added a small serving to her plate. Trey took no notice that she didn't touch it afterward.

"Yes, he wanted to go to a school on the west coast. I would have lost my mind," she said as she rested her crossed arms on the table. "Tell me Trey," she said hastily changing the subject, "what do you know about our family history?"

He took a moment to twirl stretchy cheese around his fork.

"Uh, well, Grandpa lived in Louisiana for thirty years or so before moving to Boston. Mom never told me why. I suppose I could have asked. Anyway, his family came over from Europe in the 1700's. That's about all I know. Dad told me a few stories about Grandpa's adventures before Dad, you know..." he trailed off chopping his noodles into the melted cheese and thick sauce.

Kathy sighed and her smile faded as she addressed Trey's emotional statement, "Your father is a good man. Very smart and devoted to you and your mom. Sometimes people get distracted and marriages sort of don't make any more sense. You know what I mean?"

Trey became angry and lashed out, "No. I don't know what you mean. He left us. He hasn't been devoted at all."

Kathy thought he might cry or leave or both. "I can see why you feel that way," she said softly. "You'll understand your father and his actions in time."

"Whatever," he replied dismissively. He set his fork in the plate and looked away, trying to hold back powerful emotions.

Kathy exhaled audibly before continuing. "Uncle Patrick, I mean your Grandfather, was a historian. He had a passion for discovering the truth. He studied ancient civilizations, specifically those of Africa. He travelled all over the world looking up clues to fill in the details of broken history. In fact, he discovered a whole race of people related to the ancient Egyptians that lived thousands of years ago. I know you didn't know him well, but he knew you."

"He knew me? Really? How?"

"Mostly through your dad."

"My dad told Grandpa about me?" Trey asked in disbelief.

She smiled, "Yeah. They talked all the time, nearly every day."

Trey rolled his eyes, looked away and commented, "I can't imagine the crap Dad told him. I'm sure none of it is actually me."

"I'm sure there's some accuracy in his stories."

"I'm sure," Trey said sarcastically. "I don't understand why I didn't get to meet him. Why wouldn't he come see me?"

"I don't know, Trey. Maybe you'll find the answer soon."

"What happened to him? Mom never told me. How'd he die?"

"Did your mom say he died?"

"Actually, no. No, she didn't. I think I might have just assumed. I don't remember. I didn't know him so maybe I just shrugged it off. That was around the same time Dad left."

"I know it was a hard time for you. I'm sorry. Your father is my cousin, but that doesn't mean I understand his actions." She looked at him with immense empathy, nearly tearing up at the thought of what the poor boy has gone through. She gathered herself, wiped away a tear and continued. "Anyway, your grandfather was in an incident in China about four years ago. The officials said he and a colleague were attacked one evening but no one could find either of them afterward. We had people searching for nearly a year. Nothing. We all assume they were killed."

"Killed! Why would anyone want to kill Grandpa?"

"Your grandpa dealt in many important historical items. We think someone attacked them for something they had."

"Like what?"

"Something like this." She pulled a round metal object from her purse, pushed her plate aside, then displayed it to Trey. It had a hole the size and about the same shape of a plum seed in the center. "He asked me to give it to you when the time was right."

"What are those markings?" he said taking interest.

"Hieroglyphs," she said – happy to see his lightened expression.

"Really? This is an actual artifact from ancient Egypt?"

"I believe so," she said.

He moved his plate so he could get a closer look.

"It looks like it was made yesterday. There's not a mark on it at all. Was it cleaned or restored?"

"No. This is how he found it."

"Amazing. It's not tarnished or anything."

She watched his curious eyes scour the item. "He discovered it in a shallow room adjacent to an unmarked grave in the Democratic Republic of Congo. The story goes that an ancient magical being made this for a very bad king. He said there was once a stone in the center thought to grant great powers to the one who joined it to the disk. He never did find the stone. It was told that after the bad king was defeated, the benevolent queen removed the stone, then sent each part separate ways to prevent it from falling into the wrong hands. Additionally, Uncle Patrick learned that each piece carried a spell that bound the piece to a human guardian, which was to prevent anyone from removing it unwillingly. It can only be removed by granting it to another, or by the death of the guardian, otherwise, they will be cursed."

"Death? That must be how Grandpa got it. At the grave."

"I believe so," said Kathy.

"What kind of curse? Will you turn into a zombie?" he said jokingly.

"I don't know. He didn't tell me," she replied seriously.

"Wow. There's no way any of that's true but cool to think about. Shouldn't this be in a museum?"

"Probably. Uncle Patrick thought it was too important to give up. He also said to keep it from your mom because the museum would be the first place she'd take it. So, you must keep it safe *and* secret."

"Have you carried that in your purse since Grandpa gave it to you?"

"I have. It's not very big and I... I didn't want to be cursed." She released an unsettling chortle.

"So, you're giving me the disk so that you don't have to carry it around any longer?"

"Yes. Well, no. I'm just doing what Uncle

Patrick told me to do." Her eyes shifted and she fidgeted with the metallic disk.

"Aunt Kathy, are you okay?" Trey asked nervously.

"Oh. Yeah. I'm good," she said as if she was woken from a dream. She paused a moment, took a deep breath, placed the disk in his right hand holding hers on top and said in a projected monotone voice, "I Patricia Clarise Monihand grant Olerand's Disk to Wallace Patrick Roberts the Third."

She removed her hand from the disk, then took a quick step back out of her chair as if she expected it to explode.

An image of a long-faced man with a trim beard and mustache briefly appeared in Trey's mind. A chill overcame him.

"Whoa! That was weird." Trey dropped the disk onto the table.

"What was weird?" asked Kathy.

"When you let go, an image of a creepy man appeared in my mind. Did that happen to you when Grandpa gave it to you?"

"No Trey," she said as if she didn't hear his question. "Well, that was all I came for. Hope you enjoy the lasagna. Good luck Trey! I love you! Tell your mom I said hey."

She nearly tripped over her chair exiting the house.

"Remember," she said virtually sprinting to her car, "don't tell anyone you have it! This is a serious matter!"

"Ok. I'll keep it secret. Bye, Aunt Kathy," Trey said in a low unmeaningful voice as he looked at the disk. He rubbed his finger over the cold engraved markings. He hollered out the door, "Thanks for leaving me this ancient cursed relic!"

Trey looked at the disk again, then said, "Magic spell, huh." He placed it into a pocket dismissing her warnings.

He went to his room, removed a picture buried deep in a desk drawer. It was of himself in a black and yellow baseball outfit. He was maybe five. His father stood next to him in a matching cap with a serious look, as if he were revealing the secrets of the world while they mounted the diamond.

"I hardly remember this. It seemed so long ago. Was it even real? Was he actually involved in my life? He really cared enough to coach my baseball team and tell stories about me to Grandpa, a man I've never met?"

He mused a few more minutes then placed the picture back in the desk drawer. He then tried to drown his emotions in an old video game.

Unexpected Partners

As he strolled through a crowded Dulles International Airport terminal with busy travelers swerving in front and around him, Nick Hampton was unaware of the woman matching his steps. A pleasantly toned man's voice projected throughout the facility:

Ladies and gentlemen. It is important that you keep a close watch on your baggage and carry-on items. Do not leave items unattended at any time. Do not accept articles from unknown persons to carry onto the aircraft. Maintain carry-on items to prevent the introduction of dangerous articles without your knowledge. Do not carry items belonging to others. Note that all bags are subject to search. Report any suspicious persons or unusual activity to you nearest law enforcement officer. Thank you and have a good flight.

He sat in an empty row adjacent to the gate for the next flight to Egypt and immediately pulled out his phone.

She carried herself confidently – striding as if all eyes were on her every move. Toned arms swayed within snug sleeves that fit loosely at the elbows. From lovely shoulders cascaded tight fitting black material enveloping a trim torso in wide draping layers down to sumptuous knees. The dress accentuated long muscular legs wrapped in black knee-high boots with overlarge clasps.

The phone Nick mindlessly scrolled through slipped from entranced fingers as she took a seat next to him. It clacked on the hard terminal floor. She removed rose lensed aviators revealing intensely dark blue eyes of which if an ocean, a sailor would dream to drift in aimlessly. A wavy tuft of long dark-mahogany hair escaped from the front of a knitted headdress that wore more like a beanie than Hijab and flowed low across a smooth forehead before disappearing behind a neck he fantasized pressing his lips against. Dusky skin, like smooth milk chocolate patted perfectly with powdered sugar, highlighted high flawless cheeks and sensuous red lips.

"To where are you travelling?" she asked in a deep lustrous voice with a hint of an Arabic accent.

She was aware of his rugged attractiveness but gave no notice of the observation.

Surprised by her unbelievable beauty, he was momentarily speechless. He fumbled to retrieve his phone then said in a sheepishly weak voice, "Cairo." He cleared his throat, sat up straight and tried again in a deeper, manlier tone, "I'm going to Cairo."

"Interesting. Are you travelling for business or pleasure?" she said as her eyes caressed his sculpted, recently unshaven chin.

"Well, sort of both. I've never been to Egypt, so I think that will be pleasurable, but the purpose of the trip will be, well, I suppose it will be workish."

"That's a pretty vague description," she said with a knowing smile. She crossed her legs slowly, then leaned slightly closer. Her radiating warmth encompassed his senses to the point he didn't feel the pressure on his coat pocket.

"Will you travel anywhere other than Cairo?" she said momentarily dropping her gaze only to return to meet his. "I'm from Egypt and if you have never been, you should visit the southeastern portion of the country. It is rich in history."

"No. Not this trip," he said unsteadily. "I think I'll manage to spend most of my time in the desert."

"That doesn't sound interesting at all. You should be aware the western desert can be treacherous for the unprepared."

"I have a reliable guide," he said. "I'm sure we'll be just fine." After a moment's pause Nick said, "I don't remember saying I would be in the western part of the country."

"I really must be going," she said as she rose from the seat. "It was very nice chatting with you. Good luck on your workish pleasure trip," she said casting a smile over her shoulder.

He could barely remember the conversation as he watched her sway gently away.

"It's true. He's waiting on a flight to Cairo now.

I don't know how he knows either. There's too much security here. I couldn't make a scene. However, I think there's a good chance he'll miss his flight. Plus, even if he makes it, we don't know for sure he knows where he's going. Make certain he doesn't get to the oasis. Keep me updated. I'll try to find out what I can here and meet you in Cairo if by some chance he actually recovers the eye." She slipped the phone in her back pocket, then left the airport.

Nick sat in the stiff seat adjoined to twelve others in a row, pondering the interaction he had with the woman.

"Something wasn't right about her. She seemed to be too flirty and knew too much about my trip."

"Excuse me sir," came a strong voice. A Transportation Security Administration (TSA) agent and an armed police officer were standing in front of him. The officer had a hand on his pistol as if he expected resistance – and he looked eager for trouble. "Place your hands on your head and rise slowly from your seat," he commanded.

Startled and confused, Nick did as directed. As he rose, he asked very nicely, "I apologize for asking officer, but what is this all about?"

"Come with us, sir," the TSA agent said while the officer walked behind Nick to a private room near the security screening area.

He was instructed to sit in a chair then the officer and TSA agent left, securing the door behind them. Nick checked his watch several times, nervous about missing his flight.

Thirty minutes passed before a very round police officer named Franklin who wore a thick, reddish moustache and a rather unintelligent looking skinny officer with a belt cinching pants raised too high around his waist entered the room. The skinny one said to Nick, "Please stand, Sir," then thoroughly patted Nick down.

Franklin asked, "What'd you find there, Willy?" after Willy retrieved something out of Nick's coat pocket.

Nick stammered nervously, "What is it! What did you find? I didn't have anything in that pocket! How did it get there?"

"It's some sort of small device, similar to a TV remote," Willy said as he examined the object.

"That's not mine. I don't know what that is?"

"Is that so, Mr. Hampton of 135 Wilkins Way," Franklin said as he read Nick's driver's license.

"Yes. That's so. I've never seen that," he craned his head to see what Willy was holding, "that, whatever it is."

"We had a report that a man fitting your description was mumbling something about a bomb and playing with a trigger device."

"A what?" Nick replied exasperated.

"A trigger device," Willy replied curtly.

"Really? They said trigger device?" Nick asked.

"That's what she said," replied the round one.

She? It was a woman. But why? Why would she try to get me arrested?

Nick wasn't restrained so he turned to face Willy. He looked at the man dumbfounded then snatched the object from his hand drawing surprise and an aggressive stance from both Willy and Franklin. He then said, "It *looks* like a TV remote because it *is* a TV remote." He shoved the remote back into Willy's hand who had loosened his attention toward Nick. "Can I leave now? I have a flight to catch," he said angrily.

"Oh yeah. Look at that Frank. It's a TV remote," he said as he turned on a TV in the room and started changing channels. "Judge Judy! Look Frank, Judge Judy's on," he said happily. "I didn't know she was still on TV," he said in utter amazement.

"Willy! Turn that off!" Franklin yelled under his breath. He returned to nick in forced politeness, "I apologize for the inconvenience, Mr. Hampton," Franklin said as Nick grabbed his things and turned toward the door. Franklin, as an afterthought said to Nick who was storming away, "We at the TSA take threats seriously!"

Nick rushed to his gate barely making it before the doors closed. He spent the next several hours ruminating on the airport incident coming to one conclusion – she, whoever she was, didn't want him in Egypt.

After the sixteen-hour flight with a layover in Istanbul, Nick departed the Cairo airport with no checked baggage and dark, tired eyes – still perplexed as to why the woman wanted him to miss the flight. He found a stocky man with a modest belly and thinning black hair holding a sign reading "Hampton."

"Seth Nahas?" Nick yawned as he approached the man with the sign.

"Yes! Mr. Nick Hampton!" Seth said in a jovial Arabic accent. "It is very good to meet you. We have everything prepared for our journey tomorrow. We shall leave after breakfast around nine A.M."

"That's great, Mr. Nahas."

He patted Nick on the back, took his only bag

and said, "Please Mr. Hampton, call me Seth."

"Ok, Seth," he said as he followed him out of the airport. "You can call me Nick."

"Ok, Mr. Nick," he said with a wide grin. You will be staying in my home tonight. I hope that is ok. It is on the way and I make a wonderful Kushari."

"Sounds great!" Nick replied, attempting to muster enthusiasm for Seth's hospitality.

"Right this way, Mr. Nick" Seth ushered. Nick gave him a curious look then followed the man out of the terminal.

As they turned to cross the road leading to the parking lot, Nick noticed two figures approaching swiftly from the corner of his eye. At the last second, Nick yelled, "Seth! Get down!" He then crouched and leaned into the first assailant launching him over his head propelling him painfully onto the pavement. Nick subsequently rolled from the crouched position avoiding a strike from the second attacker. Seth drove a fist into the second attacker crushing his jaw.

A woman screamed while a couple rushed a small child away.

Nick and Seth recognized each other's bewildered looks before Seth yelled, "This way!"

The first attacker righted himself, then gave chase along with three others, including the second who held a hand to his mouth trying to soothe the pain from Seth's strike.

"The brown car there!" shouted Seth flashing the lights with the remote.

Nick slid across the hood as Seth took the driver's seat slamming an attacker's arm in the door - he fell away reeling in pain. Seth quickly fired the engine as two spread out on the hood while another grasped onto the back.

The engine echoed loudly as Seth piloted the car through the garage. Tires squealed around corners. A quick turn tossed one of the hood riders into the street as they sped away from the airport. The one on the rear pulled himself to the roof.

Three motorcycles raced up from behind the vehicle as Seth zipped through the outskirts of the city. Two riders wearing black outfits and red helmets brandishing pistols pulled up to either side of the car.

"Why are they attacking us!" screamed Seth.

"I was about to ask you the same thing!" Nick's hand gripped the upper handle, the other braced himself against the console as he looked at Seth with alarmed eyes.

Bullets blasted through the ceiling of the vehicle, narrowly missing the occupants.

Seth slammed the brakes smashing the following cyclist into the rear of the vehicle tossing him onto the trunk. Seth swerved to avoid a slower car causing the cyclist to tumble off into a passing group of pedestrians.

The roof rider slid uncontrollably onto the hood. He grasped onto the original hood rider who lost his grip and slipped off to the right and skidded into the narrow, crowded street.

Blaring the horn, Seth swerved left and right avoiding tuk-tuks and spectators.

The right cyclist smashed the window with a pistol. Nick quickly grabbed his arm as bullets flew through the vehicle, narrowly missing Seth. Seth swerved to drive the right cyclist into a street side vendor causing an explosion of citrus fruits to rain all over the road and nearby people frightened by the chase.

The hood rider pulled a pistol firing five shots through the windshield.

BAM! BAM! BAM! BAM! BAM!

He proceeded to kick his way through. Seth slammed on the brakes, then turned onto a dead-end alley to the left, cutting-off the left motorcyclist who crashed into the side of the car, launching him overhead into a cart scattering hundreds of cheap jewelry items. The owner of the cart yelled wildly at the cyclist. The hood assailant lost balance and fell to the front of the vehicle. Seth quickly reversed, leaving the two remaining attackers behind.

After a few minutes of assessing the situation, they both determined the barrage was over.

Just as Nick caught his breath, Seth skidded the car to a stop and yelled, "Get out!"

"But I have –" Nick began to plead before Seth cut him off, "No! Get Out!"

"But I don't even know where I am."

Seth pointed out the window as a signal for him to exit the car. Nick got out as Seth peeled away from the stranded teacher.

Now what do I do?

The street was busy with people in a hurry to get places and sell things. A vendor held out a blue-faced mask. Nick shook his head, then began to walk. A well-dressed couple were perusing fresh fruits and vegetables to his left. A tall man dressed in a religious thawb eyed him suspiciously as he passed. He hailed a cab and shortly after, arrived at a nearby inconspicuous hotel where he paid cash for one night.

Staring into the ceiling in a single bedroom hoping to drift off to sleep after the earlier excitement, a soft knock startled him. Wary of visitors, Nick wondered who it could be.

From the other side, "It's me Mr. Nick."

"Seth? Is that you?"

"Yes. Let me in, your life is in danger."

"What are you talking about?" he said with his face close to the door.

"You don't understand. You have to let me in."

Nick opened the door. They regarded each other for an uncomfortable moment before Seth took a seat in a small chair next to the bed. Nick sat across from him on the edge of the bed.

"How did you find me? I took a random cab and paid cash at a random hotel."

Seth leaned back in the chair. He raised a hand in the air and said in a rhythmic tone that traveled from high to low, "My cousin is a driver in the district south of us. I asked him to call around to see if anyone picked up a man fitting your description. It was really easy to find you, so we can't stay here much longer.

"The man that shot through the windshield had a tattoo just on the inside of his forearm. I wouldn't have seen it had the wind not pushed up his sleeve. I haven't seen that design in many years. I dismissed it at the time but if those guys are who I think they are, you need to disappear and quick."

"So what. That doesn't mean anything," said Nick in a dismissive tone. "It's just a tattoo. Besides, how do you know they weren't after you? No one even knows me or that I'm here."

"Don't be naive, Mr. Nick. The moment you booked the flight, everyone who wanted to know, knew you would be here at that time." He paused and sat up facing Nick. "This is serious, Mr. Nick!" he said in a gruff voice. "Tell me what you are looking for in the Oasis?"

"This is ridiculous, there isn't a group of people trying to stop me from getting to the Oasis," he replied leaning back on the bed. He turned his eyes to the ceiling thinking about the woman.

"Really? Then why were we attacked today? What are you looking for?" asked Seth again in a more forceful voice.

After a few minutes Nick looked at Seth and said, "Fine. I'm a physicist. I've studied the effects of quantum theory for many years. I developed a theory of quantum teleportation and built a machine that I believe will bring this theory to life." He took a breath to assess Seth's response.

"Please continue," Seth said flatly.

"You see, the problem with today's notions is that they rely on the copy and destroy paradigm, meaning that basically a copy of you is made in the destination and the existing you would be destroyed. That's not really an optimal scenario. Plus, the computing power required would be tremendous. However, what I have created is more like the theoretical wormhole, or a door to the destination that you would simply walk through. I believe there is a geode located in western Egypt or eastern Libya that is somehow related."

"And you think that's a typical activity of

normal people?"

"I don't suppose so," Nick replied.

"Are you seeking Egyptian artifacts?" Seth said accusatively.

"No. I don't believe that is my mission," he said but began developing the notion that an artifact is exactly what he was searching for.

Seth looked at Nick for quite some time. His head cocked slightly to one side. His brow furrowed.

Nick uncomfortably adjusted his position.

"It is very dangerous where you wish to go. It has become a preferred route of terrorists and smugglers."

He paused for another unpleasant length of time with an expressionless glare directed at Nick.

Nick again adjusted his seating position.

After another moment Seth said, "I will take you as promised." He placed both hands on his knees while leaning forward. "I have a cousin that operates in the area and feel we will be relatively safe. He will also arrange passage into Libya if necessary."

"Thank you, Seth. I appreciate you coming back for me."

Seth's face softened and his jovial smile from the airport returned. "Have you ever been to northern Egypt?"

"I've never been to Egypt."

"You are in for a treat," he said with a clap. "The way along the Mediterranean is beautiful." He opened his arms and turned his hands up then brought them together in a closed handed prayer position. "We will visit my cousin who lives just outside Alexandria. But we must leave right away, it is not safe here. We will rest at my office for a few hours before we set off."

"You sure do have many cousins."

"More than fifty scattered around the world, but most live in and around Egypt."

"That's a lot of cousins. I only have nine."

Nick grabbed his pack then they walked out of the hotel onto a moderately lit sidewalk.

"What happened to the brown car?"

"It was too damaged. I borrowed this one."

"Let me guess, from a cousin?"

"Yeah. How'd you know?" Seth smiled.

They drove twenty minutes through the vibrant city night. Nick admired a tall blue-lighted tower across the Nile River shortly before Seth parked on the third floor of a somewhat crowded parking garage. They exited the opposite side of the garage on foot.

"Through here," said Seth as they turned down a narrow alley. "In here, quick," as they ducked inside an unlocked alley side door.

Nick began to question the integrity of his hired guide amid the hustle.

Seth locked the door behind them.

"Hey Seth. Maybe we should just go back," Nick said uncomfortably.

Seth looked at him without saying a word as he continued to hurry through the building.

They passed through a narrow corridor, and then exited the building to the right. Nick trailed back a little, looking around frantically. Having no idea where he was, he chose to follow his trusted guide.

"Please keep up Mr. Nick. We must get out of sight," Seth said sternly.

"Look man. I don't know where we are or

where we are going...and I just met you. Can you help me out a little?"

"We have just a little further to go. Stay close."

Nick looked around, reluctantly followed the burly man across the street, down another dark alley, and then through a door to the left into a frenzied kitchen that smelled of steamed rice, garlic and strong cheese.

It was about 10:30 PM when a sous chef eyed them suspiciously. A waiter greeted Seth as they exited the kitchen into a serving area before continuing to the dance floor. The crowd enjoyed a live DJ playing electronic dance music. Nick enjoyed the steady beat of the music in his chest as the two pushed their way through an energetic crowd.

Boom. Boom. Boom.

Nearing the front entrance, they heard a thunderous voice roar, "Seth Nahas?"

Seth cringed and mumbled, "It can't be! Not tonight!"

He turned to find his trepidation to be justified.

"Mr. Soliman," Seth said in an overly cheerful tone still moving toward the door. He continued in Arabic, "How are you this evening? I'd really love to catch up, but we're in quite a rush."

Nick studied Arabic in college and choppily followed the conversation.

Mr. Soliman motioned for two men to stop them. Several more moved in around.

The men hustled Nick and Seth to a large table which sat an imposing, slightly overweight dark-skinned man in a white fedora and matching suit. A fat cigar protruded from his teeth of which he didn't seem to be pulling – smoke swirled around his corpulent head.

As they approached the table Mr. Soliman said in Arabic, "Seth, my old friend! It has been so long. Why have you not come to see me before now?" Soliman lowered his tone in a sinister sneer, "I believe we have unfinished business. Where is my talisman?"

"Well...um, you see sir, I had it then...well it... um...was sort of taken from me in Somalia."

"Who could steal from the great Seth Nahas?" Soliman said sarcastically.

Seth hung his head at the insult.

"Tell me who!" Soliman demanded as he slammed a fist onto the tabletop.

Startled, Seth said, "By, uh..." he tried to think of a better answer but failed, "...by a member of the Order."

"The Order huh," Soliman said dryly as he stared coldly into Seth's eyes. "Do I look like a fool."

"Really, I –".

Soliman leaned forward over the table and yelled, "Tell me, Seth! Do I look like a fool to you!"

"No! No, Sir. You're no fool."

"Then why do you treat me as such with foolish talk about this Order?"

"I know it sounds crazy but it's true. They took it and I've been trying to get it back. You see, I even have this professor from America to help me. We're travelling west to recover it now."

Nick cut his eyes at Seth.

"Silence! You intentionally deceive me and then make a fool of me!" grumbled Soliman. "Where would I be if all my associates mocked me in this way. My empire would be crushed. He stared at Seth for a moment more then said dismissively, "I'm tired of looking at his face. Take him out back and make sure I never see him again."

"And the American?" the man holding Nick said.

"Him too. He's seen too much."

"But sir! You must believe me! I can get – " Seth pleaded.

The beat continued in the background.

Boom. Boom. Boom.

One of Soliman's men grabbed Nick's arm – with a flash Nick twisted the attacker's arm awkwardly, then kicked him in the back onto the table, tossing drinks and food on Soliman.

Boom. Boom. Boom.

Soliman thundered in anger as Seth punched one of Soliman's men into the crowd. Seth struggled with another of the men while Nick engaged one more, threw several body blows, avoided a wayward punch by placing one hand on the man's wrist another on the back of his elbow forcefully dislocating it with a loud crack. He thrusted a knee into the attacker's gut stepped back, then ended the man's fight with a roundhouse to the left temple sending him limply along with a table into the dance floor.

Boom. Boom. Boom.

Soliman fired three rounds into the air from a

45-caliber pistol creating a panic. People began rushing toward the exits. Nick tossed a heavy plate and a glass toward Soliman. The glass dislodged the pistol from his hand and the plate struck Soliman's throat sending him sprawling to the ground. Nick sprinted toward Seth, lept into the air and struck Seth's opponent with a precise foot to the jaw.

Boom. Boom. Boom.

"Let's get out of here!" screamed Nick.

They ran into the street with the wailing crowd then ducked out of site into another building.

Nick heaved deep breaths as he asked, "Who were those guys?"

"Oh, it's a long story."

"I have time," Nick replied.

"Not here. Let's keep going."

They passed through two additional buildings before climbing three sets of stairs. They finally entered a small room decorated with peeling wallpaper and thick layers of dust.

"We'll rest here for a few hours. We leave at six tomorrow morning," Seth said as he reclined back in a chair and closed his eyes.

Nick sat on the corner of the bed staring at Seth. "Tell me what's going on Seth. Who was that man in the club? Who or what is the Order?"

"Can't we just rest for a bit?" Seth asked without opening his eyes.

"No. I need to know what's going on. Were they the guys chasing us at the airport?"

"Arrg," Seth replied grunting as he sat up in the

chair. "They aren't the same as at the airport. I work for, well used to work, for Mr. Soliman. He is a very prominent businessman in Cairo. When he needed something to be found, he would call me to find it. You see like I said before, my family is large. I have many ears in the city and spread out across the region which makes it relatively easy for me to find stuff. Several years ago, he hired me to find an antique metal talisman with a single stone in the middle. I traced it to Somalia where it was held by a large sea tro..." he cleared his throat. Well, let's say it was protected by a big bad guy who lived in a cave near the ocean. I was able to sneak by him when he was asleep during the day. He awoke when I accidently hit him with a sword that he was also protecting. However, I was in disguise and was able to steal the talisman without being noticed but had to leave the sword.

"The problem I had was that the talisman was missing the stone. I met with a friend of my cousin who said there was a group of people in the Oasis region that knew of the talisman and may have the stone. But before I could get there the talisman was stolen from me by some old crudgy man in a panama hat."

"He works for the Order?" Nick asked. "The crudgy man?"

"I believe so. I never knew who he was or how he knew I had it, but somehow, he found me and was able to get it. I have no idea where it is today, but I would like to get it back in addition to the stone to pay my debt to Mr. Soliman. He is not a man you want on your bad side."

"Even after today, you still have loyalty to him?" asked Nick.

"Well, not so much loyalty as much as keeping

my life and name in this city. If it gets out that I failed, no one will hire me again. Lucky for me, Mr. Soliman is proud and doesn't like to admit failure. So, I'll help you get your geode and you help me get the stone, deal?"

"I can live with that. So now tell me about the Order."

"Okay. According to folklore, there was a great king by the name of Ronodan." He said this as if he didn't quite believe in the story or perhaps, he didn't believe it was folklore. "He was loved by his people. A sorcerer by the name of Khaitu appeared out of nowhere and overthrew King Ronodan. He destroyed Ronodan's army along with his loyal followers. He also took Ronodan's only daughter as his wife. The Order of Hsehk were seven ancient beings bound by a cruel curse to serve Khaitu. They turned on Khaitu after a horrific slaughter of a whole city. They afterward gave their lives entombing him in a relic, then banished him to a dimension of ghostly creatures known as the Etherios.

"Seven relics were left behind along with several other artifacts such as the talisman I am seeking. A group of mortal humans vowed to protect the relics so that Khaitu could never return. Most of the relics were dispersed across the world. If they are ever brought together again, Khaitu could become free and with the power of the relics to himself, he could conquer the world sending it into pain and destruction. That's why I asked if you were seeking ancient artifacts as well as why I believe they are after you. They want to stop you from finding whatever it is you are seeking."

A long silence was broken by soft laughter that quickly gained in fervor.

"That is one hell of a story Seth. You say it with such passion that someone more gullible might actually believe it. So, you think these mythical *beings* are after me?"

"No. Those guys are long gone. The Order are the group that vowed to protect the relics. Unfortunately, it has changed over the years. Under the leadership of the Phoenix, they have lost sight of the original purpose."

"Riiiight," Nick said patronizingly. "Ancient kings and mythical creatures. It just sounds crazy."

"I suppose it does."

"That's all you have to explain what Soliman was after?"

"Yeah. That's the story."

"Well, I understand why he was so mad at your excuse. I don't believe you either."

"That's okay. You don't have to believe it yet. Try to get some sleep. We have a long day tomorrow."

Nick laid back in a twin bed, taking in the musty apartment. His mind buzzed as he ran the day's events through his head including how Seth finished the conversation.

What did he mean by I don't have to believe it yet? That was a ridiculous story.

He thought he would never sleep. As exhaustion took over, he drifted off to horns beeping a melodic tune.

"Wake up Nick," Seth said in a whisper.

Nick fluttered his eyes and asked sleepily," Wha...What's going on?"

"Be quiet, someone is outside the window. I don't know how they found us."

Nick groggily rolled off and crouched behind the bed while Seth slunk to the right side of the window which was the only source of light emanating from the city outside. The window opened with a smooth *shhhhhh*. Nick readied himself to launch into action while Seth prepared to grab whoever was coming through. Steadily waiting, Nick trembled with anticipation. Suddenly, a wet sticky smack alighted on Seth's left cheek. Startled at the unexpected attack, he fell back into the television, knocking it off the dresser as he tumbled off to the side onto the kitchen floor.

Drawn to the commotion, Nick missed the assailant enter the room. He rushed to the window prepared to attack but found nothing. Laughter came from the kitchen – Nick briefly let down his guard.

"Mmmm, Seth, who do we have here? Looks delicious. Can we eat him?"

Nick quickly turned toward the scratchy voice to find nothing speaking.

"Show yourself and I'll show you how delicious I can be!"

"Brave *and* fast. I'm not sure you have chosen wisely, old friend," said the voice.

"Cievan! You slimy cuss," Seth said still laughing. "What in the world are you doing here?"

Suddenly, a five-foot-tall man with an overly large Cheshire Cat toothed grin appeared in the corner of the room. He wore a brown t-shirt, beige shorts and no shoes.

Clievan looked at Nick with cold, deep orange eyes and a mischievous smirk and said, "I know you only use this place when you're up to something, so I often stroll by looking for excitement." A fat slimy tongue the size of a Saint Bernard's slid across a thin upper-lip – it grazed his nose before submerging out of site.

"What gave me away? How'd you know I was next to the window?" asked Seth.

"I can recognize you from half a mile away," Clievan snickered.

"Of course, you can. I forgot about your heat sensy thingy."

"Heat? What? What's he talking about Seth?" Nick questioned scratching his head.

"Nothing Nick, this is Clievan. He's from, well, I don't really know where he's from."

"Hi, Nick," Clievan said with a moist, reptilic voice. He waved a hand with large, bulbous fingers.

"Yeah, uh, nice to meet you," he replied – trying to hide obvious discomfort with the strange looking man.

He's not grotesque, Nick thought with an inquisitive expression – he held his hand to his chin and a raised an eyebrow along with a curled nose. *He's just very weird looking. He almost looks human if he'd keep his mouth shut. What's the deal with those toes? They look just like his fingers – fat and sticky. Now where have I seen fingers and toes like that before?*

Seth continued the introduction while Nick studied his new acquaintance. "We met many years ago while I was attempting to reclaim a priceless heirloom from England. It was rarely moved and was the only opportunity I had to retrieve it while it sat in a temporary location. However, I wasn't the only one."

"Let me guess, he was also there to steal the heirloom," said Nick issuing a thumb at Clievan.

"Steal is a strong word. England stole if first, so technically we were reclaiming previously stolen property. And yes, Clievan along with two others working independently and a team of three. It was a boisterous party, let me tell you!

"We found ourselves in a real bind, two of the independents began fighting while Clievan and I watched from under cover. I had no idea he was there. I had to act fast before security arrived, so I disguised myself as a security guard. I ran in yelling at the others, 'What are you doing here!' I pretended to press an alert button in my jacket hoping they would scatter allowing me to walk away with the item. I didn't fool anyone. They rushed me. I was able to quickly subdue several, but a masked woman appeared from nowhere. She was tough."

"He was really getting his butt whipped by the girl," laughed Clievan.

"Hey! She was very skilled at several martial arts and every bit of six feet tall."

"Yeah, especially Jiu Hits You!" Clievan laughed out loud at his witty burn.

"Anyway, he helped out with the woman by," he regarded Clievan then turned his attention back to Nick, "uh, surprising her. About that time the real security came in. There were too many, so Clievan grabbed the heirloom, I grabbed the woman and we all left through the ceiling."

"And we've been best buds ever since," added Clievan.

"I wouldn't go that far but he did eventually turn into a great finder of things," Seth finished.

"You were able to just escape through the ceiling?"

"Yeah," Clievan said moving a stubby hand through the air like a kid pretending it's an airplane. "We just flew right out of there like we had wings," he chuckled.

"I'm just trying to figure out what's going on. You don't have to make fun," Nick said annoyed at Clievan's remark. "Why did you help the woman?"

"I'm not sure," Seth replied. "I just couldn't leave her behind. There was something about her that made me feel strongly about helping."

"Why didn't you take the heirloom for yourself, Clievan?" Nick questioned.

"Yeah, Clievan. Why don't you tell him what happened with the girl?"

"Oh, you are a funny guy Seth," Clievan said. "She kicked me in the eye, then ran off with the heirloom," he said holding a large hand over his right eye as if the event just happened.

"A gecko! That's it!" Nick yelled then instantly wished he hadn't said it aloud.

"What?" replied Seth.

"Oh, nothing. I thought I saw a, um, gecko in the window. I'm a scientist, I like geckos," he said as blood rushed to his cheeks. "Please keep going."

Seth released a short uncomfortable laugh then said, "For all the trouble and essentially saving her from prison, she goes and betrays us both. I haven't seen her again."

"You sure are full of stories," said Nick trying not to stare at Clievan. *He has fingers and toes of a gecko. That's so weird!*

"So, where're we going," asked Clievan?

A Trip to Egypt

Trey woke in a puddle of drool with the game looping the opening screen. Incessant bleeps and bloops of the archaic soundtrack drilled through his skull. He wandered groggily into the kitchen for another bite of Aunt Kathy's lasagna, wondering when his mom would return.

Trey stopped in the hallway. Confused in a sleepy stupor, he stared at the mysterious woman in dark jeans and an 80's style jean jacket finishing off the pan of lasagna.

"Trey!" she said in a throaty Arabic accent. "This is fantastic! You should really give Kathy my compliments," she said taking a heaping enthusiastic bite.

Recognizing her as the woman from soccer practice, he overcame the startling moment. He turned to dash back to his room for his phone, but before he could take more than a few steps, the woman subdued him on the floor.

She stood above him holding her right boot to his chest and said in a friendly manner, "Listen. I'll let you up. You do not need to fear me."

"Okay," squeaked Trey.

Catching his breath, he rose slowly never removing his eyes from hers.

"Who are you and why are you in my house?" he asked firmly.

"My name is Lyza," she said as they returned to the table. "I knew your grandfather Patrick."

She took another bite of lasagna then said, "Kathy left you something very important today. I'm here to help you keep it safe. You must never show it to anyone."

"So she said," Trey replied. "Why? What is it and why is some dumb old artifact so important?"

"That dumb old artifact is a piece of three items that together wield great power. The other two are hidden safely in different parts of the world but are close to being discovered by people that should never possess them. Your grandfather helped us recover and protect ancient relics for many years. Without him, the forces against us would have surely prevailed by now."

"What do you mean by forces against us?"

"We'll get to that later. I need to ask you a few questions that you must answer honestly and without too much emotion."

"You broke into my house, attacked me and ate my lasagna. Sure. I can totally trust you."

She sighed then asked, "Did your father ever tell you about –" Her eyes shifted over his shoulder then she screamed as she threw Trey to the ground, "Get down!" She twisted her body as a stone bladed knife nearly pierced her chest.

"What was that!" shrieked Trey.

"Stay down! Don't move unless you have to!"

She jumped up in time to intercept a hooded figure with a belt full of knives holding one in each hand. She threw lightening quick arm blocks, careful to avoid the jagged blades. She drove the attacker back with a powerful front kick. Another hooded attacker crashed through the living room window diving into the formidable woman with great force. She used the momentum to hurl the attacker against the wall. She rolled to her feet leapt into the air, then dropped a powerful axe kick onto the first attacker ending his fight.

A third entered the back and grabbed Trey by the foot while Lyza was occupied with the second.

Trey shrieked for Lyza to help then kicked the third in the forehead dropping its hood to reveal a face of crooked black teeth and pale scaly skin. The creature had thin strands of oily hair drooping into cloudy eyes.

Trey screamed in fear, then quickly stood as the creature did likewise. It swiftly attacked Trey by grabbing at his arms. Trey defensively fought off the creature then reflexively leapt into the air closed his legs around its neck, spun it, then slammed the grotesque head into the floor. He kicked up from the floor to his feet surprised at his swift actions. He then stomped it a few times for good measure.

Lyza ran to him and said, "Go! Now!"

They ran out the front door to a silver sports car parked at the curb. Two ghastly creatures stumbled out of the house joining three more sprinting at an astounding pace. One tackled Trey sending them both sprawling to the damp grass.

"Lyza!" Trey screamed.

She spun around in time to judo hurl one into the car while slyly snagging a knife from its belt. She then plunged the stolen knife into the skull of another.

Trey stood prepared to run when he was deafened by gun shots.

Blam! Blam! rang from across the yard.

The beast that tackled him lurched backward then its head exploded in a cascade of greenish gray goop.

Two more blasts targeting the others resulted in similar destruction.

"Mr. Johnson?" Trey said bewildered as he watched his elderly neighbor methodically ravage the assailants with a pump shotgun. Each shukshak signaled a new shell ready to explode into action.

Lyza extracted the knife from the dead skull then flung it into the chest of the one she tossed into the car. It staggered into the road where Mr. Johnson, with a single blast, repositioned its head into an arch pattern of blood and flesh onto the street.

He grabbed the gun by the stock, walked briskly to Trey then said with a comforting hand on his shoulder, "Son, are you ok?"

"I don't know, Mr. Johnson. I'm pretty freaked out."

Trey turned to Lyza. His eyes were as big as grandma's pancakes.

Mr. Johnson said to Lyza, "You need to get him outta here."

Sternly she commanded, "To the car, Trey. We need to leave, now."

"But I –"

"Now, Trey. We don't have time. There will be more." Her eyes were cold and dark. Shadows from streetlights cast a sinister shadow across her former stunning face turning it to something – less.

"More! What? But –"

She gently pulled the reluctant teenager to the car and opened the door.

"Get in." She commanded. He refused. She softened then said, "Please." She almost seemed sincere. He didn't move. He was scared like a small child in the dark. He wasn't just refusing, he was immobile – in shock. Then she continued bluntly, "Do you want to stick around and wait for the rest to show up or would you like to get in the car and drive far away? Hmmm?"

Trey glanced worriedly at the woman then toward the house, seeming to understand the situation. He received an approving nod from Mr. Johnson then said distantly, "Away. I would like to be far away, please." He then sat in the car, fastened the seatbelt and didn't say another word until they hit the freeway.

"What *were* those things?"

"I'm not sure you're ready for that answer," she said, glancing in his direction.

"Try me," he replied sternly.

"An evil king's roggletts."

"What the heck is a rogglett?"

"Like a minion but nastier."

"Where'd they come from?"

"Kathy told you what she knows of your grandfather's ancient Egypt story? She told you about the kings?"

"You mean the one in Egypt? The bad one?"

"Yeah. That one. There was also a good one. After King Khaitu, the bad king, was banished in a rebellion led by his seven sorcerers, a group of his loyal guard attempted to recover the lost relic that contains his essence. They must have found a way to reach the Etherios and were turned to these creatures."

"Banished king? Sorcerers? What are you talking about?" Trey said confused.

"I know," she said. "I told you you weren't ready."

"So, what you are saying is that we almost died because of this stupid thing Aunt Kathy gave me?"

"It's much bigger than that," she said. "Khaitu is a powerful being from an alternate reality. He led a reign of terror across the multiverse. Your Earth was just another stop on his long list. He raised seven ancient spirits from the Earth, then granted them each certain powers that would complete his transition to immortality: water, wind, fire, physical, time, healing and the last bound the seven to grant immortality. Witness to horrendous acts, the seven vowed to stop him at all costs becoming the Order of Hsekh. In the ceremony intended to grant Khaitu immortality, the Order imprisoned him in a relic and then sent the relic to a realm of spirits and ghostly creatures, the Etherios."

"Why didn't they just kill him?" asked Trey.

"Khaitu can't be killed with ordinary weapons, and other than those wielded by his personal demon guard, weapons were banned from the ceremony grounds. One of the Order, Commerand, was killed during the ceremony, complicating the process. A curse Khaitu placed on the seven so they would remain loyal overtook his body. The rest of the Order transferred their essence into individual relics to avoid the curse, then their relics were dispersed all over. Commerand, however, was not able to fully die. He became trapped in the curse and is now leading the effort to release the evil king."

"That sounds a little more serious than a bunch of creepers wanting their toy back."

"I wasn't aware until now that Commerand knew what your Grandfather left you. He may even know the location of the Eye of Kartho," she said distantly.

"Eye? What's that?" asked Trey.

"Nothing. It's nothing. You handled yourself well back there."

"Six years of Yondo Jiu-Jitsu finally paying off," he said proudly. "Who are you, really? You said you knew my grandpa. How?"

"I'm originally from Egypt, south of Cairo. I lived there for many years until I became a protector of the ancient relics and artifacts. I help the Order and others, including your grandfather, to keep Khaitu bound in the Etherios. We periodically find and hide the artifacts so Commerand can't acquire them."

"Did that guy kill my grandpa?"

"I don't know what happened to Patrick. I wish I knew. We're still trying to find out."

"Do you think he's still alive?"

Lyza fidgeted. She bit her lip then answered, "I don't know. I want to believe he is, but it's been so long."

Trey's voice saddened as he looked at his feet in the cramped floorboard. "I never knew him other than the stories Dad told, but now I'd like to. Dad always made him out to be this great brave man. No one could stop your Grandpa; he would often say during a story of one of his adventures."

"No one ever could. That's why I'd be surprised if he wasn't still alive." She startled herself with the comment and quickly added, "But don't get your hopes up. We haven't found him yet and he's most likely....well....you know."

"Yeah I know. He's probably gone for good."

"He knew you well. Your dad told him stories of you all the time. Always kept him up to date on you."

"Aunt Kathy told me today about Dad and Grandpa. I didn't know before. I'm not sure what to think about it."

Trey's emotions often surfaced during conversations regarding his father – angry emotions. But this time was different. His heart thumped for his lost dad like never before. His mind raced, playing back old memories – trying to make sense of who the man was.

"Yes. He hated that you couldn't know each other. He thought it was wrong. But Grandpa insisted. Which was probably the right thing."

"If you say so." Trey was silent for a minute. "Do you know my dad?"

"No. I've never met him. It was always protocol to not have contact with our own or colleagues' families."

"Oh."

Lyza thought he sounded disappointed with her response but had no further recourse to make him feel better.

"If that Katie guy is locked away in the...what did you call it?"

"Khaitu and the Etherios."

"If he's there, why put so much effort into the artifacts? What's it matter if the sorcerer dude gets them?"

"When Commerand was killed, the binding process was disrupted which left a small probability that Khaitu could free himself. We don't think that will happen, but there is that possibility. Additionally, if Commerand were to acquire all of the relics, he would be able to free Khaitu on his own. One of the artifacts could possibly give him the ability to recover the relics if he could find them. That artifact is on Earth, and he might know where it is."

"Oh. Okay. Why not just move that one somewhere he can't get it?"

"It's protected in a way that I don't think anyone would be able to recover it, including Commerand."

"Okay then. Back to why all the fuss?"

"We have to take all precautions."

"I think I understand. Better safe than sorry."

"Exactly."

"This is all so crazy. I must be dreaming. NO. This is definitely a nightmare."

"You'll be safe with me."

"Safe! With you? I haven't felt safe ever since I met you. I don't even know you. How can I trust your story is true? I can't trust you either."

"I know. But you're better off with me for now – unless you would like me to take you back to the rogglets," she said with a mischievous smile.

He jumped back and sat upright in the seat. With wide eyes he said, "NO! No thank you. I'll take my chances with you."

She looked at him softly and said, "We'll settle

some of this out and get you somewhere safe."

He calmed and said, "Ok. I guess that's good enough for now. Tell me more about you. How'd you get into the ancient relic business?"

"I guess, well you know, I don't really know." Trey thought she was evading the question – stalling. "My father was a very important person. He was aware of magical items. He believed man had no business dabbling in the enchanted and forbid them. After he died, I married a big jerk. He was always forcing people to do things they didn't want to do. It didn't last. I kicked him out ...way out. After he was gone, and considering my father's aversion for magical things, I focused on keeping the relics and artifacts away from the bad guys."

"When did you meet my grandpa?"

She smiled and looked as if she were reminiscing on a lost romance, "Oh, I've known Patrick for many years. We go way back."

Trey curled his face. "Really? Way back? Back to when you were, what, twelve? How old are you? Thirty-two? Thirty-three?"

She brought her eyes back to the road. "Yeah. I'm thirty-three. Good guess. What I mean by way back is that we've done so much together, it seems like we've known each other for a lifetime. Your grandfather was something special. He always had a joke handy. He was such a pleasure to work with. I met up with him every chance I could get."

"I wish I had known him."

"Me too. You would have loved him."

"Why didn't he ever come see me?"

"We have to work anonymously. If Commerand or anyone else working with him found out Patrick had a family, you all would be in danger."

"Like we are now?"

"I don't know how he found out. That's something I hope to learn soon."

"He didn't come around so he could protect us?"

"Yeah. That's what we do, protect those we love."

"I see. As crazy as it all sounds, it makes sense when you say it that way."

After a few minutes Trey asked, "Can you tell me a story? A story about grandpa?"

"Oh gosh. There are so many." Her eyes searched for a vivid memory. "Ah yes! You probably haven't heard this one," she said. "There was once this time when he and I were in Managua, Nicaragua. There was an attack by rebel forces on a party. Four people including the host were killed. The guardian of a relic was taken hostage along with several prominent businessmen and government officials. We hoped to rescue the guardian.

"We arrived in Costa Rica then hopped over on a couple early 1970's motorcycles. I remember racing him along the coast of Lago Cocibolca." She shivered in her seat. "That was exhilarating. There's nothing like the wind rushing past your face at 150 kilometers per hour.

"We were stopped at the border. Usually there wouldn't have been a problem, but the political situation was dire, and the weakening dictatorship wasn't letting anyone in. Patrick wasn't generally a man who backed down from a challenge. He sized the three guards up in about a minute's worth of conversation.

"I can almost hear him now," she smiled wildly and said in a lower tone as she pretended to sound like Trey's Cajun-accented grandfather, "I dell you what, slick. Ow bout you let us throo if I c'n beat y'all in a game of poker, if I c'n take dat big guy over dere in an arm wrestle and if I c'n successfully dodge ten of your best punches. If I fail at all three, I give you each twenty U.S. dollars.

"Woo Ha ha! I didn't know what he was doing. I thought for sure he'd lost his mind. I was pretty scared he just got us into a pile of trouble. These guys looked serious and carried military rifles. The lead guard Patrick was speaking to looked back at his colleagues, said a few sentences in Spanish, then turned expressionlessly to your grandfather who wore a cheesy grin. I mean, how could you not love this guy. He was negotiating with border guards when their country was in turmoil – smiling like a pig in a mud pit."

"Really? He did that? How'd it turn out?"

"Terrible. He got beat in the card game, lost the arm wrestle and was nearly knocked out on the first punch."

"They didn't let you through?"

"No! That's the funny part. They let us through. They couldn't stop laughing at this American who they beat up and took sixty dollars from. I guess they didn't feel like we were a threat – just idiots."

"Why would he risk all that if he wasn't sure he could beat them?"

"Who knows. Maybe he could've beat them. If there is one thing your grandfather knows, its people. I think he did it on purpose and he knew they would let us through after they felt like they humiliated him."

"I would have freaked."

"Like I said, he was an amazing man."

She remained silent on that last comment. Trey settled in the seat for the rest of the westerly drive on I-66. She exited the interstate highway, turned down several narrow-paved roads, then ended the drive thirty minutes along a gated overgrown path with dense forest on both sides.

"We're here," she said.

"Where's here?" he asked.

"Follow me," she said getting out of the car.

He stumbled out after her into the cool night air. An owl hooted in the distance. Frogs and insects played a moonlit symphony. A pulpy aroma comforted his heart.

"Where're we going? What about my mom? Oh my god! She can't go back to the house!"

"She's with Kathy. She'll be ok."

"Kathy? She's just a crazy old woman," he said.

"Kathy is more resourceful than she looks. Your mom is in good hands. Plus, there's nothing we can do for her here."

"What are we doing again?" he said as they approached a dilapidated well.

"We have to get to Africa."

"Africa!" he cried. "How does driving us into the middle of nowhere gets us closer to Africa? And why Africa?"

"There are other ways to travel," she said.

"What do you mean?" Trey asked getting a little excited. "Are you saying this old well is some sort of portal? We just jump down in it and it'll take us to Africa?"

"If you jump down that well, the only place you'll be transported is to the hospital. That's just an old well."

"There it is," she said squatting next to a carved stone protruding from the ground a few paces away from the well. She produced a small metal object from inside a blue locket dangling from her neck. The locket was decorated with a single white daisy flower.

"What's that?" he asked looking over her shoulder.

"A key."

After bending and twisting the key into a triangle within a circle, she said, "Hold onto me."

"What?"

"Just grab my shoulder!" she cried impatiently.

After he gripped her shoulder, she closed her eyes then said, "You may feel a little weird when we land."

"Land? What?"

She took a breath, then touched the metal object to the stone.

Whomp, Whomp, Whomp Trey felt in his ears as the pressure around him become unstable. His body twisted unnaturally, like he was an orb of silly putty being spun by a toddler. He lost his stomach in a sensation of falling then an abrupt acceleration forward came to a sudden stop.

Trey fell onto his hands and knees. He slowly raised his head, braced himself with one arm, then shielded his eyes from the bright sunlight then looked back down.

"I think I'm gonna puke," he said looking at the dry cracked ground. His throat grasped for moisture.

"That was intense," he continued. "It felt like my insides were trying to get outside." He lurched, attempting to hold back the lasagna from a few hours ago. He released several hacking coughs but didn't vomit. "Oh my god. That was terrible. Let's not ever do that again."

"You'll get better. Don't worry."

"What was that?"

"It's sort of like a teleporter."

"Really? How does it work?" he asked regaining his wits.

"I form this key into the shape of the diagram on the stone located where I want to be. See there?" she pointed to an inscription on the stone at their feet.

"And you just touch it to the stone?"

"Yes....and think about where I want to go." she added. "That part is important, especially if you get the shape wrong. You have to be careful with this magic. You certainly don't want to be fluxed out."

"Fluxed out?"

"Yeah. Sort of like being stuck in the middle. I'm not sure there's a way out. You just keep flowing without landing anywhere. The key also powers the portal. Without it nothing would happen."

"How did they get here?"

"The ancients placed them thousands of years ago, I believe in preparation for Khaitu's immortality ceremony."

"The ancients? Are they the same as the Order?"

"Yes. The same."

"This is all so cool. My science teacher would freak out if he knew teleportation existed. He's studied it for years."

"A science teacher you say? I would like to hear

more about him. Sounds like an interesting guy."

"Yeah. I think you'd like him." He looked at her carefully then said smiling, "He would definitely like you."

She smiled at his compliment.

"Where are we and why is it so bright?" he said continuing to squint.

"Egypt," she said placing the key back in the locket. "It's mid-morning here."

"This is so awesome! I can't believe I just teleported to Egypt! Wait until Marcus hears about this!"

"I think we just keep this between us for now," she said then turned away from the solitary stone protruding from the arid desert floor. "Let's keep moving. We have questions that need answers."

Trey rose quickly, instantly retook a knee then said, "Wait, I think I'm gonna be sick." He hung his head ready to gag. "Nope." He tried to force steadiness through his body. "I'm okay," he said hesitantly. "Maybe just another minute," he finally said cautiously.

Trey regained his feet, briefly wobbled unsteadily then they slowly hiked North on a paved road toward buildings in the distance.

"In that story you told me about Grandpa, you didn't get to Costa Rica by plane did you."

"No. We didn't."

"Why didn't you just port straight to Nicaragua?"

"There isn't a portal there. Usually the guardians of relics stay close to portals, but it was an important meeting that our guardian couldn't miss. In hindsight, we realized that it may have been a trap to separate him from a quick escape with an elaborate political attack to cover their real intention."

"Ah. Got it," Trey replied but didn't really understand the basis for her explanation but understood they were after the relic.

Shortly after taking to the road, a car stopped just in front of them. The driver jumped out and ran towards them. Trey stepped back, ready to defend himself. Lyza stood motionless.

The driver knelt in front of Lyza. With his covered head lowered and an arm bent above his head showing a tattoo of a long shield with wavy lines he said in Arabic, "I am Alain, how may I be of service?"

Trey looked at her with an anxious expression.

"We need a plane, and I need to make a stop in town," she replied in Arabic.

"As you wish," he replied, then opened the door for Lyza.

"This is Alain. He will help us," she said.

Alain made a brief call and then spoke to them in Arabic.

"What's going on?" asked Trey to Lyza.

"Alain has a friend with a plane, but first, we must visit the Phoenix after we get some rest."

"A plane? For what do we need an airplane? You have a lot to explain lady."

She cut her eyes and gave half a smile at him.

They arrived at an off-white stand-alone wood paneled building in a tiny town. No one was there.

"We'll be safe here. There's a room in back and a shower. Go get some rest. I'll be out here if you need me."

"Trust me. There's no way I'm sleeping after all

that."

"You need the rest we have a long day. So please try."

Trey washed off, then laid down in a soft queen-sized bed. The shades were pulled tight cutting off all but a sliver of light probing the room. After spinning the day in his head, he drifted off to sleep.

He woke to Lyza speaking with someone in the other room. Trey groggily snuck to the door to listen.

"Are you sure it was Don's office? I mean, we haven't heard from him in so long. Why would he keep it from us?" he heard Lyza say.

"I don't know, but you need to check it out. There must be something there to draw the Phoenix's attention," said a high-toned male voice.

"Do you think the Phoenix knows we know about the office?" asked Lyza.

"Most likely. I'm sure he was involved in relaying the info. He probably didn't find anything and hopes we do," the male voice replied.

"Don and the Phoenix worked closely together. Do you think Don told him?" asked a squeaky female voice.

"No. I think Don kept it completely to himself. If he told anyone, it would have been Karim," Lyza replied. "I agree we need to see what's there, but Trey cannot be included any further."

"But the prophecy! All the other signs are here. He is in the line and must go on," the male voice asserted.

"He is just a boy, Karim. He does *not* belong here," Lyza said in a more forceful tone.

Karim pleaded, "I am certain it is him! I know

it's been many years, but I'm sure of it."

The squeaky voice added, "If I'm right, which I usually am, we have to see how it further plays out. Keep him close, protect him. No one else is more capable than you."

"Thank you for your vote of confidence Malory, but I cannot take him were I'm going. We don't know what's waiting at Don's and the Oasis is too dangerous."

"My sources say Don's is clear and we have men in the Oasis. They'll be watching and ensuring his safety. Both of your safety," said Karim.

"I appreciate your help but please just keep them out of my way. I won't be responsible for their lives."

"I'll inform them to keep their distance."

"I believe someone is eavesdropping our conversation," said Malory.

"Trey. Please join us," said Karim.

Trey cautiously entered the room to find Lyza, a moderately sized black skinned man in his forties and a brown-headed woman in her late thirties who looked to be of Persian descent. Alain could be seen through a window outside, rocking peacefully in a chair on the front porch.

"Trey, come meet a very old friend of mine. This is Karim. If there's anyone on this planet you can trust, it's him. He's sort of like your grandfather – he helps us protect the artifacts and relics."

"Trey! It's you!" he said jumping up from his chair. Trey grunted to release pressure from a powerful hug. He winced when a small rod-shaped reddish-brown tinted metal charm attached to a neck chain pressed into his cheek leaving a faint impression. "It has been so many years. This is truly amazing!" When he noticed Trey's stand-off expression; Karim glanced quickly at Lyza regained his composure, released the embrace then grasped Trey's hand in one hand and arm in the other. "Lyza has told me much about you and your recent encounters. She says you are a very competent young man."

Trey had the feeling he met this man before – there was an instant connection. Lovers would call it love at first sight, but this was different – more on a friend-level than that of a father/son – like he has with Marcus. He felt comfortable in Karim's enthusiastic hug and wanted to further explore the connection. However, he kept these feelings inside considering he'd never actually met him before. Had he?

"Thank you, sir. It's nice to meet you too," he said guardedly.

"This is Malory," said Karim.

"Hi Trey," she said without leaving her seat.

"Hey," he replied with a low wave.

"You were asleep for nearly two hours. We have one stop before we visit the Phoenix so we must be leaving soon," said Lyza.

"Who's the Phoenix?"

"He's a connected businessman that helps us when it suits him," Karim replied. Trey detected obvious ambivalence.

"Karim, be nice," Lyza retorted. "You'll meet him soon enough," she said to Trey.

"Hungry? There's plenty in the kitchen," offered Karim.

"Actually, I am a bit hungry," he said, understanding the hint to remove himself from the room. "I'll leave you all to your conversation." He then walked into the kitchen where he heard lowered murmuring but couldn't make out any of the words.

He made a turkey sandwich with mustard and lettuce while looking out the window onto boats floating down the Nile in the distance.

"I'm really in Egypt," he said to himself. "This is completely nuts."

"Ready to go?" called Lyza.

"Yeah. I'll just bring this with me," he said holding a drooping sandwich.

"You better grab a plate," she smiled.

They walked back into the main room to join Karim and Malory.

"Be careful out there Lyza," said Karim. "Stay close to her, Trey."

"Yes, Sir. I'll keep her in sight."

"And Trey," Karim said. "Take this. Always keep it on you." He handed him a small gold coin about the size of a quarter. He then smiled and said, "You never know when it'll come in handy."

"Uh, Thanks," Trey said as he took the coin from Karim's hand and placed it into a zipped pocket.

"It is so good to see you, Trey. I hope to see you again soon!"

"Uh, you too, Sir," Trey said uncomfortably.

As Allain turned south, Lyza noticed Trey rubbing his cheek, "You okay?"

"Yeah. Karim's stick thingy necklace pressed into my face when he hugged me. It's nothing. You called him an old friend. He doesn't look much older than you. Like when you said you and grandpa go way back, I think you have your words mixed up."

"Maybe so," she said cutting her eyes at him and brandishing a gorgeous white, smile.

"Are we going back to the portal?"

"Yes. We must go to Shanghai."

"Yes! China! This is so cool!"

Donald Smith's Office

Alain drove them most of the way to the portal before the sand began to deepen.

"Allain, please wait here for us. We shouldn't be more than an hour and a half."

He held his hands together and nodded in acceptance.

Lyza knelt beside the stone. She blew away a thin layer of sand before removing the metallic key from her locket. She bent it into a crescent moon with an embedded half circle then looked up at Trey.

"Oh yeah," he said as he lowered to his knees and grasped her shoulder.

"Are you ready?" she said smiling.

"You know it!" he said with a big nervous smile – unable to contain his delight. His smile faded as he rubbed his stomach.

She touched the key to the stone – the crushing

Whomp Whomp Whomp consumed them.

Trey's insides twisted, his mind blurred and then everything was eerily calm – and dark. Trey fought back the urge to vomit. A crack of light shone through the underside of a far door. A *seal must be loose*, he thought.

"You okay?" she asked.

"Yeah. I'm okay."

"Stay here while I find the lights. It's been a while since I've been to the Shanghai portal. I think," she said as she walked away, "they are over here." Her diminishing voice withered with the passing distance from each echoing footstep.

Trey shielded his eyes from the brightness that soon followed. The room was completely empty – not a desk, chair, window or coffee pot. The only thing, besides the woman and kid was the smooth black stone barely protruding from the center of the white floor as if it were a misfit replacement for a broken tile.

"Let's go, Trey," she said urgently.

He followed her out of the dark wooden door onto a busy sidewalk. The warm moist air stuck to Trey's face reminding him of a time his mom took him to the popular city streets of Washington D.C. on a late summer day. A light breeze blew the reminiscent memory away before he could wrap a longing emotion around it.

Trey looked back at the thick door close behind him. He felt uncertain about stepping too far away from a reliable exit.

They turned left, traversing Old City Shanghai by foot. The colorful pagoda style structures with distinctive upturned roofs looked like enormous cubic bulls while other roofs formed smooth concave transitions. The few blocks they walked were decorated in large buildings interspersed with congested narrow alleyways. People of all nationalities occupied the streets and sidewalks laced with newly constructed buildings – some fancy Chinese style fraternizing with old Chinese heritage complete with hang-dry laundry outside of windows in some cases.

"Does everyone drive scooters?" Trey asked as they passed a lineup of various colored motor scooters parked street side opposite to various open-air businesses selling everything from bead jewelry to live food.

Lyza replied to Trey's fantastic expression with a smile.

They were greeted by a small queue at the ticket machines as they turned into the modern metro station decorated in sterile white columns and overt cleanliness. A woman's voice methodically repeated information in Mandarin. A man in an overcoat pulling a rolling piece of luggage bumped into a teenager submerged in his phone. The teen turned and spouted, most likely insults, at the overcoat man's back, but Trey couldn't understand the language. People mulled about waiting to go home or possibly a local hot spot.

The rude overcoat man pushed past them through a glass door that separated passengers from moving trains.

"Jerk," Trey muttered. The man paid no notice of his comment.

They entered a clean and quiet moderately occupied northbound car. Trey and Lyza sat a few seats down from Overcoat Man who sat in a handicap-only bench next to an elderly man who followed them in. The elderly man wore long thick forehead wrinkles and regarded them with a blank expression. His stocky stature and light skin suggested he was of North Asian descent. Trey nervously shifted his legs repeatedly under the man's glare.

Trey looked away and focused his attention on the city outside the window. The Shanghai Tower with colorful orbs and striking spire rising high into the skyline came into view across the Huangpu River. After it passed, he turned to find the man's eyes locked on his. He remained focused on Trey over several stops.

Overcoat Man began watching loud obnoxious videos on his phone.

Trey glanced at Lyza, noticing her concerned expression toward the aged onlooker.

"Why is he staring at us?" Trey whispered to Lyza.

She quickly broke her attention from the man as if she were embarrassed he caught her looking. "He is of the old day. He doesn't believe foreigners belong here. Just pay him no mind," she said as she regarded the man once more with her head down and eyes up. Her hair fell lightly over the front of her shoulders.

Overcoat man laughed audibly at his phone briefly drawing Trey's attention from the elderly man. The elderly man continued his unwavering stare.

The train slowed to a stop. Several people temporarily broke the elderly man's line of sight as they exited the smoothly opening doors. Trey's eyes shifted rapidly from the floor to the window to the cold grey eyes of the man's piercing gaze. He noticed Lyza shift slightly, bringing her fisted hands to her lap. She was looking at the floor, but not entirely.

"HA! HA! HA!" Overcoat man again laughed aloud.

The car smoothly resumed the prescribed route.

"We get off in two stops," she murmured.

He nodded then forced himself to look out the window.

The train again slowed to a stop. No one entered the cabin while two exited – only a dozen remained, most of whom were studying small electronic devices or staring out the clear windows – unaware of the stress Trey was currently under. Overcoat Man continued scrolling through videos.

The elderly man's gaze continued.

Trey could feel Lyza tense as the train resumed.

Overcoat Man laughed, "Ha Ha Heeey!"

Trey quickly glanced in the elderly man's direction, he pushed back in the seat, flooded with fear.

The elderly Asian man's eyes slowly clouded as he stood – never removing his stare from Trey. The skin of his face shriveled. Ooze erupted from open slits. He produced a six-inch jagged blade then took in a raspy breath releasing it with soggy popping sounds. Small blobs of yellow phlegm flew at them.

Before the shifting rogglet took a step, Lyza launched. She avoided a swift stomach-level jab of the blade. She swept its feet then shoved the airborne rogglet into a pole by its shoulder. Its flailing legs slapped Overcoat Man out of his seat. The blaring phone skipped along the metal floor.

On the ground, the rogglet took sight of Trey. It scrambled on all fours towards him at a lightning pace.

Lyza ax-kicked it in the back, smashing it onto the floor. It released an ear-piercing howl. Trey scrambled over the seats to avoid the calamity. Lyza jumped back in preparation for its retaliation.

The rogglet pressed up with its hands into a standing position seemingly unaffected by Lyza's initial success. It hissed loudly then slashed at Lyza with the knife, of which she countered with a kick sending the knife bouncing off the window. It reached behind its back revealing another. It slashed again but this time followed with a left maul which caught Lyza off guard, sending her stumbling backward. It quickly advanced with the sharp blade raised above its head. She thwarted the attack with a rising block then grasped its outstretched wrist with one hand then placed her other hand on the blunt edge of the knife and with a quick twist took possession of the weapon.

It blocked an immediate neck jab with two hands, dislodged the knife from her hands and twisted her away from Trey.

A woman shrieked in the back.

Trey reached for the knife. Just as he grasped the handle, the rogglet stomped the blade with a thick soled boot. Its haunted eyes tugged at Trey's soul as if it intended to rip if from his body. Trey scrambled backwards next to Overcoat man who cried profusely.

Lyza grabbed the rogglet by a back leg then whirled it into the door on the other side of the car. Her face was blood red. Anger poured from fierce blue eyes. Trey thought they were glowing but was too frightened and too fascinated by her immense strength to be sure. Afterward, he would question how she could man-handle the creature with such ease.

She pried the doors open and with a swift kick, the rogglet rocketed out of the car, slammed into the wall and disappeared from sight.

She turned to notice the remainder of the

passengers, all of Asian descent, huddled against the far end of the car. Overcoat Man laid dumbstruck and whimpering on the floor. The phone continued to blare in the background.

She released a breath, smiled and gave them a respectful bow. She and Trey returned to their original seats.

"What was that? I didn't know those things could change shapes!"

"Me either, Trey. I knew something was up with that guy, but I didn't know it was a rogglet. Commerand must have changed that one to blend in and he now knows we're here. Those things could be anywhere and anyone. We have to be extra vigilant."

"How does he know we're here?"

"He controls them – he is their mind. What they see, he sees."

"Oh. That's bad."

"Tell me about it."

They got off at the next stop then walked toward the exit of the station – scrutinizing every wayward look they received from passerby's.

A chubby Asian man in a tight-fitting black T-shirt and jeans stepped from a white sedan parked in the pickup area of the station. He casually approached them with a wide smile.

"Nǐ jiào shén me?" she cautiously asked the driver for his name.

"Xhau Pingjin, lèyì xiàoláo. Karim sòng wǒ," he replied politely indicating Karim sent him.

Lyza reviewed a text from Karim on a smartphone she removed from her back pocket and said "Xhau Pingjin," under her breath. She nodded at the man then turned to Trey, "This is Xhau, he will take us to Don's office."

Xhau bowed to Trey then turned toward the car. They both took a back seat. Trey appreciated the cool, soft leather compared to the hard train seat.

Lyza communicated directions to Xhau in Mandarin before they sped away in a manner indicating she must have specified they were in a hurry.

They drove several miles along the expressway before exiting onto a four-lane street then turned left down a one-way road. Xhau parked street side of a plain white office building located between two larger buildings. There were no signs indicating a business name or description. A small sliver of grass lined with trees separated the three structures. Xhau remained in the car as Lyza led Trey across a smooth concrete walkway. She picked the locked beige colored metal door then entered into an unlit area scattered with papers, toppled desks and random holes in the walls.

"What? He didn't leave a key under the rug?"

She ignored his sarcastic comment as she moved through the disheveled office. "What did you get yourself into Don?"

"This place is trashed. What do you think they were looking for?"

"I don't know. It doesn't look like anyone's been here in a while."

"Yeah. It's so dusty." He swiped his hand across the only upright desk in the room leaving four lines on the surface. He sneezed.

"Keep a look out for anything out of the ordinary?"

"Out of the ordinary? Like a portal that takes you across the world? Oh, never mind. That's completely ordinary to you."

She looked at him sternly then softened her expression into a weary smile.

"Who was this guy?"

"He worked with us. He was a brilliant man. Strange, but brilliant. He and the Phoenix developed an information system to track and locate the artifacts and Commerand's activities. He disappeared four years ago. Just vanished. We never heard from him again."

"This Phoenix guy seems more important than what Karim led me to believe."

"He's been integral in our mission. Karim doesn't trust anyone."

"And you? Who do you trust?"

"I'm cautious. I've been around guys like Karim and the Phoenix for a long time. I stay vigilant and it usually suits me well."

"Why's he called the Phoenix?"

"I'm not sure. No one seems to know his real name. I was introduced to him several years ago when looking for information regarding an artifact. He knew where it was, so I connected him with Don who became our liaison. I didn't have significant personal contact with him afterward – I mostly know what was relayed through Don."

"Don is the same guy that had this office?"

"Yes. Don Smith. He was American."

"Oh, God. Don't say that name. He haunts me even from the other side of the world!"

"What do you mean?"

"Nothing," he said while avoiding her eyes.

She stopped looking for clues and focused her

attention on Trey.

He looked up and said, "There's just this kid at school that picks on me. His name is Donald Smith."

"Really? Don had a son that would be around your age."

"I'm sure it's a coincidence. Donald said he'd never known his father so it can't be him."

"Must be a coincidence, because Don couldn't stop talking about his son which he always called little Don. I'm sorry you get bullied at school."

"It's ok. I'm not scared of him. I just wish he'd be nicer."

"Some kids don't understand that it's easier to be nice."

"Hey Look at this. She said handing him a torn piece of paper.

"It's some sort of hand drawn diagram, but most of it's missing."

"You're right. It's a piece of a diagram to build a portal."

"You can build portals? I thought they were magical rocks in the ground."

"Yes. They can be built with a special kind of rock. This symbol at the bottom means spirit kingdom or Etherios as we now call it. This other one is the Eye of Kartho."

"The Eye of what?"

"Kartho. It's a multi-dimensional geode. I think this is a piece of a diagram to build a portal to the Etherios."

"Multi-dimensional geode? Are you serious?"
"Yeah."

"Like as in alternate realities and multiple

universes?"

"Yep."

Trey looked down at his hands as if they held the answers to the myriad of questions blistering his mind.

"So the portals, they also take you to a parallel universe?"

"That's right."

"So, what you are saying is that the portals aren't just teleporting us to physical places on Earth. They open a dimension that connects time and space, a dimension that allows us to instantly move from universe to universe?"

"That's it, Trey."

"I don't believe it. It can't be. But how?"

"There are things about your reality you will probably never understand. But we don't have time to figure out how much you can grasp at this moment."

"Okay. But why would someone want to go to the spirit world?"

She furrowed her eyebrows and her voice became intensely sincere. "I don't know, Trey. Let's try to find out."

He put the diagram paper in a zipped pocket and continued to look around. He shifted a few papers around on the floor near a desk. He uncovered a 5x7 metal framed picture. He gasped when he turned it over.

"That's Donald! Donald *is* his son! Holy Crap! Donald's his son! He's younger and skinnier – and happier in this picture but it's definitely him."

"What are you saying over there?" Lyza shouted from the other side of the room.

"The kid I was telling you about, Donald. It's

him. The guy that worked with you and disappeared is Donald's dad. Holy crap I can't believe this?"

She walked to see.

He turned to her still looking at the frame as she approached.

"Wait! Are you the woman his mom thinks he ran away with?" he said as he looked up at her.

"What? What are you talking about, Trey?"

"The rumor of Donald's dad's disappearance was that he ran off with another woman. Was that woman you?"

"No." She looked away and said no again. "Donald and I were close but not romantic. We often met at various places within the D.C. Metro area, but we shouldn't have been noticed."

"But maybe you were. Maybe someone saw you or maybe his mom hired someone to spy on him?"

"I suppose that's possible, but none of our concern right now. Maybe Don told Little Don something or left something behind that can help us. You will have to talk to him."

"I don't think so. His mom went crazy and moved about three years ago. And like I said before, Donald said he'd never met his father, but this picture says otherwise. I wonder why he would lie about something like that? Plus, he hates me. I don't think he'd tell me anything."

She placed a hand on his shoulder, looked him in the eyes and said, "We really need to find out more about what happened here."

"Arggg! Fine. I'll try to talk to Donald. I'm sure it'll be a waste of time. But you have to get me home to do that."

"I know. I'm working on it."

He removed the photo from the frame, placed it in the pocket with the diagram and resumed the search. Lyza drifted off to search a different room.

Something shuffled in the far corner.

"Lyza. Was that you?" he said peering in the area of the disturbance.

"What, Trey? You need something?" she replied from the other direction.

He ignored her.

A piece of drywall that leaned against the wall fell as something moved behind it. Trey saw something furry scurry under loose rubble.

"Was that a rat? Are rats blue in China?" he said out loud to himself.

He inched closer, careful not to disturb anything along his path.

The mound of light rubble shifted when he approached. He stopped then started again. He slowly approached the debris.

Trey crouched next to the small pile. A piece of paper trembled against a torn box surrounded by bits of drywall. Trey slowly reached for the paper and said, "I'm gonna totally freak if a giant rat jumps out."

As he lifted the paper, a sharp spark of electricity stung the underside of his arm. He jumped back, mainly out of surprise rather than pain.

He looked down where the paper was to find an oblong furry blue object about the size of a woman's hand. Four-inch-long hair wrapped around the front and tapered together in what Trey assumed was the back. He inched closer to get a better look. As he slowly approached, he noticed the fur straighten into millions of needle-like spikes. The spherical object looked a little larger than a softball.

"What in the world? I have to get a closer look."

As he did so, the spikes waved in pulses. Miniscule white and blue electric tentacles travelled all along and throughout the spikes of the ball.

He stopped his progress to catch a thought. He pulled back to look around the room for something to touch it with. When he did so, he noticed the electricity stopped and the spikes softened back to long relaxed fur.

"Interesting."

He grabbed a toppled over lamp from the floor. He once again approached the furball. The spikes and electricity returned. Trey gradually dangled the metal end of the cord above it – careful to keep himself as far away as possible. When it reached about a foot from touching the blue ball the electric spikes aimed toward the metal plug and shot out a bolt of electricity that traveled through the cord, exploding the bulb in the lamp. He shielded his eyes as tiny shards of glass rained down.

Trey jumped back and dropped the lamp onto the floor with a crash.

"Trey! Are you ok?" Lyza asked from another room.

"Yeah! I'm fine! I just, uh, I dropped a lamp! I'm ok!"

"What are you," he said looking closer at the furball.

He crouched to where his face was nearly on the floor.

He looked closely and barely inched forward as a tiny pair of eyes peeked from under a tuft of fur, just above the floor. They disappeared when they met

Trey's.

"Oh my god it's a tiny electric furball – and it's alive!"

He looked again and waited until the tightly wrapped fur lifted just enough to expose the eyes again.

"Hey little guy," Trey said with a very soft voice.

It hid its eyes again and spiked its fur. Electricity rolled across its tense surface.

"Easy. Easy. It's okay. No one's gonna hurt you."

It showed its eyes again to reveal big black pupils with a sliver of gold iris.

"I know you're scared little guy. It's ok. I'm scared too."

The electricity died but the spikes remained.

"There. There. That's it."

Trey reached a hand toward the creature. It instantly hid its eyes and electricity returned.

Trey withdrew the hand to his side then laid his head on the floor facing the furball. It retracted the spikes and showed dilated pupils again.

Trey closed his eyes and remained completely motionless. After about a minute he reopened them slowly to find the little guy's eyes less dilated which showcased splendid gold irises. He also revealed a kitten-like nose and mouth with wispy whiskers.

"That's it, little guy. I won't hurt you," Trey continued softly.

Trey closed his eyes again. When he reopened them, he found the blue ball still looking at him but several inches closer. He closed them again. After a few seconds he felt his hair stand like he had been rolling around on a trampoline. He heard a diminutive *tick-tick-*

tick as it approached but kept his eyes closed. His hair stood full on end when he felt something soft press against his forehead. He held his eyes closed for just a few more seconds. When he opened them, he looked upward to meet the golden eyes of a tiny blue creature that was crouched against his head staring back. From this distance, Trey could see thin vertical streaks of electric blue mixed within golden eyes.

Trey thought the little thing was so scared. When it didn't react to him opening his eyes, Trey said, like he would to a puppy or a baby – not expecting a response, "Are you scared?"

It made the cutest, tiniest little sound somewhere between a bird whistle and a chick peep – seemingly in acknowledgement. The sound transitioned from low to high.

"Are you scared of me?"

Its eyes shifted left then back to Trey as if it were processing the question. It then made a different sound from high to low.

Trey thought it was uncanny that it seemed to respond to his questioning but dismissed the thought and continued trying to comfort the creature.

"Are you hurt?"

Again, a sound from low to high.

Trey was certain it was exactly the same as the first response. He questioned whether it could understand what he was saying. He began to test the theory, as would any reputable scientist.

"I'm going to move now. Don't be scared."

Its eyes shifted nervously then back to Trey's as if in acknowledgement.

Trey slowly rolled onto his stomach. The tiny creature inched back but didn't seem too alarmed.

Now looking eye to eye with it he said, "Show me where you are hurt."

It looked down then back at Trey. The lower area of fuzz lifted on the right side revealing a tiny little foot.

"Amazing," he said out loud at the creature's response. "You understand what I'm saying?"

It made the low to high sound as before.

"Low to high means 'yes' and high to low means 'no.'"

It made the low to high sound.

"Ha ha! Excellent! You have the cutest little feet. Just like a tiny little bunny."

He then looked closer. A tack was caught between his toes. It shook its foot a little to show it was stuck good.

"Oh gosh, little guy. That must sting. Can I help?"

It held out the injured fuzzy foot and made a low to high sound.

The tack was awkwardly positioned.

"I'll have to use something else. My fingers are too big."

He slowly pushed himself away before standing to search the surroundings. He found several pens on the floor, grabbed two and returned to the previous position on his stomach facing the injured furball but resting a little further away so he could use his arms. Bringing his arms above his head he attempted to wiggle one pen under its foot. It jumped a little then yipped in pain but seemed to understand what Trey was doing. It looked at Trey then down then placed the injured foot on the pen and returned its eyes to Trey's. Trey then used the writing tip of the other pen to gently pry down on the tack until it loosened and fell out.

The tiny foot wiggled then its eyes widened, looked at Trey then it began hopping up and down. Tiny pops and sparks emitted from its furry body. It peeped and whistled as it performed a sparky dance.

"Ha Ha! Look at you go!"

It swiftly ran to Trey and much like a cat would by walking back and forth, pressed his body against Trey's forehead. Trey brought a hand toward it. It let him touch it. The furry body didn't quite feel like fur – it had a stiffer feel but soft all the same – like a stiff silk, if there were such a thing. He slowly scooped it into his hand then lightly stood, looking the little guy in the eyes. He couldn't tell he was holding anything. The tiny thing seemed to have no mass at all.

"I will call you Sparky. Is that okay?"

It answered affirmatively.

"Trey," Lyza casually called to him.

"Yeah?" he said as drew his attention away from his new friend.

"You don't have to talk to that kid anymore."

He turned his gaze back to Sparky and replied, "Who Donald? Great! Why?"

"I figured out why Don had this place. Come take a look."

"I have something to show you too," he said as he began to walk toward her voice.

Sparky then made a high to low sound indicating his disagreement with Trey.

"What? You don't want her to know about you?"

It answered affirmatively.

"Ok. We'll keep you a secret for now." He then

looked at Sparky with a very serious expression and said, "Do you want to stay here, in this place?"

It made the high to low whistle indicating it didn't want to stay.

"Okay. Do you want to go with me? I may be doing some very dangerous things. You might get hurt again, even worse than before."

It thought about Trey's question then answered with the low to high whistle.

"Okay. You can stay with me. I'll take care of you."

It made a soft whistle. It then sparked and disappeared.

"Sparky! Sparky! Where'd you go?" he said in a low panicked voice. He bent over to search the floor thinking he dropped him.

Several sparks popped on the floor in front of Trey then Sparky appeared. He sparked and disappeared again. Several pops to his left drew his attention just before Sparky appeared on his left shoulder.

"That's an amazing trick!"

Sparky made a playful peep then sparked away again.

Trey was unsure where Sparky had gone but confident he was still with him.

Trey carefully walked in Lyza's direction, dodging overturned waste cans and large empty boxes that could have held the reams of paper scattered about the floor.

"They even looked in the ceiling," he said as he crunched pieces of collapsed ceiling tiles.

"What is it? What'd you find?" he said curiously

as he approached.

She ran her finger over a smooth six-inch by six-inch flat stone sitting next to a larger stone housing encased in what looked like a podium made of copper wire. Two large copper rods exited the structure into the wall.

"What is it?" he asked again. He glanced to his shoulder, expecting to see a blue fuzz ball looking back.

"A portal."

"Really? A portal like the one we used to get here? Can we use this portal to get back to Egypt or better yet, home?" His posture softened and his shoulders inched together as he thought about home. He knew he wouldn't be going there anytime soon.

"No. Don miraculously built a one-location portal. Well, he almost built it. This stone here must be somehow joined to that one."

"And look at that," Trey said pointing to a chunk that had been forcibly removed from the corner of the housing. "It looks damaged."

"Someone must have used the blunt end of this to smash it," Lyza said inspecting a wooden handled ax lying behind the portal.

"What good is a one-location portal, anyway?"

"They are very rare and only used for very specific purposes. I've only heard of one, and it isn't on this Earth"

"Where does this one go?"

"To where we discussed earlier, the Etherios."

"The Etherios? Didn't you say that's were ghosts and Khaitu reside? How do you know that's where it goes?"

"This space here," she said pointing to the small indention in the otherwise solid stone surface, "is where the user would hold the Eye of Kartho. Only with it can one open the portal to the Etherios. Since it was designed one way, the user doesn't have to use a key or worry about getting fluxed."

"Why would he build it then try to destroy it?"

"I've known Don for a long time. He never struck me as someone who would intentionally build a portal to the Etherios. I think what happened was that he was misled to build this portal but tried to destroy it when he realized what he almost built."

"But someone stopped him before he could complete the job," Trey finished.

"It looks that way. Then they ransacked the office looking for the diagram to finish it. The piece we found earlier must be what's left. I bet he destroyed the instructions."

"Probably." She regarded him solemnly then said, "I believe this portal was built for Commerand to use to bring the relics to Khaitu. It is through this portal that they intend to free him."

"Then we should smash it now!" Trey said. He picked up the ax and charged the metal and stone structure.

Before Lyza could stop him, he raised the ax overhead then leveled the blunt end against the stone surface of the housing. The ax bounced off, violently shaking out of Trey's hands – just missing his head as it fell wildly to the floor.

"That thing's robust!" Trey said huffing. "No wonder he was only able to chip off a small piece.

"The stone is nearly indestructible. Come on. There's nothing more to see here."

"We can't just leave it there!" Trey cried.

"It's okay. We now know it's here. We'll send a

team to dismantle it."

"Okay. But you better send them quickly."

Just as they turned toward the exit, four men busted through the front door – not four separate men, four of the same man. They entered in a single file line then spread out blocking the only exit.

"Those are some crazy quadruplets!" Trey exclaimed.

"Those aren't men, Trey."

"Of course not. Why would normal humans attack us when we have these pleasant guys," he replied gravely.

The men's faces melted into bloody, oozing disgust. Their bodies swelled into muscular forms, ripping ill-fitting clothing. Claws emerged from the tips of their fingers.

"Lyza! These are not ordinary rogglets!"

"No, they aren't Trey," she said calmly.

"What do we do?" he said as he moved several feet behind her.

Trey was scared. He was surprised when they were attacked at his house – he reacted out of terror but Lyza and Mr. Johnson did all the work. She also single handily defeated the one on the train while he sat motionless in fear. He now stared down four gruesome formidable beasts and was petrified.

"I'm not sure, Trey. Give me a second to think."

"What do you need to think for! They're right there!" he said as he cowered steps behind her.

She glanced at him – worrisome terror etched on her face. She contemplated a decision that would ensure his safety. But they were trapped. The only way out was through that door – through those monsters.

She prepared to fight for their lives.

The rogglets brandished long knives in each hand as they slowly proceeded in a unified formation toward Trey and Lyza.

Trey heard a popping sound then leveled the palm of his hand in response to the sparks. Sparky appeared.

"What are you doing," Trey whispered. "You can't be here. Go away before you get hurt."

Sparky looked at the ghastly quartet then popped and sparked.

"Yeah. We're about to die! Go away!"

He looked again holding a foot toward the rogglets then looked back to Trey.

"Those guys are trying to kill us!" he continued in a low voice so Lyza wouldn't hear as she was focused on the approaching hoard.

Sparky then made a high to low whistle then sent a bolt of electricity into Trey's hand.

"Ow! Why'd you do th... Oh. You want me to throw you at them so you can do your little sparky thing?"

Sparky hopped and answered affirmatively.

"No way. I'm not sacrificing you so you can try to hurt them. No way. You get out of here!"

Sparky replied.

"What do you mean no? No, you don't want to do it now?"

It answered no.

"You mean you won't get hurt?"

It answered yes then popped onto Trey's shoulder, rubbed itself against Trey's neck then popped back into his hand.

The rogglets continued to steadily approach as

Trey and Lyza retreated.

"Lyza can handle these guys," Trey said to Sparky. "You go away now. Stop fooling around."

He knew Lyza was good but didn't think she could stop all four. Her indecision confirmed Trey's thoughts.

Sparky said no in his whistle language.

"You know she can't win this fight on her own don't you and you think you can help?"

He answered affirmatively. His golden eyes exuded confidence.

"If you think you are such a tough guy, why do I have to throw you? Why don't you just pop over there, do your thing and pop back?"

Sparky looked down and made a sad low sound.

"You can't go that far can you?"

He answered affirming his inability to travel that far.

"So, throwing you is the only way? And you are our only hope?"

Sparky made a low to high sound and hopped again with big beaming eyes.

"Arrrgg! Ok. You better not get hurt. You get out of here when your trick doesn't work."

Sparky beeped in excitement.

Trey and Lyza ran out of room. They had to make a stand. Trey looked into his hand at the cute blue fuzz ball that was quite possibly giving his life for Trey only to have them slaughtered by the rogglets anyway.

Two of the rogglets bared black teeth. They snarled as if victory was already a reality.

Trey held Sparky at his side, unsure if he could actually toss the helpless creature to his death. Trey hoped something else would save them.

Suddenly the rogglets sprinted toward them in full attack. Trey reflexively underhand tossed the tiny creature and yelled, "Lyza! Get down!"

They both fell to the floor as the blue ball sizzled in an ill thrown arc. Trey watched in dismay, knowing he mis-threw Sparky, ending their chance to escape with his help. The bright side, Trey thought, was that Sparky would land out of harm's way.

Suddenly Sparky sparked mid-air then disappeared. Instantly, an immense flash of light erupted amid the rogglets, momentarily blinding Trey.

When his vision returned, he found Lyza regaining her feet and approaching the fallen rogglets. The air was filled with a horrendous odor from burning putrid flesh.

"What was that!" she said in astonishment. "Trey! What was that!"

"I, I don't know!" He stammered. He looked around frantically for Sparky but didn't see any sight of him.

"Let's go while we can!" she yelled.

She led them out of the building. Trey hurtled a downed rogglet.

Trey whispered, "Sparky. Sparky," periodically as they ran.

They rushed out of the office to the white sedan. Trey fell into the back while Lyza took the front passenger seat, startling Xhau who had been asleep.

"What? Huh? Oh!" he spluttered in mandarin.

"Xhau! Drive!" they both said in unison.

Trey silently cried in the back while Xhau drove

them all the way to Old Town Shanghai, rather than attempting the Metro again. He sent Sparky to his death. Had he known Sparky would have died, would he have still thrown him? Trey couldn't get this question out of his head. He felt horrible. The little guy saved their lives. He was a hero. He reminisced on the beautiful big golden eyes of the little creature and how playful he had become when Trey removed the tack. He held his head in his arms pretending to sleep so Lyza wouldn't see his tears.

"Karim," Lyza said on her mobile phone. "It's worse than we suspected."

"How so?" replied Karim.

"He built a portal, but it wasn't complete."

"How?"

"I don't know where he learned how. Karim. It is to the Etherios."

"That is bad. That means Commerand believes he is close to acquiring *all* of the relics."

"Exactly. You have to send a team to disassemble it."

"Okay. I'll do that right away."

"There's another thing. The rogglets – they take the form of people. They could be anyone."

"You saw one?"

"Yeah. It tried to attack Trey on the train and there were four at Don's."

"So, they know Trey is involved. Do you think they know who we think he is?"

"I'm not sure. All I know is the one on the train was definitely targeting Trey."

"How's he holding up?"

She glanced over her shoulder to the back seat.

"He's handling it all really well considering the circumstances. He looks pretty shaken up but is asleep in the back right now."

"Good. He needs to rest. I'll send a team to Don's. You be careful and keep him close."

"Ok. I'll call you later."

She set the phone to her side, laid her head back and closed her eyes amid tumultuous thoughts on how to proceed.

Xhau drove them to the front of the building that housed the original portal from which they arrived. Lyza thanked Xhau for the ride with a courteous bow. After they entered the empty building, she bolted the door behind them. She formed the key into a triangle within a circle and returned them to Egypt in a nauseating flash.

"What's wrong?" Lyza asked noticing Trey's sullen demeanor.

"Oh. Nothing," he softly replied. "Just a little nauseous," he added, hoping she would drop it. He was immensely saddened by the loss of his tiny blue friend and was having a hard time hiding it.

She lowered onto a knee, placed her hands on each of his shoulders and looked deep into his eyes. With a caring voice of a mother to her child she said, "You've had a long day. However, we have much more to do. Hopefully, the remainder of today will be uneventful."

He sighed and looked down and away.

"It'll be ok, Trey. We'll figure this out," she said in a comforting manner then turned toward the car.

They walked the short distance and found Allain reading a book in the car. Lyza rapped on the window, startling him. They drove north with the great black river to their East. Trey noticed when they passed the road that led to where he met Karim and Mallory, looked again to his shoulder then closed his eyes.

After a lengthy drive, Alain brought the car to a stop in the parking lot of a white stoned building fronting a large warehouse surrounded by freight trucks. Trey noticed several armed security guards walking the lot and outside the front office. He thought it was strange to have such tight security at a trucking company.

After they exited the car, she stopped Trey outside the front door and said, "The Phoenix is on our side but don't say anything that might give him more information than is necessary."

"Okay," Trey said with a troubled look.

They entered the drab building and then with a nod, continued past the front desk attendant and several members of security. At the end of the hall, a bulky guard in a navy suit courteously opened the door as they approached.

The room was conservatively decorated. A modest wooden desk occupied the center-back upon entry, a coffee table surrounded by three chairs sat to the right and a big leafy plant stood near the only window. Trey detected a hint of vanilla in the air. A well-dressed man in a grey suit and neatly combed hair greeted them as they walked in.

"It's a pleasure to see you again Lyza," said the Phoenix. He walked to meet them at the side of the desk. "It's been such a long time. You are as stunning as ever – as if you haven't aged a day," he continued and kissed her hand.

"Thank you," she said in an obligatory tone as she pulled her hand away. She nonchalantly wiped it on a pant leg.

"And you must be Trey." He turned and reached out a hand of which Trey took. "Your family's history in our shared endeavor goes back many decades – maybe even much longer." He slowly regarded Lyza then continued addressing Trey, "It is very exciting to finally meet the grandson of the great Patrick Roberts."

"Thank you, sir. It's nice to meet you too." Trey respectfully pulled his hand away, thankful to be released from the uncomfortable handshake.

"Tell me, Trey, how much of your family's involvement in protecting priceless artifacts do you know?"

"I uh, don't really..." Trey nervously looked at Lyza.

Lyza spoke up drawing his focus away from Trey, "He knows very little. The less he knows the safer he is. Patrick kept the family's involvement a complete secret. I suppose you know why I'm here."

"Yes, of course. Don't I always," he said through a Styrofoam white grin. "It is unfortunate that you were attacked in your home, Trey. We are evaluating all information sources to determine how you were discovered." He turned to Lyza, "Commerand is growing stronger. He seeks the artifacts."

He indicated them to sit in the two available chairs. Lyza opted to lean against his desk. Trey took the left chair.

"I don't think Commerand is after the artifacts quite yet, but he is definitely seeking the relics which means the eye may be in danger?" she said.

"Speaking of the artifacts, the sword is no

longer in Somalia."

She furrowed her brow and stood from the desk, "Do you think Commerand already has it?"

"I don't think so. The troll said it was there one minute and gone the next."

What? Did he say troll? Trey was loosely following the conversation prior to the mention of a troll. He was at full awareness now, tossing his attention between the two as they spoke.

"That's coming from a sea troll. He's probably just defending himself," she said.

Trey couldn't believe his ears.

"True, but he wouldn't be around to tell a lie if Commerand came for the sword," the Phoenix replied.

"I suppose you're right. He doesn't leave survivors. I think I know where the sword may be or at least will be and lucky for us we're already heading in that direction. We'll go for the remaining pieces as soon as we leave here."

"That's good. I assume once you acquire them you will re-disperse them around the globe?"

"Of course."

"And the eye?"

"It's safe for now. We'll need a few things," she said.

"Come this way, I have just what you're looking for," he said with a broad closed lip smile.

He slightly pulled a hanging wine glass, opening a small brightly lit room behind the bar. An assortment of weapons and military gear were neatly organized on above ground shelving. Lyza chose a knife she placed in her left boot and a semiautomatic pistol in a shoulder holster. While she filled a pack with ammo, she glanced a small rack of tiny bottles.

"When did you get into potions?" she asked.

"I've been collecting over the past few years. They are from all over the world and some from different worlds."

Looking them over, she said, "I'll take two energy, these two levitation and do you have any fireproof?"

"I believe so, yes, I have three of them."

"This one came from a shaman in central China," he said as he held a tiny green glass bottle for her to see. "It is a cloaking potion. I think it will be handy if you are attempting to recover the eye," he said.

"We will not disturb the eye. It is well protected. Commerand himself wouldn't be able to retrieve it. However, I'll take the potion anyway. Cloaking could be useful."

"Indeed. I would like to add that the eye has been at rest for a long time. It might be wise to relocate it," he replied with an overly anxious face.

"I appreciate your concern; however, we won't be moving it anytime soon. There are more pressing matters at hand."

"Understood."

The Phoenix removed the bottles, then packaged them in a pouch that Lyza immediately fastened to her belt.

"Remember, Energy and Fireproof are to be consumed, levitate should be sprinkled on whatever you want to levitate. Do not, I repeat, Do Not drink the Levitate," he said sternly. "Once applied, it should begin working within thirty seconds. The cloaking potion is actually a gas. When you open it, it will visually blend all that surrounds the gas so that everything contained in the gas will look like the surrounding area," he said urgently as he walked them out. "I will send a few of my men with you. You could use the assistance. Jessie is still really upset. I hear he has a twenty-four-hour lookout for you."

"All the better to stick with just the two of us. I know the area very well, probably better than Jessie. We'll be able to sneak in without being noticed," she said.

"And what about the teacher? He gave my guys a lot of trouble at the airport."

"Let him go. We'll catch up with him in the Oasis."

Trey's eyes grew large, but he didn't say anything. The Phoenix took notice of Trey's changed expression.

"Will there be anything else I can do for you?"

"No. You have been generous with your time and resources."

"And you Trey. Is there anything I can do for you?"

"Actually, yeah. I was wondering what type of stuff you store and ship from here that requires so much security."

"Certainly. This warehouse and trucking company operate as a government contractor. We oftentimes have sensitive and dangerous material here that can be a target for militant groups. We rarely know what we store. The government regularly comes and goes with their issued security protocol." He looked questionably at Trey then continued, "But that's not why you asked the question. As you may already know," he said glancing at Lyza, "I operate a network of, let's call them Information Specialists who gather information regarding the artifacts and relics Lyza has most likely informed you about. I aggregate that information here in our offline databases. If I or our databases were to be compromised, the very important mission the Order was created for, could be thwarted. I retain an expansive guard regiment to protect that information."

"I see. Thanks."

"If that is all, I will walk you out."

He walked them from the building to the car. At the car Lyza turned and said, "Thank you Phoenix. Your assistance is noted and will be rewarded."

"You know I'm not looking for a reward," he said proudly.

"Right. You're more of a power guy," she said smiling as she ducked into the car.

Allain pulled away leaving the Phoenix at the curb.

Trey immediately turned to Lyza. "What teacher were you talking about? My science teacher is in Egypt. Does he have something to do with all of this?"

"We've been following Nick Hampton for some time now, but we can't talk here. We'll talk about it when we land."

"Who was that Phoenix guy? He knows my family?"

"Yes. He works closely with us. He never worked directly with Patrick but acquired information for several of his missions."

"Do you think he had anything to do with Donald's dad's disappearance?"

"No. I don't think he had anything to do with that. While I don't fully trust him, I don't think he would do us harm. He likes to think of himself as the leader of the order. He's a very useful person and is constantly gathering information on the whereabouts of the relics and artifacts. He's also aware of the movements of those that serve Khaitu. To be in his position, he walks a very thin line on what team he plays for. Do you know what I mean?"

"Yeah. He's like a double agent?"

"Something like that."

They continued a northerly route. Trey beheld the sun settling over the western desert, casting brilliant colors onto the clouds above. He drifted off dreaming of holding the hand of beautiful wavy headed girl who reaches for a playful kiss but just before their lips connect, the car came to a stop waking him from the reverie.

Trey looked out the window into a moderately lit area to find waiting a single propeller airplane.

Assauf, a medium sized clean-shaven thin man knelt before Lyza, then greeted them in Arabic.

She turned and said, "Thank you, Alain." She then addressed Trey, "This is Assauf. He will fly us to the Oasis."

She kissed Alain on the forehead before taking a pilot's seat. Trey climbed in back followed by Assauf who sealed the aircraft then sat in the remaining pilot seat. The plane was a four-seater with sizable cargo space behind the rear seats. The engine sputtered to life briefly sending the scent of burnt aviation fuel through the cabin.

They taxied onto the runway after a brief systems check. The plane roared as it picked up speed. It bumped and swayed then gracefully lifted from the runway. Assauf steepened the ascent then banked to the left, steadily rising into the dark night.

Two hours into the noisy turbulent flight, Trey was startled by an unexpected silence. The only sound was that of the wind rushing over the wings of a powerless plane hurtling through a black sky.

Lyza looked calmly back at Trey's wide-eyed pale expression and said, "There's a strip of dry flat land just north of the city. I'll take it down under no power to avoid detection."

"And you've flown a plane before?" Trey asked. "Yes."

"Without engines?" he replied more desperately trying not to show immense fear.

She gave him a thumbs up, then took over the controls.

Trey looked out the window unable to see anything in the darkness – he tried not to panic. Breathing a bit harder than usual, he thought, a *small plane like this probably has a glide ratio of 10:1 and if we are roughly 12k feet in the air we could be on the ground within twenty minutes.*

The steady whir of the wind was unsettling. His stomach tingled and his ears popped as Lyza made several consecutive quick descents – he clinched the arm rest each time.

About eighteen minutes later, she made a final descent leveling out smoothly onto the hard-packed desert floor. Trey was thankful to be safely on the ground. Lyza pulled the aircraft to a stop while Trey released a comforting breath.

"Just a minute. For the dust to settle," said

Assauf as he flipped switches and turned knobs.

Moments later they all exited into the dry cool air.

Trey kicked at a soft layer of sand.

"Leave if anyone other than us approach," she said to Assauf.

He nodded, then waved to them as they walked south in the west Egyptian desert.

After a few moments of walking Trey said while looking at the clear sky above, "To think, billions of gigantic fireballs blast light billions of light years so that we can see just a tiny glimpse of their magnificence. I've never seen so many. The Milky Way is beautiful. I've only seen it in pictures," he said in amazement. "Look! Canis, and Orion! They seem so close out here. Did you know that ancient Egyptians used the star Sirius to predict seasonal flooding of the Nile?"

"Yes," she said smiling. "I have heard that one a few times."

"Of course you have," he said feeling a little silly.

He brought his gaze from above to Lyza. "Tell me how Mr. H fits into this puzzle."

"You're pretty close to him, aren't you?"

He looked at her, trying to decide how much he should share. "Yeah. He's like the father I wish I had."

She looked at him with perceptive eyes before continuing the conversation about Nick, "He seems like a really nice guy."

"He is. He's helped me out more times than I can count."

"We think Nick is looking for the Eye of

Kartho."

"Why would Mr. H be looking for an object to power a portal to the Etherios?"

"I don't know. Possibly the same reason as Don."

They walked a few steps before Trey asked, "How does the eye work?"

"The eye is an artifact Khaitu used to travel between worlds. With this key," she pointed to her locket, "and the eye, one could travel anywhere they please if the holder is powerful enough – no portal needed. Only one with formidable magic could do it effectively without the eye and the key together. Khaitu didn't need a key. With the eye alone, Khaitu's sorcerer Commerand could probably open the portal but would not be able to choose where to go. He would randomly drift until he arrived where he wanted to be. He could also get fluxed which I don't think he wants to do. We do not believe he's powerful enough to will the eye to open the portal to the destination of his choosing. However, he is growing stronger by the day and we can't risk the eye falling into his possession. With it, he could find the relics of the Order and free Khaitu."

"Didn't you say before the key will also power portals?"

"Yes. Just like we have done. But the holder has to know the exact shape or can manipulate the magic of the portal to take them to the destination in their mind."

Trey looked up at the stars as his mind overtook his sense of purpose.

"I think it's time you send me back home. This is over my head. I'm all about the adventure but I almost died three times today! My mom could be in danger and I just learned this world is a whole lot scarier than I could ever imagine. Just take me home please," he pleaded.

"You can't go home. It isn't safe," she said sympathetically.

"What about with Kathy? You said mom was safe with her."

"*She* is safe. No one is out to get her. You, however, are not safe."

"Lady, I haven't been safe since I met you. It couldn't be worse there." He intentionally kicked up sand as he took a few more steps. "It's this metal thing isn't it. I'll give it to you!" He said hopefully. He clutched her hand and said, "I grant this, the disk of uh of Oleradada to Lyza!"

The disk remained in his hand.

"It doesn't work that way, plus, I can't carry it," she said. "We don't have time for this. I agree it is too dangerous for you to be here, but we don't have a choice. We must go on."

He lowered his head, placed the disk back in the pocket and continued walking.

"We don't know why Nick is searching for the eye, how he knows where to find it or why he even knows about it at all. I hope he can clear some of it up for us when we see him later today."

"Really?" Trey said excitedly. "He's here?"

"Maybe," she said. "Did he say anything to you about where he was going?"

"Actually, he did. He said he was travelling to an Oasis in western Egypt and possibly eastern Libya. That's here isn't it?"

"Yes. Anything else about where he was going or what he's doing here?"

"No, we were interrupted before I could ask more questions."

"Has he mentioned any other travels lately?"

"Yeah, he went to China over the summer and Costa Rica before that."

"Costa Rica? Are you sure he said Costa Rica?"

"Yes, he meditated with a wierdo named Che."

"Che! Of course!" she said startling Trey. "That's how he knew to go to China. Did he say how he met Che?"

"No, we didn't get into that. Who is he?"

"Che is a medium. Someone was using him to communicate with Nick."

"Who would want to do that?" asked Trey.

"Someone looking for the eye, needs a properly-built portal and who can't do it themselves," she said.

"So, most likely the same person that convinced Donald's dad to build his portal?"

"Probably."

"But when Don bailed on the task, they had to find someone else."

Lyza gave him a confirming glance. She looked toward the sparkling sky and continued walking more briskly.

"Why are you and Nick so close?"

"What do you mean?"

"In our surveillance we've noticed you spend a lot of time with him. He takes you places, he's at your house often and the way you lit up when I said he was here tells me you are closer than just a teacher/student relationship."

"Oh. Yeah. I really like the guy. I guess it started when he was a judge at my first science fair. I was in fourth grade then. I built this awesome fusion reactor replica. I spent nearly all year designing and building it. Had it not been made of Styrofoam and cardboard, it would have held the plasma as well as any of them," he said proudly. "My dad helped me a lot with it. It was the last thing we did together. Not a week after the fair, he left. I've barely had contact with him since."

Trey became quiet. He rubbed his eyes.

"Go on," she said softly.

"Mr. H worked it out so I could talk about my project to his science classes. I was overly excited about nuclear fusion at the time and would talk to anyone about it, especially middle school kids. So, I agreed. Afterward, he and I spent an hour or so talking about science and performing simple experiments in his lab while my mom waited. It was a ton of fun. We did the one where you mix hydrogen peroxide, yeast, soap and food coloring in a bottle for a fantastic colorful eruption."

"I don't know that one."

"Oh. Well, you should do it one day. It's pretty cool. Anyway, several months after the science fair he asked mom if he could take me to a robotics challenge. She agreed. We've gone every year since then. After that he gradually started doing lots of stuff with me including helping me with future science fair projects. He also helps us around the house, you know, lifting things and moving stuff around. I guess mom thought he was a good role model for me. She must have known dad wouldn't be coming around anymore. I've gotten to know him well and really like him. I was super excited when I finally made it into his science class."

"Do you think there could be more to it between your mom and Nick?"

"No. Nothing like that. At least nothing that

I've noticed. Why do you ask?" He looked at her playfully. "Are you interested? I can talk to him for you if you want." He smiled and they both laughed. "You don't have any competition with my mom. She's at least ten years older than him."

"Yeah," she said looking off distantly. "That age difference can cause problems."

"It's just not like that. Mr. H seems to be a friend rather than someone mom wants around permanently."

"I see. What's permanent anyway. Everything goes away eventually. Change is inevitable."

"Yeah. I guess."

After a few moments of silence Trey changed the subject, "What's the deal with the sword you and the Phoenix were talking about?"

"It's a piece of the three that complete a powerful weapon. It was Khaitu's personal weapon he used to," she looked away - her voice became harsh - angry he thought, "to defeat King Ronodan," she looked back and regained her smooth mezzo-soprano tone, "as well as wreak havoc on many innocent people. However, only a being of great magic can wield it. If ordinary people like you or I try to use it, we will be instantly consumed in flames and die a horrible death. The pieces must never be joined."

"And you know where it is?"

"Maybe. It is most likely with an old friend of mine in the very city we are heading. If this is true, the pieces are too close together. We must find them first, then scatter them across the world.

"The town is just over this dune," she said. "Let's take a quick break before we go any further."

"Who's this friend of yours?" Trey asked as he stretched out his legs while sitting in the sand. "And if he's a friend, why do we have to sneak into town to see him?"

"Well, Jessie isn't really a friend."

"Yeah, I guessed that. Who is he?"

"He's not a nice guy. However, everyone around here loves him."

"If he's not a nice guy, why do people love him?"

"He takes good care of those he lives with. They love and protect him for it. He's in all sorts of illegal activities such as drug and weapons smuggling as well as human trafficking."

"Why doesn't the government come and stop him?"

"The governments are unconcerned with Jessie. He's racked up quite the business with the political unrest of Libya and Egypt. They've made it easy for him to move his goods around as well as provided the necessary environment for his particular services. He's currently in high demand."

"So, what you're saying is that this bad guy is flush with cash and weapons...and we're just going to sneak in and take something from his house?"

"Yeah. That's the plan."

"You're crazy, you know."

"Trust me, Trey. We'll get through this if you do what I say."

"Ok. Sure." He fidgeted with his shoe then took one off. "My shoes are full of sand. I wish I brought boots," Trey said dumping out one of his shoes. "We're here to get the sword?"

"That, and to have a good conversation with your science teacher. He must not attempt to get the eye. It is much too dangerous but more importantly, if he were to somehow succeed, it would be much too dangerous for the entire world."

After a few moments she said, "Let's get moving. The sun will be up soon."

Trey and Lyza summited the dune then snuck into the quiet sandy town. The early morning sun had yet to crest the horizon.

"Follow me closely," she said. "Don't make a sound and keep your movements clean and concise."

"Clean and concise? What's that mean?"

"Just follow me and be careful to not make noise."

"Why didn't you just say that to begin with?"

She gave him a *don't be a smartass* look, then continued slinking around town - careful to stay in the shadows.

She stopped against the wall of a building on the street corner holding out a closed hand indicating Trey to be still. She peeked around the corner to spy two men talking outside a gated residence. One of the men smoking a cigarette, laughed as he playfully pushed the other. The other, shorter and stouter than the lanky smoking man, seemed to be put off by the comment from his cohort.

"Stay here. Don't move unless you have to. Got me?" Lyza commanded.

"Yeah. Just like last time, huh?" he whispered with a grin.

"Just stay here." She handed the pouch she received from the Phoenix to Trey. "Remove the green one and hold onto it." She then continued to study the guards.

"He unzipped the bag containing neatly organized bottles. He took out a green capped bottle. "This one?"

"That's it. If you get into trouble, sprinkle it around you to hide."

Trey looked curiously at the small green bottle then fastened the pouch to his waist.

Lyza studied the guards closely. The men stood facing away from the compound continuing lively banter for nearly thirty minutes before one turned around. Just as the other began to turn, Lyza erupted from her crouch. Trey gasped at her quick movements. In less than five seconds, she launched from behind the building, struck the base of the cigarette guy's skull with the heel of her right boot which propelled her just enough to exert brutal force behind a cross to the second guard's temple. Both men fell to the cold sandy road, unconscious. A soft breeze blew strands of hair across her face. She stood tall with cinched fists at her side as she examined the outcome of her swift actions. After securing the guards, she effortlessly hurled herself over the fence.

Who is this woman? Can I really trust her? Trey thought in amazement as he sat at the corner waiting for her to return. *What am I doing here? This is maddening. What do I do? What if she doesn't come back? What if she does come back? Where will she rush me off to next? I could have died tonight. Mom could have died. She might be in trouble now! Aunt Kathy couldn't protect a poodle much less Mom. God help me!*

He sat for several minutes wallowing in his

thoughts.

"Marhabaan ya tifl," a voice behind Trey stated.

Startled, he turned to find a skinny guy wearing a yellow shirt with an AK-47 in his grasp.

"Ma aldhy tabhath eanh?" the man asked as he looked toward the compound. Seeing the guards down he raised the weapon toward Trey and yelled, "Aaeal maeay! Alan!"

The man rapidly approached and grabbed Trey's wrist, pulling him toward the gate. Trey twisted free from his grip, spun with the twist, then hammered a side kick into the left knee of AK Man. Trey bolted down a side street.

BAM! BAM! BAM! echoed from the automatic rifle. Trey fell to the dusty ground.

Jessie's Girl

Lyza snuck across the desert lawn, careful to draw no attention. She intentionally followed the shadows from the early morning sun. To avoid a guard, she grasped the ledge of a balcony, tossed herself up, then entered an unlocked window.

Getting in was the hard part – everyone inside seems to be asleep. She thought to herself.

She found a familiar meeting room that contained a large table and a dozen rolling chairs. Three large original paintings donned three walls. But no sign of the sword so she continued the search to other areas.

She heard someone approach as she crept down the center carpeted hallway. She quickly and quietly entered a random room. She glanced over the empty bedroom as the footsteps passed.

She slid out carefully and continued down the hallway toward Jessie's office. Suddenly a man opened a door she was passing. She stunned him with a slap to the face, reached past and grabbed his hair, then pulled the door violently smashing his head between the door and the frame. She rammed a front kick into his sternum, propelling him into the room. She closed the door and quickly continued to the office undisturbed.

The office was dark and heavily decorated in hardwoods and shiny indulgences. Knowing Jessie's mammoth ego, he would have surely prominently displayed the sword. However, it could not be found with a quick search.

Looking around the desk she eyed a few open letters addressed to Jessie of no concern. Inside a side drawer she found an oil and gas contract between Jessie's West Oasis Oil Company and that of Phoenix Industries. *This is disturbing. I'll address this with him later.*

Shots rang outside the building. She quickly lunged to the window in time to see Trey fall in the street.

"Trey! No!"

A man with a pistol entered the room. He screamed at her in Arabic.

She quickly tossed a letter opener at the man which he easily deflected with the pistol, but he was too slow for the left cross from her leap off the desk that followed. He stumbled as she quickly disarmed him with a hammer fist sending the pistol to the floor. She kicked the firearm away simultaneously dodging a left hook with a timely straight legged lunge. He caught her with a right jab, then threw her into the wall knocking over a bookshelf decorated with several glass keepsakes. Priceless glass shattered sporadically on the marble floor. Lyza kicked up onto her feet, hurled a book toward the man and quickly followed with a flying side kick. The book missed crashing upon the wall, but the kick was on target, knocking the man through the open door. She followed with a brutal elbow to the right temple which crumpled him onto the floor.

A single heaving breath is all the time she depleted before continuing the search of which was rapidly becoming an escape.

The extravagantly decorated hall of exquisite paintings opened into a restaurant sized greeting hall. A man busted in from across the room. Lyza hurled a small vase toward the attacker, then blitzed him as if she were an all-star linebacker. Without losing momentum she rolled off the downed guard into a sprint, then descended the staircase continuing her escape.

~~

"What's going on?" Jessie said in Arabic to AK-47 man – South African was prominent in Jessie's accent.

Jessie flaunted a deep red robe donning a silver crest on the right chest. Disheveled black shoulder length hair, morning stubble and a look of confusion completed his appearance.

"I found a boy outside the compound. He was looking at Jeffe and Gordon. They were attacked and bound. He tried to run."

"So, you shot him?"

"No. Just scared him. He's locked in a room."

Jessie scowled, "Good. We don't need any dead kids around here. Has the person who attacked them been subdued?"

"No. We haven't found them yet. It had to be at least 3. No one can take Jeffe alone."

"Ok. Get out there and find out what's going on!"

The doorknob jiggled. A slide lock clicked. Jessie entered the room.

"What are you doing here, boy?" Jessie said as he squatted in front of Trey who sat unbound in a chair.

"Nu...Nothing. I was just outside when your goon tried to kill me!"

"So, wrong place wrong time, huh?"

"Yeah! That's it! Can I go now?"

"I find it implausible for an American kid to be all alone on the streets of *my* town, outside *my* house at the very time it is compromised. Don't you find that a little beyond coincidental?"

Trey looked at the bag Lyza handed him on an adjacent table. The green bottle laid undamaged on its side. "Possibly. Or maybe I'm just a curious teenager on vacation with my parents, heard a commotion and followed the sound to where your guy found me."

"That's some attitude for someone in your position." He leaned in really close to Trey, then said in a softer more threatening voice, "I'd watch my mouth if I were you."

Morning breath and whisky dominated his statement.

Trey took the opportunity Jessie gave him by thrusting his hand into the man's adam's apple. Jessie went to his knees gasping for breath. Trey stood then smashed his wooden chair onto Jessie's back taking him completely to the ground. He grabbed the bag and green bottle then fled the room looking for a way out.

Trey rushed past an intersection, AK-47 man yelled, "Walad! Tawaquf alttayira!" He turned in pursuit. Trey crossed a common area with a theater sized tv, marble tables and elegant chandelier. He hurdled a gaudy couch, then punched through a doorway nearly knocking Lyza over on the other side.

"Trey! I thought you died! The man with the gun! What happened! Are you ok!"
"Yeah! I'm fine but we have to get out of here quick!"
"Follow me!" she screamed.
She led them to the garage which held five of the most beautiful cars Trey had ever seen.
"Quick! Find one we can use!"
He searched two Italian sports cars, then said, "I can't get in either of these!"
"Over here!" she said standing by a white convertible Rolls Royce Phantom.
Jumping into the drop top Trey said, "You really have discerning taste!"
She smiled as she brought the car to life. The luxury engine roared as it smashed through the garage door ripping it from its hinges. Taking no heed of the elaborate driveway, she hurtled the car across the yard avoiding delicately placed palm trees and targeting the front gate.
"Get down!" she yelled as three men fired automatic rifles at the approaching vehicle. She lowered her head as she shattered the front gate which ripped off the front bumper and finally released them into the city.

Tiny Island

Nick, Clievan and Seth left early in the morning toward Marina El Alamein on a route south of Alexandria in a clean four-door sedan Seth procured from yet another cousin. The car provided a comfortable ride with plenty of room for the band of misfit adventurers.

"Hey, uh, Seth."

"Yeah Nick?"

"You think you could go any slower? I mean, we're not competing for a racing trophy or anything."

Seth navigated the sedan around a tight corner prompting Nick to grasp the handle as the tires signaled the upcoming end of their grip on the aged road.

"What's wrong with my driving? You weren't complaining when we had those motorcycles after us yesterday." He chuckled then looked at Nick through the rear-view mirror. Nick returned a frown.

"Fine. We can take a break with some

breakfast." He hurtled the car into the parking lot of a rundown diner.

While waiting on the server Clievan said to Nick with a smirk, "So you're looking for a big rock in the desert?"

"I believe it's a crystal geode."

"You believe? You aren't sure what you're looking for are you?"

"Not exactly. But I'm pretty sure it's there."

"Check this guy out, Seth. He comes all the way from the states to search for a rock in the sand that he's *pretty sure* is there. What a doaf. You need to get your head checked."

"Why'd we bring him?" Nick asked Seth.

"Give our new friend a break will ya?" Seth replied to Clievan.

"Ah, yes! Breakfast! Finally!" Clievan said reaching for the plates as fast as the waitress could serve them.

Nick had a coffee and croissant sandwich, Seth a plate of pancakes and juice. The waitress returned three times with Clievan's order. He had two stacks of pancakes, four fried eggs, three scrambled eggs, a heap of breakfast meat, smothered hash browns and a pina colada flavored milkshake.

Nick barely sipped his coffee as he watched in awe, the precision and efficiency of the odd shaped man devour the mass of food. He was surprisingly well mannered – not a smack was heard during the exhibition.

When Clievan was finished with his portion he looked over at Nick and said, "You gonna finish that?"

As if woken from a daze, Nick said startled,

"Oh. No. You can have it." He handed his sandwich to Clievan who replied, "No. The syrup, but I'll take the sandwich too. Thanks!"

Nick passed him the blueberry syrup with which Clievan chased the sandwich. After the sandwich was gone, he finished off the remainder of the bottle of syrup. Seth paid the spectacle no mind as he blankly stared forward, slowly forking in soggy pieces of fried batter.

"I think we've been here long enough. Let's get back on the road," Seth said as he removed himself from the table leaving behind a stack of Egyptian pounds.

Thirty minutes into the drive Clievan held his stomach and said "What's there to eat in here. I haven't had anything since breakfast."

"How can you possibly still be hungry – and so skinny?" gawked Nick.

"High metabolism," He said with a sharp grin.

In just under three hours, they arrived at Emil's.

"You weren't kidding, Seth. The Mediterranean coast is beautiful. I'll have to come back one day for vacation," Nick pondered.

Nick looked out over the white sandy beach to the clear blue sea while Seth and Emil caught up over a cup of coffee at his coastal cottage near Sidi Abd El-Rahman.

"This would be a great place to take your old lady," Clievan said to Nick.

"No old lady for this guy."

"You mean a striking human as yourself doesn't have a woman back home?"

Nick looked at him strangely, "No. But if I had

one, she would love to come here. It's beautiful isn't it?"

"Ehh. I prefer the city. People are more fun when they're stressed out and overly concerned about unimportant stuff."

Nick gave him a sideways look and said, "You're a weird dude, Clievan."

"You know it!" He then strutted off toward the beach leaving Nick to relax in a chair on the back porch – enjoying the brisk morning breeze.

"Really? The Order attacked you?" asked Emil as he sat heavily in a cushioned wooden chair. His light blue button up shirt decorated in multi-colored flowers bunched around elastic waisted white pants. He wore a thick black moustache that seemed more like a filter for the foamy coffee than an aesthetic facial feature.

"I believe so," said Seth to Emil. "At least one of them had the mark."

"That's unbelievable, cousin. They haven't been active for centuries."

"I know! I was also surprised. But this guy, Nick, there's something about him. Something a little interesting but mostly naive. I'm not sure he understands what he's looking for. He's very confident and can handle himself in a fight. He's also super smart. I know he can help recover the stone. But what is it that he's looking for that has the Order out to stop him?"

"The order, maybe. But most likely it's a directive of the Phoenix. Whatever it is, I hope you don't find it," said Emil gravely. "It might be easier for you to look for the stone separately. Leave this American to his business. At least you won't have the order or the Phoenix to deal with."

"Well, that's not exactly true. You know what the stone is. The Order doesn't want that to fall into the wrong hands either."

"True. The stone also doesn't need to be in the possession of the Phoenix. You're screwed either way so you should just work as a team, find out what he's searching for and deal with it then. Why do you think Soliman is looking for the talisman?"

"I don't know. I don't think he knows what it is. I get the impression he is acquiring it for someone else, but I don't know who."

"Who else could possibly know about it? Do you think it's the Phoenix?"

"I don't think so. Why would he be seeking out the artifacts. That would go against all protocol. He would surely be discovered. However if so, I hope I find it before they do."

"You know, you two look alike. Not quite twins but very similar," Nick said entering the room.

Seth and Emil shared a chuckle.

Emil responded, "What are you talking about? We look nothing alike. His, er, feet are a completely different shape."

"Mine were always bigger and more spectacular," Seth added.

"But mine are stronger and faster. You never could beat me in a race."

"Pshhh, whatever. You only wish your, uh, feet were as beautiful as mine."

"Hey guys, can we stop comparing feet now? Shouldn't we be moving on?" added Nick then turned toward the car.

"Yeah, let's get going," said Seth. "Where's

Clievan?"

"Clieeevaaaan!" Seth yelled. Nothing. "Clieevaaaan!"

"Yes Seth," Clievan said about three inches from Seth's ear.

"Jeeess! Stop doing that," Seth exclaimed.

Clievan walked toward the car snickering.

"Is it time to go yet?" Clievan rebuked. "I'm tired of waiting on y'all," he said with a sly smile and terrible cowboy accent.

"It's been a while since you've been down there, Seth. Things have changed dramatically with all the political drama in Cairo and Tripoli. You should have no trouble moving around in the city. However, if you are to get stopped, tell them you're looking for Jessie, but by no means should you seek him out. If you can avoid interactions with him, you will be doing us all a favor."

"Note taken."

"Hopefully this ride won't be as exciting as the one from the airport," Nick said jabbing at Seth as they pulled away from Emil's house.

"Only If you think sand is exciting," Seth replied.

Indeed, sand was all they saw. Once they turned south from Garawlah, all he saw were miles and miles of maddening sandy road broken by the occasional rock formation that gave way to more sand.

Several hours later, they rolled into the Oasis village, which was of no surprise to Nick, comprised of sand-colored block buildings scattered palm trees surrounded by a vast desert. The sun beat down on the travelled sedan. In the center lay an ancient fortress which held a temple to the Egyptian god Amun Ra, now eroded by years of harsh desert weather. The wind blew furiously as they passed women and children scurrying for shelter.

"What are we looking for Nick?" asked Seth.

"It's a shop with a sign hanging that displays a long shield with wavy horizontal lines." Seth gave Clievan a concerned glance.

"Alexander's home is just around the corner. We must take cover to let this sandstorm to pass."

They pulled up to a commonly made sand brick structure. The three rushed in protecting their heads and eyes from pelting particles. Upon entering the home, they met a tall, burly man with a thick, black beard. He wore a purple accented beige turban.

"Cousin!" the man exclaimed joyously upon seeing Seth. They grasped each other strongly.

Seth pushed arm's length away, removed one hand from Alex's grasp then said, "Nick this my cousin, Alex. Alex, this is Nick from Washington D.C."

"Good to meet you, Nick from Washington D.C.," Alex said in a deep Arabic accent. He then released Seth to offer his hand to Nick of which Nick took. "My English, not so good," he said as he nearly crushed Nick's fingers with a powerful grip. Nick slightly bent at the knees trying to withstand the handshake.

"And you know Clievan," Seth continued with the introductions.

"Hello, Clievan! It is nice to *not* see you again. Eh! Hahaha!"

"Back at ya, buddy! What ya have to eat around here?"

"Help yourself to whatever is in kitchen, old friend."

"Thanks, bud!"

Clievan strolled into the kitchen, hoping to stave his insatiable hunger.

Alex addressed Seth, "Welcome to Oasis! May I ask, what is reason of visit?"

Seth explained in Arabic that Nick is looking for a specific shop but left out the details of the shield and stripes.

"We also seek the center stone," he whispered so only Alex could hear.

Alex gave him an approving nod.

"We look for shop tomorrow," said Alex. "I have heard of this stone you seek, cousin. But is not here. A woman three year ago, a massive woman standing six feet tall, long dark hair, very lovely, brought stone to city. This amazing beauty meet with Jessie. He no help her and try to take stone. There were more than twelve men in building. Only Jessie escape. To this day, he has lookout on all corner of city watching to kill on site. Oh my she ... so enchanting. I see her in my dreams, you know." He bumped Seth on the arm.

"Seth? What up cuz?" said Alex. "You seem," he took a moment to think, "jumbled."

"A woman...six feet tall," Seth said under his breath. "She really fought all those men...by herself?" he asked.

"Yes, at least twelve."

"You say just three years ago?"

"I am certain of time."

"It couldn't be," he said in a whisper.

"Is something wrong Seth?" asked Nick.

"Oh, no. Nothing is the... No. Nothing is...wrong. No one saw her leave, and no one knows what she did with the stone?"

"Not that I know. People look for days. Say she ran to desert. Everyone assume she perish. Some say she drown in salt lake. No one know."

"Salt lake?" Seth asked.

"Yes. Lake on west side of Oasis."

Suddenly a tiny decrepit old woman rasped, "She didn't die, she can't die. Ask Amun Ra."

"Shut up old woman," Alex yelled toward the antique woman in the corner. "Don't listen to her. She lost mind decades ago. She think woman was a god. Been going on many year, ask Amun Ra what to do, she say. You know how old people get when end is near." He shrugged, "They hang on to silly idea."

Clievan returned with a large turkey leg.

"Ask Amun Ra! He knows everything! Put the gift in the bowl!" she said louder before closing her eyes and losing consciousness.

Startled at the outburst and subsequent limpness of the woman, Nick asked, "Is she ok?" He looked closer then said, "Is she still alive?"

"Amun RAAAAA!" she bursted as her body flailed before finally tipping over to rest on the bench.

Clievan who was creeping toward the woman to check jumped back with a shriek. He dropped his mostly eaten snack. "What the heck is with that crazy old lady?"

"Just ignore her," Alex replied. "I don't know how to help you. But you welcome to stay as long as you want."

Clievan picked the turkey leg off the floor, examined it with a bulging eye then finished it off.

"Maybe just a day or two to give us time to think about what to do next," said Seth.

"Ok. It is good to have you back in my home."

"It's great to be back, Cuz."

They exchanged an embrace.

Seth turned to Clievan, "You sure did scream like a little girl."

Defending his actions Clievan said, "What that? No. I was just, uh, you know I was preparing to...arrrgg!"

Everyone had a good laugh.

They all caught up over a dinner of a crisp flaky pie stuffed with a salty meat of unknown origin and a layer of crushed cinnamon toasted almonds. Afterward, Nick and Seth sat together with a cup of tea.

"I can't stop thinking about the woman," Nick said.

"I know, she creeps me out too."

"No, not that. Well, yeah, she's creepy, but it's what she said that I can't get out of my mind. Ask Amun Ra, gift in the bowl. What does it mean?"

"It means you are jetlagged and need to rest, my friend. She's just a senseless old lady. Let it go," Seth said.

"Maybe you're right. I'll try to get some rest. Can't go anywhere at this time anyway."

He made his way to the couch which was prepared for him with a handmade quilt and comfy pillow then closed his eyes and slept.

"Ask, ask," Nick heard as he felt something bumping his arm in his sleep.

He opened his eyes to find the old woman

squatting next to him saying, "Ask, ask, you must ask."

She handed him a bowl, then said, "gift".

Confused, he took the bowl and said thank you. She smiled, then disappeared into the dark.

Nick's eyes brightened. He hurried over to Seth.

He shook him then whispered urgently, "Seth, wake up!"

Seth slowly opened his eyes.

Nick stood over him and said, "Maybe the old lady is daft but what if she isn't? I have an idea, get Clievan and Alex, we're going to the Temple of Amun Ra!"

As they left the house early that morning, Nick dropped a few dates into his pocket. Clievan dropped a few into his mouth along with the other turkey leg, a sandwich and a glass of camel's milk.

They walked to the center of town toward the dilapidated old fortress worn from years of desert erosion.

"Temple recently improved but overall, badly eroded," said Alex. "Many tourist come and go from area. What could possibly be here that will help find what you look for?"

"I'm not sure, Alex. I just have a hunch," he replied as he scoured the decaying ruins.

They entered the fortress, then traversed a courtyard. They turned left into a crumbling stone structure then entered the open court.

"Where would one go to speak to god?" Nick asked uncomfortably.

"Maybe sanctuary?" questioned Alex unsure of himself.

They moved through two rooms when Alex

said, "This is sanctuary."

Feeling along the walls and sweeping away debris the group looked to Nick for answers.

"No, it's not here," said Nick.

They also found no clues elsewhere within the temple.

"Is there nowhere else people once used for worship?"

"Yes. Is other place. I should have thought in beginning," Alex said excitedly.

-Alex rushed out of the room, then ran to an area with several large stones surrounding one standing wall. The rest followed close behind.

"This wall," Alex said using wide sweeping arms, "all that stand of alter to Amun Ra. Many year ago was destroyed for the stone."

"That one," said Nick pointing to a large stone. "Help me stand it up. This looks like an alter stone or perhaps a pedestal of some sort."

Three of them were unable to budge it. Once Clievan stepped in, they easily lifted and steadied it on a makeshift base.

"Look at that, it can't be," said Nick in amazement.

He pulled the bowl the old woman gave him out of his pack and placed it in an indenture in the surface. It fit perfectly. The four stood waiting, but nothing happened.

"Oh yeah, the offering!" Nick remembered.

He removed the dates, then placed them in the bowl. Nothing happened.

"Date? You think he like date?" Alex asked mockingly.

"I saw them on the way out. They looked tasty. I thought they would make a nice gift," said Nick.

"That right! She said gift," said Alex. "Date not great gift here. We in desert. What is best gift to receive in desert?"

They all said together, "Water!"

"Give me your water," Nick urged to Seth.

He grabbed the dates from the bowl, started to throw them on the ground, then looked up at Clievan.

"Yeah, I'm famished dude. Send 'em this way!" Clievan said in response to Nick's implied offer.

Clievan plucked the dates one by one from Nick's hand and tossed each into his mouth successively as if he were a juggler finishing a routine.

Nick slowly poured the water into the bowl. They all waited in anticipation.

The bowl sank into the stone which drew a resounding "Ahh" from the group.

Gradually, the water drained from the bowl. An image slowly appeared on the stone surface as if the draining water carefully etched each precise detail.

"Look, that City Lake, and smaller salt lake to west I mentioned before," said Alex.

"And that must be where the geode is located," Nick said, pointing to a cluster of buildings far west of the image of the Oasis with water spewing from a small hole in one of the structures.

"That is the city on the Libya side of the border. It will be tricky getting us all there," said Seth.

The water irregularly spurted from the hole making a sound like a water hose as it prepares to fulfil its purpose. It then spattered and spewed a thin stream. The stream rose higher and broadened. Suddenly, it stopped and became silent. The group edged in to see what happened just as it rushed out high above the onlookers in a massive gush – narrow at the bottom and wide at the top. Clievan pointed and looked around as if he were the only one to notice that the water wasn't coming back down. The surge wobbled and wafted in several ill-defined forms. Then, like it had been there all along, the vertical flood took the shape of a thick flying serpent that from its watery mouth violently sprayed them with a gush of warm liquid before bursting like a water balloon. The group reactively jumped back as it rained out over the stone eroding the entire podium until it completely disintegrated before their eyes.

"That was freaky!" Clievan exclaimed. "Did everyone else see that?" he continued looking at the group individually.

Nick fought to catch his breath. "I'm the only one that needs to go," he replied still startled by the serpent's warning.

Seth responded, "Okay. You and I can go. But first, let's check out the lake on the way."

Nick nodded in agreement.

Alex pulled Seth aside and spoke to him in Arabic. "You must not search for the item. This was a grave warning. It is unwise to continue."

"I'll be careful, cousin."

"I know you will, but you are messing with old magic unseen for millennia. This is more serious than you let on earlier."

"You knew these days would come. We must continue." Seth then walked a few steps back to Nick and Clievan and said, "Let's get back to the house."

"You got any more of those dates in your pocket?" Clievan questioned to Nick as they all exited the ruins.

Back at the house, Seth removed a sword from the back of the vehicle.

"We're going to a tiny lake, not to a medieval battle," said Nick.

"Yes, I know," said Seth excitedly examining the sleek flawless weapon. "But this is the sword from the sea troll's cave. It was with the talisman I lost to the old man. You see here at the pommel? That hole is the exact size of the talisman. I think it goes with the sword. That's why I tried to get both the first time. I recently went back for the sword."

"Sea troll? What?"

Seth replied evasively, "Nothing. I just meant cave."

"No. You clearly said sea troll.

"It's, ahhh, you know... just an expression. In our folk tales, sea trolls protect items for humans, so we sometimes use the term in that way."

"As expressions go, it's a strange one. I can't see how a sword will help us retrieve the stone if it's there, but I guess we can bring it anyway," said Nick. They joined everyone else in the house except for Clievan who wandered aimlessly outside.

"We must be leaving," said Alex. "Is twelve mile to lake. I arranged passage to boarder for you two but we no leave til morning.

"Ok," replied Nick.

Clievan busted into the room, "Hey come look!"

They all rushed outside to find three trucks of

armed men in black turbans barreling after a woman and a teenager in a very expensive, damaged white convertible Rolls Royce.

"That Jessie's Rolls! Who would dare steal from Jessie?" said Alex excitedly in Arabic. He took a closer look at the driver, then said with a large smile, "Ah yes, it is her."

Alex ran back into the house.

The masked men were aggressively firing on the car with automatic weapons.

Alex emerged from the house with a large weapon which drew frightened looks from the others. He loaded a rocket-propelled grenade then launched it with a deafening boom. The rocket ignited a second later, propelling the explosive warhead into the leading vehicle sending it into a fiery somersault.

Nick, hit the ground, then shouted, "Where the heck did that come from!"

"A birthday gift from cousin," Alex said smiling. "I wait many year to play with."

He fired off another at the second vehicle narrowly missing. Chunks of asphalt and dirt rained onto the assailants.

As the car passed, Nick's mouth dropped. "Trey? It can't be." "Let's go! Get in!" Nick yelled furiously.

Seth tossed the sword into the trunk. They all piled in with Seth at the wheel, then sped off toward the chase.

"What's going on, Nick? Why are we chasing them?" Seth asked as he raced down an alternate dusty road avoiding street vendors and onlookers.

Crunch, crunch.

"The boy! I know him. We have to help!" Nick said worriedly following the caravan with his eyes.

Crunch, crunch, crunch.

Nick turned to Clievan. "Chips! You thought to grab a bag of chips on your way out?"

Clievan shrugged with his hands near his shoulders – a bag of tortilla chips dangled from thick fingers.

Seth entered a drift in a round-a-bout sliding precisely onto the third exit. The tires threw a thick mixture of sand and pebbles into vacant storefronts. Seth took a hard-right to squeeze the car in between the two pursuing trucks and the convertible.

Nick climbed out of the window, onto the hood. Bullets pinged off the sedan causing Nick to reflexively duck. He balanced on his feet in a crouch with a hand on the hood for added stability and signaled for Seth to get closer to the Rolls. Just as he readied himself to jump into the convertible, Seth's vehicle was rear ended. Nick awkwardly flopped onto the trunk of the Rolls and barely grasped the convertible roof housing. He pulled himself up into the narrow back seat.

Seth made a slow turn left drawing the following truck with him. He led the truck back through the round-a-bout. The trailing truck plowed through the center without attempting the circle, shattered a statue in many pieces and just missed several palm trees. Shots rang off the car.

"Can't this thing go any faster?" Clievan yelled as he shoveled chips in as if it were popcorn and he were at a movie. *Chomp, crunch, crunch.*

"I don't need to go faster," Seth said calmly. He

quickly locked the brakes skidding the car sideways before thrusting it down a narrow alley. The truck completely missed the turn, smashing into a building. Seth gave Clievan a self-satisfied smile.

Clievan said, "Don't get too cocky speed racer. Let's get back to Nick!"

Nick took a deep sigh of relief when he laid back in the seat. He sat up with his head between the front seats. "What are you doing here!" said Nick to Trey.

"Mr. H! You're here!"

"Yeah! Now tell me what's going on?" he said angrily.

"Don't look at me!" he replied.

"You!" Nick said recognizing Lyza. "You're the woman from the airport! Why are you following me!?" "What a bunch of crap you were giving me with your big boots and suggestive sexy dress. You tried to get me arrested! Why?"

"What do you mean sexy dress!" said Lyza. Nick would later remember that angry voice to be romantic and soothing. "That was traditional attire for Egyptian women," she said in a matter of fact manner.

"Don't play coy with me. You knew exactly what you were doing," he said crossly.

"I had to be sure of where you were going," she replied defensively.

"Why do you need to know where I'm going and why did you try to stop me?"

"You don't belong here. You must go home as soon as possible."

"Well, let's just get through this ordeal and I'll see what I can do about it. Why'd you bring Trey!?"

"Mr. H! You should have seen the things that attacked us! They had this gnarly face, creepy eyes and Oh My Gosh What's that!" Trey said pointing at the car that pulled up next to Lyza.

Nick quickly looked in the direction. "That's just Clievan eating a bag of chips. Don't worry about him."

Clievan waived with a big toothy smile.

Lyza gave Clievan an *I can't believe it's you* look. She took a better look at Seth, then immediately remembered when they last met. Seth bowed his head humbly with a fist raised to his forehead when her eyes met his.

The road widened as they headed out of the small town.

Alex tossed the RPG launcher into the convertible, then said, "Use this on the truck!"

Nick acknowledged Alex, then turned back to Trey, "Let's get you out of here."

But Trey was no longer in the passenger seat. One of the men yanked him out of the car when the truck pulled alongside during Nick's conversation with Lyza. Trey struggled with the man in a choke hold in the bed of the truck.

The driver of the truck pelleted the side of the Rolls with a submachine gun. Seth swerved behind the car, then pulled along the far side of the truck of which Clievan and Alex climbed into. Clievan disappeared, threw a guy overboard and then reappeared.

"Holy crap you can go invisible!" Trey screamed in excitement at Clievan. Clievan grinned and nodded just before taking a punch to his wide jaw. Alex took a roundhouse to the right temple and went down hard. Trey elbowed the guy in the ribs then pushed him off the truck onto Nick in the convertible.

"Sorry, Mr. H!" Trey said apologetically.

The man in the turban and Nick gave each other surprised expressions. Nick punched Turban Man in the face.

Trey leapt onto the top of Seth's car and grasped tightly.

Nick yelled to Seth as he held Turban Man down who was grasping wildly at Nick's arms, "Get him out of here!"

Seth nodded, then pulled away from the chase.

Nick took a fist to the jaw then fell into the narrow floorboard. Turban Man rose with a knife intending to flop on top of him. Nick quickly tucked his knees to his chest so that Turban Man would land on them rather give him access to do real damage. Nick propelled Turban Man out of the car with a rapid extension of his legs as if the two were performing an acrobatic demonstration.

Clievan cleared his assailant then easily tossed Alex's large unconscious body into the Rolls before following him in. Lyza turned, away from the truck which matched their direction a distance behind.

After making a few more well-timed turns, Lyza said, "I think we lost them" as she continued to speed back toward the small town. Alex awoke and said, "Did we win?"

Suddenly, the truck appeared on a perpendicular street ahead of them – it blocked the exit.

"No Alex. Not yet," Lyza said as she slammed

the breaks navigating the car into a 180-degree skid just avoiding buildings on either side of the narrow road. More shots rang off the car, with several piercing the front window.

"They're still behind us!" Nick shouted.

"You ready Alex?" said Lyza. "

"Yeah. Yeah, I'm ready," he replied unsteadily.

"Ready for what?" asked Clievan in an anxious tone.

"She gave Alex a nod, then spun the elegant car around facing the oncoming truck. She stomped the gas targeting the approaching vehicle. Bullets from automatic weapons peppered the car.

"Anytime now!" said Lyza.

"Just a second," Alex replied.

"Holy roses, you aren't doing what I think you're doing!" shouted Clievan.

"Now, Alex! Now!" screamed Lyza.

Clievan disappeared.

"Just a second!" he said. "This is not as easy as it looks!"

Alex glanced to insure no one was in the rear blast radius. He released the last RPG. The launch explosion shattered the remnants of the front windshield. The ordinance found its mark. The truck blasted skyward as the convertible skirted underneath. The car bounced roughly in the newly made crater. Several confused black turbaned eyes met theirs as they flew above upside down. The truck slammed onto the road putting an end to the chase. She drove as far as she could before the car died amid heavy smoke just on the other side of town.

The car looked like it had been at the forefront of a military assault or contestant in a demolition derby.

The hood and bumpers were gone. The windshield panel dragged the ground on the passenger side. Scrapes, scratches and a multitude of dents scarred the previously flawless paint.

This is as far as we go," she said kicking one of the three flat tires.

~~

Seth gently stopped the car to let Trey in.

"Hey. Thanks for getting me out of there. You think they'll be okay?" Trey said looking back periodically as they drove away.

"Yeah. They'll be fine. They just had the one truck and most of the men were thrown off in the chase."

"I don't know about that. Trouble seems to follow Lyza."

He looked at Trey as if he'd misspoken. "Lyza, huh?"

"Yeah."

"Are you sure the trouble is following her?" he said with a glance.

"I don't know. She said they may be after me. After something I – "

"You what?"

"Nothing. Something about my family has them mad at me...I guess."

"Your family does business with Jessie? Maybe you're the trouble?"

"No. No. Not Jessie. We've been having all sorts of trouble since yesterday." He looked out the window at the passing desert. "Crazy stuff."

"Sounds interesting. We have a few minutes. Tell me about it," he said excitedly. "I do love a good story."

"I better not."

"Really? Okay. Fair enough." Trey thought he was genuinely disappointed.

Seth and Trey drove along a beautifully calm Lake surrounded by palm trees with a serene Great Sand Sea backdrop.

"I'm Seth, by the way."

"Trey."

"Good to meet you, Trey."

"How do you know Mr. H?"

"You mean Mr. Nick?"

"Yeah."

"I'm his driver. He hired me to get him here."

"What's he doing here?" asked Trey.

"Says he is looking for a geode to power a teleportation device." Seth expected a reaction.

"Really? He said teleportation device?"

"Yep."

The Eye. That must be what he's building at school, Trey thought to himself. *I can't wait to tell him.* A smile crept upon his face.

"How do you know the...um, Lyza?" asked Seth.

"I don't. She showed up at my house yesterday and we were attacked by, well, I don't know what they were. And now we're here running from a guy that wants her dead."

Seth was quiet for a moment as he drove them along a placid waterway. His expression became serious.

"Can you tell me what exactly attacked you?"

"No. I shouldn't."

"They were rogglets. Right? Lyza told you they

Trey Roberts and the Ancient Relics

were rogglets didn't she?"

Trey was startled. His eyes lit up as he stared at the stranger driving the car.

"How'd you know?"

"There's only one reason she would bring you with her."

"What's that?"

"Because you're safer with her than without."

"It sure doesn't feel that way."

"Listen carefully, Trey. If you are who she thinks you are, there's significantly more danger to come."

"Who does she think I am?"

"I can't say. You'll have to talk to her about it because I'm not sure why she brought you. That's just the only logical reason I can think of."

"Believe me. None of this is logical."

Seth laughed heavily at Trey's bewildered expression.

"Can you tell me why she came back to Jessie?"

"She thought he had a sword of some sort and she wanted to find Mr. H. We snuck in early this morning and looked all over for the sword. One of his guards discovered us, so we stole the car to escape."

"A sword huh? You're lucky to be alive."

"Tell me about it," replied Trey. "That was the fourth time I almost died in twenty-four hours."

"Third for me," he replied.

"Really?" Trey said with a surprised look.

They looked at each other and laughed. Not a ha ha funny joke laugh, but more of an I can't believe we're in this situation sort of uncomfortable laugh.

The road turned northwest a few miles before Seth turned southward through rows of date palms, olive trees and pastures of alfalfa. Seth stopped near the shore of a large lake and took an extra moment to exit the vehicle. He met Trey at the front of the car then walked out onto a small salty peninsula.

"This is where they'll meet us," said Seth.

"Why this lake?" asked Trey.

"We all agreed to meet here just before we rescued you from Jessie's men," Seth said as he stared at the mound of barren land protruding from the water.

"I figured that part out, but why did you all agree to meet here?"

"Oh. Yeah. Jessie tried to steal an ancient stone from Lyza several years ago and afterward someone saw her at this lake. I would very much like to recover the stone."

"And you think she swam to that island to hide the stone?" Trey said observing the lapping ripples in the tranquil water.

"Maybe. Plus, it's on the way to the Western Oasis. Let's check it out."

"Shouldn't we wait on the others?"

"We can't wait on the others," urged Seth.

"Can't wait for what? Why are we in a hurry? Maybe she hid it there for a reason." replied Trey.

Disregarding Trey's comments, Seth removed the sword from the trunk, then said to Trey, "Put this on."

"Is this the sword we were looking for at Jessie's?"

"I believe so," replied Seth.

Trey strapped the sheath containing the sword Seth handed him to his back. He looked out at the island in the lake and said, "How will we get out there? Should we swim?"

Seth seized Trey around the waist, then swiftly lifted them both off the ground.

"Whoooaaaa! You can fly!"

He gave Trey a smile knowing the kid was awestruck. Moments later, they set down on the tiny island.

"How'd you do that?" Trey asked excitedly.

"Take a look through this."

Seth handed Trey a round object. It had a hole in the center and was smooth and black. It was larger than a ring but smaller than a monocle. Trey looked around through the loop. Seth slowly crossed into site. Trey jumped back with a yelp, nearly tumbling into the water.

He pushed himself to the edge of the island and said shakily, "Wwha, wha, what are you?"

Seth remained steady as Trey looked again. Standing in front of him was a furry creature with a body of a man, head of a cat and a mostly white face with black accents. Broad golden tipped black dragon wings opened wide then tucked neatly behind his back.

Trey stood and said, "Your wings are beautiful."

Trey moved the ring away from his eye and back several times.

"Thank you for the complement. What you see through the ring is my true form. I can disguise myself as nearly anything."

"So, you are some sort of shapeshifter?"

"No. I can only disguise my true form as I'm doing now."

Trey lowered the ring and looked at Seth like Seth just asked him to solve a complicated equation.

"You're telling me you can disguise yourself to look like anyone and a fat, balding man is what you chose?"

"What? I'm not fat," he said looking down at his sizable gut.

"Okay. Whatever. I'm just saying, I might would have chosen something a little different."

"Like what? Like this?" Seth's facial features began to move unnaturally. His hair lengthened then faded to a sandy blonde that hung just below his ears. His stomach slimmed as his chest swelled. His traditional work clothes were replaced with jeans and a tight-fitting t-shirt that accented muscular arms.

Seth spun around slowly and pushed thick wavy hair behind an ear and said, "Is this more of what you would go with."

Trey's eyes widened as he said, "You are honestly the most beautiful man I have ever seen. Seriously. Oh my god I can't believe I just said that."

"Ha Ha!" Seth chuckled. "This gets too much attention. I need to stay incognito. I'd never be able to leave the house like this."

"Yeah. I can see why. Girls would fall all over you."

"As you saw through the loop, my kind don't mix well with your women."

"I guess you're right. It would just cause problems."

"Exactly."

"Where'd you come from? Are there more like you?"

"Do you know the story about..."

"About the evil king and banishment? Yeah."

"Great! That makes this easier. We were created in secret by the seven sorcerers before the temple ceremony that banished Khaitu. We fought along-side the humans disguised as humans. Olerand didn't take any chances. He ensured we looked like everyone else just in case we weren't successful. Afterward, we dispersed across the world when Queen Raferti, Ronodan's daughter, took over. She didn't even know we existed. Many of us remain in Egypt and surrounding countries. You're one of the few humans that know we exist."

"That's astounding," is all Trey could muster. "This whole story about the king and fantastical creatures is completely unbelievable. If only I weren't living it then maybe I could enjoy it."

"I've been at it for a long time and it never gets boring, but it's been exceptionally exciting lately. There was that span of maybe 250 years during the Persian Empire when everything seemed calm."

Trey's look of bewilderment was all Seth needed to move on.

"We need to see if she left the center stone here," Seth continued.

Trey fingered the disk in his pocket but chose to keep it hidden.

"So now what do we do?" Trey asked.

"I don't know. It doesn't look like anything's here. There should be something. If Alex was correct, she wouldn't have swam all this way for nothing."

Kicking his feet around, Trey said, "Hey, take a look at this."

He bent over, then brushed away layers of salt and dirt. With his finger, he dug an outline of a metal object in the ground.

"Look," Trey said. "It looks like it's firm in the ground and possibly goes far down. I can't budge it."

Seth crouched down beside Trey to take a closer look. He fidgeted with the object, then removed a copper colored metal cap, revealing a long narrow hole.

"What'd you think that is?" asked Trey.

"I don't know, but it's all that's here. It must be related to what she came for."

"I have an idea," said Trey.

He grasped the sword with a hand, gracefully bringing it to his front – as if he were an ancient samurai preparing for battle. He carefully placed the tip into the metal opening then lowered to his knees.

They briefly looked at one another.

"What are you doing, Trey?" Seth said nervously. "I don't think you should – " he tried to say before Trey rammed the sword fully into the hole.

"Trey! Trey! Where'd you go!"

Seth found himself immediately alone on the island. Trey was gone.

Airhame

Hands still on the handle of the sword, Trey felt nauseous but not as bad as when he travelled to Egypt.

"Where am I?"

The small damp cavern felt starkly different from the dryness of the desert. Light seeped through several deep holes above casting eerie shadows when he moved. He yelled for Seth but received no response other than a faint echo. He removed the sword from the stone portal and retained it in his hand. He proceeded cautiously down a low ceiling tunnel avoiding large boulders and stalagmites. His feet squished upon each step on the soppy floor.

The walls and ceiling were dotted with curious yellow marks. Trey neared a group to take a closer look. Just as he reached out, a long slug-like creature protruded slowly from the wall to meet his hand – then another until about 10 were competing in a leisurely race to reach Trey first. He withdrew his hand and they reacted likewise.

Trey pushed his hand closer and they reached out to meet him again. However, when he retracted his hand, they kept moving forward – very slowly. He stepped back maintaining his eyes on the wall slugs. He felt something on the back of his head and when he turned, thousands of wall slugs hung low from the ceiling and protruded from the walls – all reaching for Trey with long slimy neon yellow tentacles.

He yelped just before dozens draped over his face and ankles. He thrashed wildly but their grip was tremendous. He began to suffocate as they entered his mouth and wrapped around his throat. He then lashed above with the sword, freeing his head – goopy yellow slug guts plopped onto the floor. He gagged several times as he spit out the bitter foul-tasting creatures. He slashed again several times around his feet then sprinted toward freedom.

The slug tunnel opened into an enormous cavern where he stopped to catch his breath and to ensure he was clear of the yellow onslaught. He turned to perceive the cavern. On the adjacent wall was a narrow slit through which light emerged. The cavern was significantly drier than the tunnel. He slid down a small embankment, then advanced toward the middle of the vast expanse where he sat on a rock to rest from the harrowing slug eating experience.

"Ahhh yes. *There* you are," said a voice that seemed to come from everywhere. Each syllable was carefully enunciated. "But *where* are you? Very interesting," the voice continued.

"Who's there! Show yourself!" said Trey standing with the raised sword.

"Andressen's sword. Remarkable," the voice said slowly.

"So sad it is missing its most important decorations," the low intentional voice said sarcastically. "You are here for something, but what?" A brief pause. "Ah yes. There it is. So, *you* must be him. Curious," said the deliberate voice. "I no longer have what you seek. You should return from where you came – while you still can – Grandson of Patrick."

Trey nearly fell over as he was broadsided by the revelation.

"What! What did you say? Did you know my grandfather?"

Nothing

"Are you still there? Can you hear me? How do you know my grandfather?"

Nothing

"While I still can? What do you mean?"

Nothing

"Tell me what you know about my grandfather!" Trey demanded.

"Aren't you a persistent pest," the voice calmly replied. Why should *I* tell *you* anything? There is nothing *you* have that *I* require. I can merely take what you have should I develop the desire."

"My grandfather disappeared four years ago. I thought he was dead. Is he here? Is he still alive? Please tell me what you know!" Trey spun around as he spoke, not knowing from where the voice came.

"I could tell you; I could eat you. Either way, I believe, would be just as pleasing."

Trey took a step back, the trembling sword still raised.

"Make a funny move and I'll end you!" Trey

said shakily.

"Really? With that tiny sword?" the voice said unimpressed. "I *still* can't see you. Let's take a closer look," said the surrounding voice.

The ground trembled – small pieces of debris fell from the walls and ceiling. Trey flinched then crouched in a defensive position with the sword ahead. A truck sized glossy charcoal colored ball-shaped object with evenly spaced orange horizontal lines emerged from a cave in the far wall. It rolled slowly down a decline – defying the expected effects of gravity on the orb. It turned left to avoid a rock formation. It rolled a few paces forward then made a right – never altering the tedious pace. A crunching sound filled the space as it rolled over the gritty floor.

Trey felt anxious but not totally fearful – mostly mesmerized. He watched in disbelief as the lumbering object navigated an invisible maze. It settled ten meters from where he stood – blocking his escape back to the portal. It rapidly opened into an enormous pill bug shaped millipede that swiftly crawled with rapidly undulating legs in a wave fashion before coming to a stop just short of Trey. Trey screeched as he stumbled backward over a few small boulders.

Half picking himself up, half hiding behind the rocks Trey said shakily with the raised sword, "You stay right there! Don't come any closer!"

The bug crawled uncomfortably close to Trey and wriggled, no vibrated Trey thought, two thick antennae hovering just above the ground positioned below two large dark eyes. It then spoke directly into Trey's mind beguilingly, "There you are. I *see* you now, just barely. Yes. You are interesting indeed. Four years ago, you say?"

"Yes," Trey said out loud.

"I cannot be certain of his demise."

"Then tell me what you can be certain of."

"If you *must* know, an aged human bested me in a match of riddles. The prize was the stone you seek. However, I made a mistake for he did not come through the portal."

"Was that man my grandfather?"

"Yes."

"How do you know he was my grandfather?"

"There are hints of similarities in minds of relatives."

"What do you mean by our minds are similar? Can you read my thoughts?"

"You are challenging to read which is likely the reason you remain alive."

Alex said Lyza brought the stone here three years ago. If this bug is right, my grandpa has been here since then. He might still be alive!

"Indeed, Mr. Roberts. He may still be alive."

"You *can* read my mind."

"Indeed."

"If he didn't come through the portal then he didn't have the sword. How did he get here?"

"There *is* another way. Through Airhame."

Trey detected humor in the bugs response but continued the probe, "Please, tell me how to get there. I have to find him."

"You do? It is a necessity to you?"

Trey didn't understand the bug's rationale for the question. *I think it's trying to trick me. I didn't like how easily it mentioned how grandpa got here.*

"Trust is a hard thing to master," the bug

replied to Trey's thoughts. "I intend you no harm - at the moment."

"Stay out of my head!" Trey yelled holding his ears tightly.

Ignoring Trey's command, the large bug said eagerly in Trey's mind with its two long quivering antennae, "Let's play a game. Answer my riddle correctly and I'll show you from where your grandfather came. Answer it wrongly, I will eat you."

"How about plan C where I drive this sword through you, then leave the way I came!" Trey said with a little hysteria in his voice.

"Yes!" the voice in his mind said more energetically. "That sounds like a fun option."

Trey reconsidered his aggressiveness, then said, "What kind of riddle did you have in mind?"

"Does this mean you accept my offer?"

"Yes. I suppose I could use the sword option if I get it wrong," Trey said with an uncomfortable laugh.

"Excellent!"

"You know *my* name, who are you?"

"I am Simon. It is a pleasure to play riddles with you, Mr. Roberts."

"If I guess this riddle it will also be nice to meet you."

After a brief pause Simon said, "When you have your answer, please begin with 'My answer is' and then give your answer."

"I got it."

Simon stated his question,

"I beam, I shine, I sparkle white. I'll brighten the day with a single light. I'll charm and enchant all. I'll bring the best in you all. What am I?"

After a few seconds of silence, Trey began murmuring, "Beam, shine, white, bright, light, happy, warm, sun. Sun. Could it be?" He wiped edgy moisture from his forehead and said, "I wish Marcus was here. He's super-good at riddles. I'm sure he'd crush it." He continued his previous open thoughts, "Enchant, bring out the best. Sun? No that's too easy. Flashlight? Does he even know what that is? Arggg! This is nuts. I'm having a riddle contest with a huge bug!"

Simon's antennae quivered, "Are you ready to give your answer?"

"Not yet," Trey said anxiously. "Give me a minute. Light, charm, enchant, all, all people, all, uggg! I shine, I beam, I charm, I enchant."

Trey looked down then scanned the area hoping for a hint that would miraculously save his life. Simon stood motionlessly – like a statue. Even the once vibrating antennae were frozen in a fixed mannequin-esque position.

"Brighten, sparkle white, charm." Trey sighed.

"Do you give up?" Simon said in an overly cheerful tone.

"No!" Trey yelled in distress, fearful of the consequences of losing the ill-fated game. "Charm, brighten, sparkle white, teeth. Smile. Smile! My answer is you are a smile!" Trey screamed.

"That is correct!" Simon said with more excitement than Trey expected.

"You are a very good riddler. Nearly as good as your grandfather before you. Now I will take you through Airhame to the Keeper's Burrow.

"Take me?" Trey said as he released a deep breath. "Don't you think you could just draw me a map? I don't really travel well with gargantuan bugs. Plus, you are too large to fit through the only exit I see."

"It is too complicated to draw a map. Besides, you will need my help and I haven't been out of this cavern in ages."

"But you're still too big to fit."

The bug curled up and then as he rolled toward Trey, became smaller and smaller until he was larger than a normal sized pill bug but small enough to fit into Trey's hand. Trey lowered his finger so that Simon could crawl on. He then raised the tiny bug to eye level.

"Ok. Fine. But first..."

"You would like to bring Seth to the burrow," he said completing Trey's sentence. "Who is Seth?" Simon asked curiously.

"How are you doing that? You have to stop," Trey whined.

"It is how I communicate. Reading your mind is a bonus. Besides, I only get bits and pieces of *your* mind. I find it very interesting that you are so hard to read. You have nothing to worry about."

"I'm sure there's nothing to worry about travelling in an alien world with a size changing mind reading bug that would be happy to eat me."

"Your friend cannot bring me out of this cavern. For only the one who won the challenge can I fulfil the agreement."

"Wait. What? You mean I have to go – alone?"

"Or I can eat you. Either way is fine with me."

"You aren't as scary at this size, you know."

Trey traversed the cavern then squeezed through a large crack to exit into a lavish pasture.

"Ahh yes. That feels good. Welcome to Airhame," said Simon.

Trey stood in intense wonder at the site.

To say it was gorgeous would be a wretched understatement. To say it were merely heaven would be like using roses to wipe away excrement.

Airhame was more beautiful than the most amazing descriptions of the most amazing natural wonders man has ever envisioned. Airhame was peaceful, serene, and wildly colorful.

There were blossoming, bushy trees all about. Large pink and white flowers covered congested limbs. Fluffy red and blue birds flittered in tall lush grass. Millions of tiny rainbows seemed to garnish the land.

Trey set Simon on the fertile ground. He grew to about four feet in height.

"We will need to navigate Ravenger's Forest."

Simon turned looking down toward a dark forested area far on the horizon. Clouds, which looked to Trey to be in the shapes of hearts and stars, rose in the sky but not directly over the forest. A stream zig zagged across the land diagonally to the forest entering on the eastern side just after a splendid waterfall. Rising grassy hills gave way to thriving valleys full of more color and life.

"You see it there in the distance. We should arrive within a few hours."

"This place is remarkable! I've never seen anywhere so beautiful. Not even in pictures. I'm sure Sarah would love it."

"Yes, it is quite lovely. I had nearly forgotten. We must move on."

"Right," Trey said admiring a large silver bulbed flower with a tall green leafy stalk. Its yellow center shone like polished gold. Suddenly, but slowly, a black caterpillar with hundreds of bright red spots emerged from behind a sparkling silver petal. Trey reached a finger toward the winding creature.

"Not that one, stupid boy. Do you touch everything you see that you do not understand?"

"What?"

"The caterpillar. All places have their share of dangerous creatures. Airhame is no different."

Trey withdrew his finger and eyed the creeping creature as he rejoined the journey.

Red and purple winged grasshoppers crisscrossed their path as they trekked across lovely terrain. Something like a ladybug with blue spots on a white body with dragonfly wings hovered near Trey's face for just a few seconds.

"Good thing the bugs here are normal size. I'm not sure what I'd do if they were all like you."

Simon shuttered. Trey didn't notice.

They walked in silence while Trey remained in quiet amazement.

After a while, Trey became curious, "So, tell me Simon, how did you get the privilege of guarding the center stone?"

"The cavern has been my home for at least a hundred years."

"A hundred years?" asked Trey astonished. "How old are you?"

"Let's just say I've been around a really long time. I made a mistake, hurt someone badly and was exiled."

"But you can change sizes. Why didn't you just leave?"

"There was a spell placed on the cavern. I could only leave if I could convince someone to take me out. If I could do that, I would be bound to do what they asked of me. You asked for guidance, so I am helping you get to the burrow."

"What did you do?"

"I would not like to discuss it. It was a long time ago. Just keep up," snapped Simon.

"Okay. Okay. Don't get hostile."

"What will you do after you help me?"

"Go home."

"Where is home for you?"

"It's a place we call Land's End."

"Is it on this world."

"Yes. I do not have permission to use the portals."

"Neither do I but here I am."

"Indeed."

"So, you know there are more than the cavern and keeper portals?"

"I know many things. I have the privilege of knowing."

"You mean spying on other's thoughts."

"It's all the same, isn't it?"

"No. One is asking and receiving the answer, the other is invasion."

"Merely semantics."

Trey frowned at the comment.

"So, you've been around for hundreds of years, hiding in the corners, eavesdropping on the thoughts of others?"

"And I remember everything."

"But you don't know if my grandpa is still alive?"

"I haven't been out of the cavern and no one since your grandfather has visited, so if you would forgive me, I am a little behind on recent events."

They passed over a multi-colored flowered hill revealing an entrancing full circle rainbow in the distance.

Trey stopped and said, "That is the most amazing rainbow I have ever seen. How is it even possible?"

Simon didn't stop.

After Trey caught up to the quick paced millipede he asked, "How did you get in possession of the center stone?"

"It was entrusted to me for safe keeping by your lady friend."

"You mean Lyza?"

"Yes. Lyza is what you call her. If I were human, she would be my prize," he said distantly.

"Back over here Simon."

"Yes. She brought it to me several years ago in a desperate rush. She said someone very gifted would come for it. Naturally, I assumed she meant the one who won it from me, but I was mistaken."

"So, she thought that since you weren't going anywhere and being what you are, you would be a good protector? Why didn't you protect it better? Why did you play the game and give my grandpa a chance to win?"

"For fun."

"Fun?"

"That *is* why we play this game isn't it?"

"What game is that," asked Trey confused at Simon's inferences. "Riddles?" he said taking a guess.

"The game of life, dear boy. Why else would anyone do anything if it wasn't fun?"

Trey paused on the comment then continued, "Is that what happened? You were playing a game and someone got hurt?"

Simon swelled. His antennae quivered. He quickly turned glossy fixed eyes toward Trey and projected, "I said I didn't want to discuss it!"

Trey sensed a tremendous amount of guilt, sadness and regret. But what he felt next shook his core – icy cold undeniable deception.

They walked for some time in silence. Mentally, Trey attempted to break Simon's mind intrusions (mostly due to a newly found fear of the creature and partly curiosity). Thinking he identified the window, he opened it to see what would happen.

Almost immediately Simon appeared in his mind, "You have been unusually quiet. Are you attempting to block me?"

"Without speaking, Trey projected for the first time, "My dear bug how would I possibly do that?"

"Your smugness is annoying, boy. We need to be in constant communication. We must trust each other, especially while in the forest."

"I understand," he thought with a mindful chuckle.

But he didn't trust Simon and successfully hid those feelings from his projection.

"You know Lyza. Who is she?"

"You may find out soon enough."

"Really? You won't tell me anything about her? What about that guy she said is trying to free the bad guy, Commerand? What do you know about him?"

"Is that what she said he was doing?"

"Yeah."

"You may not be as clever as I initially surmised."

"What do you mean? Is he doing something else? Did she lie to me?"

"Again, you may discover that soon enough."

"What good is the information if you only keep it to yourself?" Trey said frustrated with Simon's constant evasions.

"It's more fun this way."

"Arrg! You're impossible."

They descended into a small valley spotted with tall stemmed yellow petaled flowers. Trey brushed one with a shoulder-level hand, releasing a purple bee from its depths.

A thunderous noise approached from the west.

"What's that, Simon?" Trey said anxiously.

"In your pocket quickly! You must not tell them our destination!"

"Okay," Trey said nervously. "Who's they?"

"They respect confidence!" exclaimed Simon as he shrunk to a miniscule size.

"What?" Trey asked tensely as he picked up the curled insect, then placed him in his pocket.

Simon didn't respond.

Gangly tendrils of panic wrapped Trey's racing heart.

He first saw the heads of men rising over the hill – abnormally large men judging by the size of their heads. Several wore thin hide vests while two were bare skinned as they rose. As they continued to advance, Trey's mouth dropped. Their lower four-legged, hairy bodies came into view. Large powerful legs propelled them rapidly toward Trey.

The half horse half man beings came to an immediate stop, flinging dirt and muck onto the seemingly solo traveler. Trey shielded his eyes to avoid the blast. Surprisingly, none of the flowers seemed to be trampled – Trey wondered why he had noticed.

"I am Toman, leader of the Rosh Clan and protector of the outer lands. Who goes there!" said one of the easily eight-foot-tall, broad-shouldered centaurs in a powerful voice. The thick, black hair on his lower body produced a shiny dark blue hue as it waved gently in the breeze. He wore a short full beard that extended into a thin point.

Trey replied in the most confident voice he could muster as the other centaurs surrounded him. A voice that may save his and the lives of his friends in time to come. "I am Trey, uh, of the Roberts clan."

Muscles bulged from Toman's shirtless upper body. Spidery veins pulsed in double time with his heaving chest. "Why are you here?" boomed Toman.

"I'm lost and trying to get home."

"Lost with a magical sword? Unlikely. You will come with us."

Toman motioned with a silver lance to a dark red-haired centaur who grabbed Trey. Toman held back to observe the surroundings as if he missed something while the rest galloped off.

They rode energetically on a westerly course for what seemed like hours to Trey but probably only a little more than one. The ride was surprisingly smooth compared to Trey's past experience on horseback.

Trey recalled a time when he saddled an old stallion by the name of Shady Wanderer. Shady Wanderer was his former racing name but Trey most of the time just called it Whoa Horse! The old horse had a bum leg that caused him to stumble about every third step but that didn't keep him from giving it his all.

That horse was crazy, Trey thought.

However, in this instance, he was held effortlessly on a shoulder.

"Put me on your back. I've ridden horses before. I'll be just fine," he yelled over galloping hooves.

"I would rather die than shame myself by carrying you on my back."

"Really? Why? Wouldn't it be easier?"

"Quiet human child. We're almost there."

Trey found himself surprisingly offended at being called a child.

A lush valley opened into a magnificent city tucked neatly within a perimeter of large grassy hills topped with guard towers. Oversized stone buildings separated by soft well-manicured roads accommodated preoccupied centaurs of various colors.

The procession trotted pompously through grass streets. Several pedestrians released surprising awes upon discovering their cargo. Trey heard one mutter, "A human," as she pointed at the group. Trey thought she may have never seen someone like him before.

Trey's captors climbed a gently sloping rise which, upon reaching the top, revealed a splendid lake in the distance that was every bit as large as the city.

They turned up a wide ramp to enter a building that resembled an old town courthouse with doors as tall as a giraffe. Traversing the lobby decorated in white marble, Trey thought his whole house could fit in the expansive space. Hanging on high walls, Trey admired large paintings of important looking centaurs in triumphant poses. Finally, Trey was transferred into a circular room occupied by five elders awaiting their arrival.

"Toman. What is the meaning of summoning us this day?" said an elegant, dark-grey thin-haired female standing in the center of the room.

"Madam Charise," replied the haughty voice, "We intercepted this human boy travelling toward Ravenger's Forest. He said he is lost but possesses Andressen's sword. Considering recent activities, I thought it best to consult with the high council on what to do with him."

"Andressen's sword? Yes. You have acted responsibly. Dark days are ahead, and this boy's presence must be related. Say you, human boy, how did you come into possession of the sword?"

"Madam, your Honor," Trey said not sure how to address her. "A guy back home had it. I don't know how he found it, what it is or even who he is. I used it accidently to get here. There's some weird stuff happening where I come from and I heard a man came here that might can help."

Trey wasn't sure why he kept the identity of Grandpa from them. He didn't feel threatened. Actually, he felt safer here than any time after meeting Lyza. The Centaurs exuded trust and honor. He felt they would always do what's right.

A large black male with grey speckled throughout his coat interrupted, "It has been years since a man has walked this land. That man was killed in the forest. He will not be able to help you."

Trey's heart sank to his feet on the comment. He built a ship of hope that he would find his grandfather. That ship was rapidly taking on water.

"Are you sure he was killed? Maybe there is a chance he's still alive?"

"He was seen entering the forest. No one leaves that wretched place."

"So, you didn't actually see him," he paused trying to build the nerve to say, "dead? You didn't actually see him?"

"No one is allowed in the forest," replied Toman harshly.

Remembering Simon's advice on confidence he said sternly to Madam Charise, "I must find him or find out why he was here. You will help or let me go."

"I admire your courage, Trey of the Roberts clan. However, we cannot allow you to enter the forest. It is too dangerous for you and if you were to upset its inhabitants, it would be grim for us all." She turned to Toman, then said, "Make him comfortable in the lower chambers until we decide our next course of action."

"Shall we confiscate the sword?" replied Toman.

"No. The human boy is not a threat and we do not want possession of the sword. Considerable harm may come to us if we are not careful with such items."

"Yes, Ma'am."

"Walk with me," commanded Toman to Trey.

Trey looked back warily at the elders as he and the dark-haired centaur left the room together. Trey found it difficult to keep up with Toman's long-legged pace. He jogged most of the way. They turned down a stone tiled hallway decorated in paintings of what Trey believed were images of the beautiful natural surrounding landscape. The hall descended at a ten-degree angle turning at each corner of the building until they entered a door to the left.

The room was big and mostly empty. It had a bear-sized mahogany desk with various writing instruments but no chair.

"I'll come for you when we decide what to do with you," Toman said then left the room.

Trey heard a series of locks, then silence.

"I sense he is gone. Am I correct?" projected Simon.

"Yes."

Trey gently placed his hand in his pocket, then pulled it out with Simon attached to a finger.

"We must find a way out, Simon."

"Yes. They will not help us."

Simon grew to his previous size. The sight of the large roly-poly-like insect still made Trey shiver.

Trey examined the only window. "Locked with a key. There's no way out." He sat nearly in the center of a single navy rug which covered a majority of the square floor.

Simon's spindly legs moved in a hypnotic motion while propelling him around the perimeter of the room.

Trey traced his fingers along the swirled design of the rug as he said, "What was all of that about the forest...you know...danger and all? Was my grandpa killed as they say?"

"It is dangerous in the forest, I already told you. But I can get you through safely. As you have seen, I have certain advantages over others."

"But do you think he survived?"

"As I said before, I do not know his fate. However, from my brief experience with the man, if any human can survive the forest it is him. My guess is that if he got past the Keeper the first time, then he must have been working with him somehow. There!" Simon said as he scurried toward the far wall. "This vent will get us out without being noticed."

A rattle of the doorknob prompted Simon to diminish. Madam Charise entered seconds later.

Many years adorned Madam Charise. She was elegant in a way someone would view a priceless painting – a beautifully aged and well-kept work of art. In her younger years she would have been, quite possibly was the most attractive.

She approached Trey, who still sat on the rug in the middle of the room.

"Please don't rise," she said ushering Trey back down. She gracefully lowered down, front legs first to sit next to him. She was smaller than the others but towered over Trey so much he had to lean back on his hands to look her in the eyes. "You and I find ourselves in a difficult dilemma. While you have done nothing wrong, we cannot let you leave."

"What do you mean? I can't stay here," he replied in a panic.

"I understand your concern," she replied calmly. "However, releasing you with the sword may be construed as helping you and your cause. Retaining the sword may bring unwelcome conflict upon our people."

"What do you mean by my cause? I just want to find my grandpa and get back home!"

"The man you seek was your grandfather? I now understand your urgency. Losing a loved family member to the forest would be quite disheartening.

However, that places you on a side and we do not choose sides."

"What do you mean, chose sides? Are you talking about Commerand and Khaitu? Did you know my grandpa?"

"Commerand is a current issue for your world and is a growing but not immediate concern for ours. However, we anticipate his imminent acquisition of the eye of Kartho which will give him the power of dimension travel. Once that happens, we will be at his mercy. We must separate ourselves from those opposed in order to protect ourselves. The Keeper is in league with them and assists in their quest to free the evil king. In fact, the Keeper bequeathed to Commerand a certain power that will enable him to acquire the Eye."

"And you won't do anything about it? You'll just stay neutral?"

"It is our way. We have existed in peace for many millennia, even after the Keeper settled in Ravenger's forest. We have kept this peace by following the rules and by staying out of the way. We keep to ourselves, protect our kind and mind our own business."

He stood to look her eye to eye.

"Sounds cowardly to me."

"Your opinion is of no concern," she continued peacefully after Trey's insult. "But you should watch your words if you would like to keep your pleasant surroundings rather than the shed."

He sat back down fidgeting with the fabric – wondering what the shed was and if he had a better chance of escape from there.

"Patrick disrupted our peaceful order when he came to us a few years ago. He stayed several days. We didn't know who he was. We mistakenly assumed he was a traveler. We sent him away once we discovered he was attempting to recover information regarding a stone – the very one that once adorned the sword you carry. Concerned of his motivations, we had him followed to Simon's prison and then to the forest. We didn't see him afterward. We assumed he perished at the hands of the Keeper."

"So, he might still be alive?"

"Indeed, he may."

Trey's stomach fluttered with hopeful excitement, "You have to help me find out!"

"Releasing you would seem as if we are aiding in your mission, whatever that may be. If your mission is that which will upset the Keeper, then we mustn't take the chance to experience his wrath."

Feeling extremely frustrated he replied, "Like I said before, I don't have a mission. Aren't you listening? I'm here by accident. I just want to know what happened to Grandpa and go home."

"You seem like a good human boy. I don't sense harm in your intentions. We are a highly intuitive race – I would know if you were lying. I believe your unfortunate story. Though, considering his allegiance with the Keeper, I suspect he is not someone you wish to find. Nor is it advisable for you to carry the sword within the Keeper's territory. Should it fall into the wrong hands all could be lost significantly faster than expected."

"There's no way Grandpa is on their side," Trey said confidently but secretly questioned his wavering certainty.

"Believe what you will."

She stood just as gracefully as she laid indicating

their time was up. He rose in response.

Before she turned to go, maybe as an afterthought she asked, "Tell me, what is the fate of Simon? I assume he tricked you into granting his freedom."

Trey's pulse increased. His stomach churned. He remembered what she said about centaur's advanced intuition. He responded with as much truth as he felt was necessary. "Yes. He gave me an easy riddle, then told me to carry him out so he could show me where Grandpa went. Once he did that, I set out on my way." She sensed uneasiness, but his vagueness was enough.

"What a wonderful coincidence for him that a naïve human boy would stumble into his prison. That scenario could not have been foreseen. While I personally like you and am not interested in holding you against your will, we cannot let you leave until we relocate the sword."

"This sword is how I got here. I may not be able to leave without it. I will not give it up unless you can promise me another way home."

"I cannot make such a promise. We do not have the ability to use the portals. I assume we are at an impasse."

"Yeah. I guess so."

"You will remain in this room until further notice. I'll have someone bring you a meal. Good day Trey of the Robert's clan."

She left with the sound of a locking door. For the first time, Trey felt hopeless. He couldn't see any way he could escape this room.

Trey walked to where Simon was and said,

"Simon? You still here?"

"I thought she would never leave. That was smart of you – your ambiguity is appreciated."

Simon crawled from the grates of the vent then grew to his former size.

"They won't let me leave."

"I know. I have found a way out."

"Really?"

"Indeed."

Trey placed a hand on Simons shell then said looking through the grate, "I'm much too big to fit through there. We'll have to find another way."

The room, to Trey's disoriented mind, instantly grew many times its original size. "What's happening!" he screamed.

Then a semblance of normality remained – but not quite.

"Get on my back. We have to be quick while we have time."

Still in shock, Trey climbed onto Simon's ridged back, then through the vent they proceeded.

Trey regained some awareness and asked, "What did you do? Did you shrink me?"

"Yes."

"Awesome!" he exclaimed with a raised fist.

The ventilation system was dark and breezy. Light shone periodically through grates along the metal shaft. After slowly navigating for a short while, they overheard a heated discussion. Simon stopped to listen.

"...but the boy may be part of it. We have to help if we can," said the voice of Madam Charise.

"She literally just said she wouldn't help," Trey said quietly to Simon.

"I heard."

"No. We can't be involved. We have to protect our kind. Humans are of no concern to us," said Toman.

"This is beyond race and worlds even. If Khaitu is released, we will all suffer just like the old books describe."

"We don't even know if this human child is the one or even if the prophecy is true. It doesn't mean anything that he has the sword. He said so himself. He got it from someone else. Maybe the other guy is the one."

"Perhaps. I suppose it is possible he's here by mistake. Nevertheless, we cannot let him go. We must know more in order to proceed."

"Yes. I'm glad we can agree on that."

"We must move faster," said Simon.

"What were they talking about? Prophecy? Who do they think I am?"

"I don't know. Let's just keep going."

Trey didn't like the uneasiness in Simon's thoughts and suspected he wasn't being forthcoming.

They passed several vent openings stopping at each to look.

They came upon another, "This is it," Simon said.

They crawled into the empty room, then approached a wall with a window slightly cracked open.

Simon grew them to normal size. Trey couldn't budge the window.

Simon said, "We'll have to shrink again. How's your grip? Think you can hold on all the way up?"

"My grip is pretty good, but can't you just make me small while you grow taller to lift me up to the ledge?"

"No. You can only grow and shrink with me."

"Oh. Okay. Then my grip will have to be good enough."

"Climb on my back, grasp the front of my shell and hold on tightly."

"Okay," Trey said unsteadily as they shrunk to the size of a roach.

They began the treacherous ascent.

"This isn't so bad," Trey said about a third of the way up as he dangled from the bug's ridged shell.

Simon continued to climb higher and higher. While only a few feet from the ground, at this size it was more like a hundred to Trey.

"My fingers are getting pretty tired now."

"We're about halfway."

Higher and higher. Trey began to doubt his ability to hold on. He wriggled his fingers individually to release tension. He tried to relieve the pressure with his feet but found no grip.

Anxiously he said, "I'm really having a hard time. My fingers feel like they'll break off any minute now."

"Not much farther."

It was as if he were sixty stories high – about two football fields. His pinkies were no longer able to grasp the shell. His grip slowly faltered. Blinding pain clouded his judgement. He tried to pull himself up, but his right hand slipped off leaving him dangling by four fingers.

"Trey! Stop moving! Hold on we're almost

there!"

His grip slipped to the middle knuckle.

"I'm slipping Simon!"

"Just a few more inches!" Simon pushed his many legs to their limits as he hoisted the dangling boy up the vertical obstacle.

Inches seemed like miles to Trey.

Trey slipped to the last knuckle, barely holding on by the tips of his fingers. Reaching desperately, futilely trying to dig his fingernails into the hard, smooth shell.

Simon apexed the vertical climb just as Trey slipped off falling to the windowsill in a crouching ball, breathing rapidly with eyes wide open, holding aching fingers to his chest.

"Lets – not – ever – do – that – again!" Trey said gasping for air.

"Get up. We must keep moving."

Trey slowly rose, still clutching his fingers as they climbed out the window onto the outer windowsill.

Trey looked over the side fearfully and said, "There's no way I can hold on all the way back down."

Simon ignored the comment and became silent. His antenna wriggled rapidly for several minutes.

"Simon. What are we doing?" Trey said while looking out over a bell tower in the distance.

Simon remained quiet.

"What's the plan? I can't go down the way we came up."

No response.

He looked worriedly at the mostly immobile bug. His antennae seemed to pulse in a slow rhythm.

"Simon?"

Airhame

Just before everything went black, Trey thought he saw something large descend upon them from behind. He never imagined that he would be eaten by a blue jay that day.

Deception

"AAAAARRRRAAAHHHHHH!" yelled Trey.

He calmed down after a moment, opened his eyes then said, "Where are we?"

"Inside the beak of a bird."

"What! Why isn't it eating us?"

"I am in control of her."

"You mean you're telling it what to do and where to go?"

"Yes. Now be quiet. It isn't as easy as it may seem."

The bird didn't fly a straight pattern. It ducked and rolled, stopped and started tossing Trey all about. Simon seemed to be unaffected by the violent turbulence. The jarring flight ended when Trey tumbled out of its mouth into a wide meadow. Simon casually crawled onto a giant blade of grass. The bird quickly stooped and turned its head. It eyed him intently then lept into the air. Trey shielded his eyes as it beat its huge wings to disappear into the distance.

Trey laid back amid the large grass. He held his face in his hands and said, "Can I please just go ahead and die! I can't take much more of this! I'm hungry! I'm tired! I just want to go home!"

"We have to keep moving. We can't risk getting caught again. Touch my shell."

"Arrrrggggg!"

Trey touched the shell, returning them to their normal heights.

They spotted Ravenger's forest which seemed about half as close as when they started. After a while hiking open meadows and thin bushy-treed areas, Trey said, "I'm pretty hungry. I can't remember the last time I ate. Do you know of anything here that's safe?"

"Why yes, the bumble berry is very good. The leaves are also tasty. Keep a lookout for a tall bush about your height covered in dark purple berries with tiny white spots. We should find some on the other side of that stream ahead."

They crossed a clear stream of leaping fish with small wings that hovered above the water for just long enough to snap at passing yellow and black flies. Making their way a few more paces down the stream they came upon a group of bushes with purple berries. Simon rose on his back legs, then began moving leaves and berries into his mouth. Watching Simon carefully, he determined the berries were safe. Trey timidly picked a berry. He squished it in his fingers, sniffed it, then touched his tongue to it.

"Not so bad," he said. "Looks like a blueberry but tastes like a grape."

He ate several more, mixing in many sweet tasting leaves.

"We must not linger," said Simon. "Daylight is short."

Trey gathered many berries and leaves for the trip ahead.

After another twenty minutes of walking, they summited a small hill. A herd of furry brown two-legged animals, each with a pair of large horns, ran together in an adjacent meadow.

"I'm not feeling so well," said Trey. Are you sure those berries were safe?"

"Of course," replied Simon.

"But you're a bug from this place, maybe they affect you differently?" he said groggily.

"You are very smart. They are safe – for me."

Trey detected a sinister tone in Simon's telepathy and thought he sensed him say "I'm not a bug," as darkness overcame him.

The Keeper's Burrow

Trey awoke feeling the sensation of floating – as if in a dream – lightheaded and dizzy. Confused, he watched trees and colorful flowers pass by.

Are plants mobile here?

"Hey little guy," he said in a sleepy high-pitched voice to a grasshopper that landed on his chest.

It leaped off onto a passing bush.

"Wakey wakey," from a voice in his head.

That doesn't sound like me. Who is that? Did those berries make be insane? Berries.

"The berries! Simon! How long have I been out?"

"About three hours."

"Where are you taking me?"

"To the burrow as we agreed."

"Why can't I move?"

"The berries didn't sit well with you. It should wear off soon."

"And you've been carrying me all this time?"

"Yes."

"Uh, thanks, I guess."

"Where are we?"

"Ravenger's Forest."

"It's beautiful from this viewpoint." He passed under a brilliantly decorated tree with vividly red and white flowers resembling carnations. Various pink and blue bugs buzzed around the large petals.

"Yes. That is what he would like you to believe."

"What do you mean?"

"What you see is not real. The forest is a gloomy and dangerous place. Can't you feel it?"

"Yes. It doesn't feel right. It's cold and damp, but I see the sun shining brightly. I can't feel warmth at all. And the stench. What is that?"

"Death and decay."

"Who would make such an effort to hide the real forest? And how?"

"The Keeper controls this forest and the magic within."

An abnormally large butterfly, about the size of a Cardinal with similarly red wings accented by blue tips flew next to them. He certainly did a good job. It looks so real. Trey tried to touch the insect but couldn't move his arms. It raised up revealing a beautiful yellow colored humanoid female figure.

"Whoa, what's that?"

It smiled at him with dazzling white teeth as they passed under the forest canopy

"That is a Dandrelierden."

"A what?"

"A fairy."

"She's beautiful," Trey said hypnotically still

looking at the tiny girl. Several more flew in to encircle Trey.

A green one with golden wings that shimmered in the sunlight hugged a blue one with silver sparkling wings. Another yellow one with white and light blue wings rested on Trey's forehead looking at him at an inverted angle.

"Dandrelierden's were the occupants of this forest before The Keeper arrived. It looked very much like what it does now but smelled of jasmine and melted caramel. They were astounding keepers of the beauty and life of this land. Not only personally full of love and loveliness but they also shared their magic with anyone worthy who happened to venture into their forest. It was an amazing place to be."

"You came here before? When they ruled?"

"Yes. Many times. She is Coméllula. I know her well. Always excited about meeting new friends."

"However, she is not herself today. None of them are."

Coméllula gave Simon an angry glance before turning back to Trey resuming her precious smile.

"She has been transformed, just like the rest of the light creatures of this forest."

"Transformed? Into what?"

"Slaves. Slaves to the will of The Keeper. Her job is to distract you from what is coming."

Coméllula's smile wavered.

"What do you mean distract me?"

"Just as you are now. Unwary that the forest has shifted."

"Shifted? What?"

Coméllula's expression transformed to anger as she shot Simon an evil glance. Her face and body distorted into a grotesque grey form with a crooked long nose and crinkly bent appendages like a zombified mosquito. Darkness exuded from around her tattered black wings. She hissed, then gave Trey an atrocious scowl before flying off into the dark menacing woods. Trey's eyes widened as his limp body was unable to reflexively move away from the frightening fairy. The others all hissed and scowled at Trey as they left in progression.

"That was so horrifying! I couldn't get away. I feel helpless. How long will this last?"

"I don't know."

"I think you did it on purpose."

"I think you walk slow."

"So, you poisoned me? I could have sped up."

Trey sensed Simon's rationale wasn't truthful.

"It didn't kill you and we made great time."

"Whatever."

Trey was angry. He felt Simon was dishonest and manipulative. He feared and needed him at the same time.

After Trey calmed from the terrifying fairy experience he said, "Those poor fairies. They were once so beautiful and happy. I could feel it in her."

"That is merely what she wanted you to feel."

"No. It was her. Maybe her former self trying desperately to be free of the curse. The Keeper did this?"

"Yes. He tricked them into sharing their wonderful light magic, just as they always did to those deserving of it. But he is very powerful and hid his true intent. Once they began to share, he trapped them and took it all. He uses the magic to transform this place into the dark and callous prison you now see and feel."

"I don't understand. Why go through the trouble recreating the forest as it was?"

"Why would anyone come in here if it looked like it felt?" replied Simon.

"Clearly I'm not catching on. Why would the Keeper disguise a gloomy forest to look like a beautiful forest just so others will come?"

"Food. Trey. The Keeper likes new and interesting food."

"And we're going right up to his house?" Trey exclaimed.

"Yes, Trey. That was our arrangement."

"Our arrangement was to get me to where Grandpa went, not to take me to some magical Keeper that might eat us!"

"Not us, Trey. He doesn't like - bugs," he said with contempt. "Besides, the old guy got past the Keeper once, maybe twice. If he can do it, certainly you can too. It shall be very interesting to see what happens."

"See what happens?" Trey could only express his panic with wide terrified eyes. "You're not going to help me?"

"Bringing you to the Keeper will build favor for me with him. That could prove very valuable."

"Arggg! You have got to be kidding me! Wait till I get my legs back!"

Trey immediately shut Simon out of his mind as Simon's many legs carried him to possible doom.

Trey focused intently on moving his fingers.
Nothing. *Come on toe! Wiggle!*
Nothing.
For nearly an hour, Trey attempted to will every

part of his body to move but to no avail. All nonessential muscles remained completely motionless. Only his mind and eyes seemed to be functioning.

Ok Trey. Think. We're travelling approximately four miles per hour at a 330-degree angle to the sun. The sun was directly behind us when we were on a straight path toward the forest so we must have angled to the left when we hit the forest. Simon said I was out for three hours and another has passed. The hill with the two-legged animals was maybe six miles from the forest. It's possible Simon moved faster in the open, maybe at five miles per hour. That puts us about thirteen miles into this forest assuming we've been on a direct course since entering. So, escaping to the meadow where the bird left us, I would need to travel at 150 degrees to the sun or 180 from our current direction to the edge of the forest then directly away from the sun until I reach the hill, assuming the sun moves in a manner similar to the one on my Earth.

The loose plan made him feel better about his dire predicament. He took a labored breath, then again attempted to move his fingers.

The forest became eerily silent. No grasshoppers, no ladybug dragonflies or scary fairies. Nothing but cold grey dampness surrounded them.

Trey opened his mind, then projected, "Why doesn't he hide this part of the forest?"

"Once you get this far, there is no escaping. You understand? He already has you by now."

"He knows we're here?"

"He's known we were here since we entered the forest. We've been followed the last eight miles. Haven't you seen?"

"No. How can I see from this position? Oh. You mean in the trees. I haven't seen anything. Wait. What was that?"

"You haven't seen because you weren't looking."

"You mean like quantum theory? It only exists if I intentionally observe it?"

"No reason to make things so complicated. They are merely disguised."

"I see something but only if I indirectly look at it. Sort of a shadowy thing out of the corner of my eye. What are they?"

"I think it's best you didn't know."

"No really. Tell me. I'm curious."

"They are a manifestation of the Keeper. It's how he keeps surveillance on the forest. He can manifest hundreds of them."

"They're just images of him? That's not scary."

"You don't understand, The Keeper is from the Etherios. He escaped thousands of years ago. Each of the wraiths have his ability to consume the essence from a living body just as if it were the Keeper himself. That's how he is able to stay in this world."

"The Keeper is a demon?"

"Something like that."

"How'd he escape?"

"No one knows."

Trey wiggled a finger. In his excitement, he nearly allowed Simon to sense the accomplishment.

"What is it that you are keeping from me?" said Simon.

"I don't know what you mean. You're in my head. I can't keep anything from you."

The lie seemed to pacify Simon for the moment.

Now a toe. Trey began to sense the remainder of his muscles coming under his control. He continued to keep his progress from Simon.

A rock archway passed above that narrowed into what looked like the roof of a wide tunnel.

"Is this the burrow?"

"The entrance."

The passageway was lit but Trey could see nothing straight above. He made a significant effort to resist turning his head to look around.

Unlike Simon's cavern tunnel with rough shaped stalactites and stalagmites, this was solid stone. Not a crack or uneven surface. It seemed completely smooth.

Trey admired the mostly glossy black and grey ceiling that contained veins of greens, golds and silvers. In a different setting, he thought, it would have made handsome countertops. Trey's stomach churned as they continued deeper into the gloomy passageway.

The tunnel twisted and turned. Trey could not determine if they were in the original tunnel or made turns into others. Mentally noting each change was increasingly arduous as his mind became cloudy and dim. A penetrating fog overcame his thoughts. He felt he no longer had control over his awareness. He fought harder to contain his sanity.

The tunnel opened into a wide cavern. A geometrically symmetrical convex ceiling glittered as they came to a stop near the center. A roaring fire burned to the far left. The room smelled like cinnamon and apples. A tremendous urge to vomit nearly overwhelmed him. His mind blurred. He wasn't sure where he was – disorientation added to the lack of cognizance.

A strong voice with a hint of a Scottish accent said, "Trey Roberts! How nice of Simon to bring you to my burrow."

Trey felt the demon probing his murky mind.

He is so much stronger than Simon, Trey thought.

Trey was unable to completely block the Keeper but felt confident he effectively hid the fact that he could move and possibly that he was in possession of the disk.

"Let's make you more comfortable, shall we?" said the Keeper.

Trey made his body as lifeless as possible has he prepared to be moved. He rose gently into the air.

He must be using telekinesis or something, Trey thought.

His head flopped limply to the side then faced down. He would have received a Tony for the outstanding performance. He felt a forceful pressure on his forehead slowly raise his head. He hovered upright for just a moment in front of a man with a clean-shaven face dressed in a casual grey suit wearing a D.C. United cap.

Trey did all he could to hide a surprised expression at the demon's appearance.

This is a demon? Not at all what I was expecting. He even has a DCU cap. Clearly, he wants to befriend me.

The Keeper raised his hand, the sword followed off from Trey's back.

"Very interesting. The sword wasn't entrusted to you? Which dead person did you steal it from? Or did you commit murder? No. Of course that's not you. Either way you won't be needing it any longer," said the Keeper as the sword floated away.

Trey was placed in a sitting position in a large chair. He faked a limp lean to the side of the chair, resting on a narrow sloping armrest and for more effect he angled his head in an awkward upward facing position.

"Bumble berries," interrupted Simon.

"You have strong control over your mind, much like your grandfather." The Keeper said telepathically to Trey. "But I think I got what I needed before you closed me out. Ah ha, Marcus. He is close to you. And yes. She is lovely? Is Sarah your girlfriend?"

"You leave them alone! They aren't important to you!"

"All information is important to me, boy."

"You knew my grandfather?"

"He and I had a brief dealing. He brought me something in return for a favor."

It can't be. I hoped Simon was lying. Grandpa would never deal with a demon. He wouldn't. Would he? Maybe that's why he never visited? Maybe Grandpa is one of the bad guys?

Returning his attention to the Keeper Trey asked, "A favor? What type of favor? What did he bring you?"

The Keeper's mental tentacles searched out more information.

Argg! It feels like long needles stabbing my brain. I think I am keeping him out. How are they (the Keeper and Simon) getting into my mind? I wonder what he thinks I know.

"You struggle so much. Why fight me? This doesn't have to be so difficult," the Keeper said in a soft inviting voice. "Continue to struggle and it will get *much* more painful," he said.

"I....I don't know anything," Trey said fighting off the pain.

"We will see. As for your question, Patrick brought me a very special stone," the Keeper resumed.

No! Grandpa! He did do it. Simon was telling the truth. He probably thinks I'm the same. That's probably why he brought me here. Lyza was close to him. She's probably been lying to me all along. Damnit! I can't trust anyone!

"That's right, Trey. You can't trust anyone," the keeper whispered in his mind.

Trey was disheartened and got caught off guard. He closed his mind as thoughts ricocheted around his brain. He felt like he should pay for his Grandpa's offence - or avenge his actions.

I have to get free. I have to do what I can to help. I can't believe my own family is one of them. At least he keeps talking – I'm sure hoping I will loosen my thoughts again.

"So, Grandpa was able to get to and from here because you let him pass? He didn't have the sword. How did he get here?"

"I let him through. Only the sword and I can unlock the portal."

"Why was the stone so important to you?"

"Let's say it helps me see things I wouldn't see otherwise. It as well as the sword will serve as payment for good favor in the new world after the Great King rises."

"The Great King, you say?" Trey said sounding indifferent. "This deal you had with Grandpa, how did you know he would beat Simon?"

"My, you are full of uninteresting questions. Simon is a very cunning creature but simple-minded."

Trey felt a sense of anger rush over him.

That wasn't me I'm not angry. Was that Simon? I must be feeling his anger. The Keeper must have struck a nerve with him.

Trey didn't notice a reaction from either, leading him to the assumption that he effectively hid the thought from both the Keeper and Simon.

Trey paused for a minute. He had an idea – the first of a string of unwise impulsive ideas.

"Simple-minded? How?" Trey replied to the Keepers comment about Simon.

The Keeper paused a few seconds – silently regarding Trey. Trey thought for an instant that the demon perceived his plan. A growing uncertainty budded in Trey's confidence. The Keeper then replied, "I knew his focus would be to escape imprisonment. I knew his challenge would be a weak attempt at deception at best. Much like with you."

Trey felt a pull to the disk in his pocket. He felt like he should be holding it.

Not now. I can't give up my advantage just yet.

"Bugs like him are easy to read and control," derided the Keeper.

Trey wearing an inner smile thought to himself, *More anger. That's it Simon. You're almost there.*

The Keeper continued, "And to think, he brought you here thinking I would grant him a favor. He should have known better."

A sense of panic overcame Trey – but again, it wasn't Trey's panic. *That's it, Simon. Hang on just a little longer,* He thought to himself.

"Plus, none of this matters any longer," The

Keeper said triumphantly. Commerand has grown more powerful than the beast guarding the eye. It will kneel at his feet. He will use the eye to gather all the relics. Once that happens Khaitu will be freed. You must choose your side wisely, boy. But yes. I sense you have already done so. Oh," he projected laughing, "and your brave teacher, Nick Hampton, is about to die in a little desert town."

Shaken Trey said, "What! What do you mean about to die!"

The cap wearing demon twisted his face as he pushed deeper into Trey's mind.

"Tell me what you are hiding!" he said.

The pull from the disk was now almost unbearable. Trey continued to fight the urge as the Keeper approached.

"Tell me, boy, what are you hiding!"

Oh god he's growing. No. He's getting longer and growing!

The grey suit faded into a translucent core with a light in its center.

The stone! It's inside him!

The Keeper's head bulged, and a third eye emerged from within. A lanky tail whipped from behind as the Keeper took the shape of a three eyed serpent that curled in front of the chair Trey was flopped in. It's head, facing downward, stared Trey in the eyes. The stone dimly shone before him through the opaque form.

"Youuuuu will teeeeell me what you knooooww," he said in a nasty whisper.

"Simon! You filthy bug! Now!" Trey screamed in Simon's mind.

Simon rolled, then instantly grew into a ball

nearly as tall as the room. He raced toward the milky snake.

Startled, the Keeper looked up. He flattened Simon against the wall with a whip of his head. Spindly legs raced for traction. Undulating tendons urged to contract in hopes of folding an impenetrable shell around it's frail underbelly. Simon seemed to be stuck, unable to move. That's all the time Trey needed.

Trey seized the disk, then thrust it into the serpent as if spooning through a thick pie.

"The disk! That's what you were hiding!" screamed the Keeper.

Not quite reaching far enough inside, the stone moved, attaching to the disk as if it were magnetized, momentarily emitting a magnificent light upon the connection. A surge of energy rushed through Trey.

Ripping the disk from the astonished Keeper, Trey rolled out of the chair away from the globulus fiend. The Keeper flailed on the ground but quickly regained himself. Trey leapt surprisingly high and further than expected off a small table only to be stopped in mid-air.

"That was a sneaky trick. You will pay dearly. I intended to kill you and your bug friend quickly but now I believe I will make it last for as long as possible. Yesssss. I will feed for days from your near lifeless body."

The snake tossed Trey into the wall. He rose to his knees just before he was whipped back down by its enormous tail.

"We shall get to know each other very well while you suffer a grindingly gruesome death."

Lifting him up telekinetically, the slimy snake brought him close. The beast's nostrils just inches from

Trey's face. He lashed a forked tongue across Trey's forehead. Trey winced in disgust and fear.

Pop, Snap, Pop sounded – both were startled. A ball of electricity quickly formed adjacent to Trey's right shoulder. Trey's heart jumped with joy. Just before a blinding bolt of electricity exploded from the object, the Keeper recoiled toward the flash enveloping Sparky in an impenetrable energy field causing the blast to be contained within a small radius surrounding a tiny blue creature.

"Sparky!" Trey said excitedly.

Electricity sizzled inside and around the invisible sphere but not outside of it. Sparky looked confused. Golden eyes bulged – then saddened at the failure of his attack. Tiny little bunny feet pressed against the imperceptible surface as he floated helplessly next to Trey.

"Well, Trey. Aren't you full of surprises? With his mind the Keeper crushed the sphere and its contents. He then made a tossing move which propelled a tiny misshapen blue object across the room.

"Sparky! No!" He reached out for his friend as if a touch would bring him back.

"He was such a brave little guy," the Keeper mocked.

"No, no, no. Sparky." The words were barely perceptible as he wept.

"Now it's your turn," the Keeper snarled.

Copious tears rained from Trey's eyes as shadowy apparitions poured into the cave. They rushed onto him from all sides. Trey felt life leaving with each wretched attack. He almost welcomed death in his depressed state.

"Yes! You have much to give, boy! Just like your dear old grandpa before I sent him to a place from which he will never return."

"What? You killed Grandpa?" Trey said weakly.

"You stupid boy. I merely sent him to where he asked to go."

A shadow plunged into Trey's mouth momentarily choking him before it escaped from the top of his head. He could barely comprehend what the Keeper was saying.

Staring at Trey through a wicked yellowish orange eye he scowled, "You will not die today, but I will feed. Yes! I will feed! Ha Ha Ha!"

Bloody and bruised, bearing ruthless assaults from demonic phantoms, mournful of the loss of his innocent friend who he promised to protect – Trey felt he couldn't take much more. He gave up.

The disk urged him, but he ignored it. It urged again. *It's too painful. I don't have anything left. Just let me die.* It urged him again, and again. A cold wraith sailed through him – sucking away precious life. He wearily looked in the direction of the pull. The one useful eye brightened. With the last of his will he raised the disk forward. The sword shot across the room finding Trey's hand. The disk sunk into the pommel.

Trey instantly burst into raging flames.

Western Oasis

"We must get far from this car," said Lyza.

"I get us to safe place," replied Alex.

He led them toward the City Lake, snuck down several streets, then moved through more than one building.

Wait, Alex signaled with his hand. He motioned for them to get down. Jessie's men seemed to be everywhere. They waited for a group to pass before turning down a dusty dirt road heading out of the main area of town. He directed them north through a palm grove to a tiny structure on the edge of the parcel.

"We safe here. This friend grove. He away on holiday," said Alex as he sat heavily in the only chair.

"Give Seth a call to let him know where we are," Nick said to Alex.

Nick pulled Lyza forcefully by the arm then said, "Why is Trey here?"

"I was informed he was in possession of an artifact entrusted to his grandfather. I went to see if it was true. We were attacked and now we're here tracking down the remaining pieces to ensure their *and* his security."

"Attacked? By who? Who would want to attack Trey regardless of what he possessed?"

"Hey lady, just tell him. He already knows most of the story," Clievan butted in.

"He knows about Khaitu?"

"Yeah, Seth told him right before I showed up."

"Yes. Before you showed up," she said giving Clievan a cunning look. "You and your flying partner are the ones that interfered with my recovery of the stone from England, aren't you? He was dressed differently, disguised, but you, not much reason to disguise someone who can disappear."

"Yea about that. I owe you one for my eye," he replied. "I couldn't see straight for days. Is that how you repay us for saving your life?"

"I'm confused," Nick said. "Flying partner? Disappearing? What are you talking about?"

"Yes. Clievan can disappear and Seth can fly. Now let's get on with it," she said curtly.

Clievan gave him a lazy nod while he peeled a fruit.

She continued, "My life wasn't the one saved that night. Had you left with the stone, you would have been dead within hours. I've been protecting it for ages. Khaitu desperately wants the weapon complete and back at his side."

"Weapon? What do you mean? Seth said Khaitu was trapped elsewhere and wasn't able to escape," said Nick.

"That is partly true," she replied. "He was partially trapped in the relic, but the ceremony wasn't complete. He must have maintained the ability to communicate with Commerand. That's how he's able to control the roggletts. He's using them to gather the relics as well as other artifacts such as Andressen's Sword and the Eye of Kartho. Trey has one of the pieces to the sword, Olerand's Disk. The stone is protected, but we lost the sword years ago."

"Sword? Is it about four feet long with an open pommel and some sort of inscription on the cross guard?" said Nick.

She nearly fell down by the surprising fact that he knew about the sword, "Yes! How do you know?"

"Seth has it in the trunk of his car."

Her tone lowered and spoke emphatically, "If it's here, the pieces are too close together. We must get them as far away as possible. We cannot let them unite."

"And the Eye. What's that?"

"I feel I should be asking you that question?" she replied.

Taken aback Nick replied, "What do you mean? I've never heard of it."

"But isn't that the reason you're here? To retrieve the Eye so you can complete the portal?"

How in the world does she know what I'm building? Nick thought to himself clearly shocked at how much she knew about his secret project.

"What exactly do you think you are building?" she continued.

"Nothing. I'm not building anything. I'm here looking for ancient artifacts," he lied unconvincingly.

"Trey told me about Costa Rica and China. I

believe Che was used to help you build a portal to another world. I believe it was Khaitu himself speaking through Che. Khaitu drew you the map to Don's office where you found his instructions but somehow overlooked the unfinished portal. I believe that's what Khaitu intended you to do, complete Don's portal and retrieve the Eye."

She paused with the gravity of her thought, then continued, "Of course. It makes sense. He knows how close you are to Trey and knew you would have his trust. You're highly motivated. He also sensed you were clever enough to follow the breadcrumbs and build the portal. But more importantly, he realized you may be smart enough to retrieve the eye." She held her finger to a plump succulent lip. "Yes. That's it. Commerand would have an easier time getting it from you than the Protector. But what I don't know is how he was able to access your mind."

Nick, slightly offended by her comment, steadied his voice and said in a beefy tone, "So, you think I'm just a pushover?"

"Compared to the Protector, Yes."

"Oh, and what if I weren't successful?"

"You're expendable, buddy," Clievan butted in again as he chewed the rinds of a melon which drew odd looks from the crowd.

"What? It's a melon," Clievan said defensively.

Lyza continued, "He's right. Khaitu can't afford to lose Commerand. With the portal complete, Khaitu could secure his freedom. If he gets free, acquires the power of the seven relics and regains the sword, he will be unstoppable. Your world and all worlds as they exist today will be destroyed."

"So, what you are saying is that the geode I saw

in my dream is the Eye of Kartho which powers a trans-dimensional portal?" Nick questioned unbelievingly.

"No. The eye itself *is* a trans-dimensional portal. We cannot let them get it. It's in a safe place. I don't think it's possible for them to remove it, nor do I think you can. So, don't even try."

"The dreams, the visions, Che and China...they were all Khaitu manipulating me to help him escape?"

"Yes. I believe so."

"Holy crap! This just keeps getting weirder. What makes you think they can't recover the Eye?" asked Nick.

"It is guarded by a puzzle, spell and a Protector," she replied.

"The Protector wouldn't be a dog by any chance would it?" Nick said shakingly.

"It takes many shapes. Why do you ask?"

"No reason."

She continued, "The roggletts aren't smart enough to solve the puzzle and even if they were, they wouldn't be a match for the Protector. Commerand though, could solve the puzzle and possibly thwart the spell. But I'm confident in the Protector's ability against the sorcerer."

"Couldn't he just use magic to defeat the Protector?"

"No. The Protector is in a sealed realm, meaning only the magic created within the realm is allowed. No other magic can exist."

"And the spell? What's that?" asked Nick.

"I was told it is either a confusion or incapacitation spell. Meaning, you will either be unable to determine why you are there or you won't be able to proceed. Either way you will die from exposure."

"Exposure?"

"The environment within the realm is harsh, but in what way is not known."

"Sounds like fun either way," Nick said chuckling uncomfortably.

"He gone! The kid gone!" Alex yelled from the chair.

"What do you mean the kid is gone?" yelled Nick.

"They went to lake. Seth say he disappeared."

"That makes no sense," said Nick.

"Tell me Nick. What about the past couple days has made any sense," replied Clievan.

"I know where he is, but I must move fast. I fear he is in more danger than ever now," said Lyza.

"What do you mean more danger?"

"If he knows the stone is gone then he is with Simon in Airhame. He will be safe with Simon only until Simon completes his obligation to Trey. I must reach him before that happens."

"What is Airhame?" asked Nick.

"It's a very unsafe world for Trey. Trey must have used the sword to access the portal."

"I thought you said the Eye was the way to access other worlds? I'm totally confused."

"There are several natural portals on this Earth that can only be accessed with special keys. Others are located in Shanghai, Yaroslavl, Kinshasha, Sau Paulo, Quito and Las Vegas. The sword is the primary key for the island portal. The key I have in my locket allows me to access them all, as well as control the Eye."

"So, you're telling me Trey is trapped in another world with a dangerous creature?"

"Sort of. He's in another world with a creature that isn't necessarily dangerous. Simon is mischievous and indifferent to human life which makes the threat real. But he has a chance if I can get to the Vegas portal before he reaches the Keeper's Burrow."

"Seth's here!" yelled Clievan.

"Get back to the states," she urged with oceanic eyes that burned like a fierce flame. "You do not want to be a part of this any longer. I will contact you as soon as I get Trey." She gently placed the tips of her fingers upon his masculine chest, moved close, looked deep into his eyes and said, "There is nothing more you can do." She rushed out the door then into Seth's car. They hastily sped off kicking rock and sand onto the doorstep.

Nick stood several seconds watching the car cast a trail of dust. He felt empty, unsure and lost.
"Will someone please tell me what the hell is going on!" Nick yelled exasperated.
He sat on the floor, leaning against a wall with his head in his hands.
"What do I do now?" he said quietly.

Trey's in trouble. What if Lyza doesn't make it? What if he's trapped like she said before? I must get the Eye and complete the portal. Maybe that will give Trey a chance to get back home.

"Alex! How do I get to the western oasis city?" asked Nick
"You heard gorgeous lady. You no get eye."

"I have to. I have to help Trey."

"She can handle it, buddy. Just relax."

"Shut up, Clievan!"

"Ok. Ok. It's your funeral."

With as much force as Nick could muster without physically assaulting the man he grumbled, "Just get me there, Alex. Finish your part of the deal."

"They all looked at Nick like he was a wild animal. No one could figure out how to approach him.

Alex spoke up gravely. "Road very dangerous. I take you to boarder like I promise but you on your own after. From there you travel west sixteen mile into Great Sand Sea. If you survive, you then turn northwest 40 mile. It should take little less than two day by camel."

"Camel. Are you serious?"

"Yes. I arrange two fine camel. Ride, very smooth." Alex, with a big smile, moved his arms together in a gentle sway.

"Fine. Clievan, you up for an exotic camel back excursion through the Sahara?"

"Sounds perilous to me. Just how I like it. Let's do it!" he replied.

They gathered a few necessary supplies, then set out westward.

"Seth probably back at house by now," Alex said as they passed the southern side of the salt lake where they assumed Seth took Lyza.

Anguish overcame Nick each time he thought of Trey. Worrisome whispers spun in his mind accompanied by a tremendous sense of helplessness.

I hope she gets to him. I shouldn't have let him out of my site. How could he have gotten into this mess?

They drove through rough arid land, crossed

dehydrated valleys, passed towering wind etched buttes until Alex pulled to a stop, seemingly in the middle of the desert. Alex looked over at Clievan then said, "Maybe you stay unseen for now."

Clievan nodded in agreement then vanished.

"That's amazing. You *can* disappear." He reached his arms slowly to were Clievan once sat. "Clievan? Are you still there? Clievan?"

Suddenly Clievan's head reappeared in front of Nick. "Yeah! I'm still here."

Nick lurched backward with a scream. Laughter poured from the slowly disappearing head – bellowing like a ghostly apparition.

"Enough fun and game. Let us meet the camels," said Alex.

Nick exited the vehicle onto hard ground to find a very short man holding two huge camels.

How did this man get here? There's no way he was able to get on one of those massive beasts.

Speaking in Arabic the short man said, "Brahim will find you. Give him the camels and walk away." Nick nodded in acknowledgement.

Gesturing to the camels with his foot, both of them lowered onto their knees.

So that's how he did it.

Nick approached one. It let out a loud gurgling noise. Startled at the animal's greeting, Nick took a quick step back. It looked distraught at the thought of a passenger. The man urged him on.

Alex made a negative motion with his hands indicating no one would ride the other. The short man handed the reins of the spare camel to Nick, turned away, then entered the car.

"West sixteen miles, northwest forty miles,"

reminded Alex.

Nick tipped his keffiyeh to Alex, then prodded the camel into the vast desert.

"They're gone now," Nick said to Clievan.

"Good. This sand is scorching."

Clievan clutched one of the leads, then crawled up the side of the creature with little effort.

Nick noticed his inhuman fingers grasping the reigns and how he used fat grippy toes to climb aboard the large ungulate.

"Tell me Clievan, what's the deal with your hands and feet?"

"What? These precious bobbies?" he said wiggling them rapidly. "They're just like yours, right?" he finished with a chuckle.

Nick understood Clievan was kidding but answered, "No. You're nothing like me – or anyone else I've met. Ever."

"That just makes me special. Mama use to always say, *You're my special little boy.*"

"No. Clievan. That's not what I'm saying. Normal people can't throw a full-grown man into a car – nor do they disappear. All this business of portals, creepy monsters and evil trans-dimensional beings has me believing there's more than what I've grown to believe."

"Boy do you not know the half of it. You guessed it. I'm not from here."

"Yeah. I figured that. Where do you come from?"

"My home is called Halidais. I arrived on your Earth by accident and have been searching for a way to return ever since. I met Seth a long time ago and stayed in touch helping him find things. I generally keep to myself. It's amusing, though, when people see me appear from nowhere. I sometimes do it for fun," he said laughing.

"I've noticed you're quite the joker."

"If you can't have fun what can you do?"

"Maybe take some things a little more seriously?"

"Pblpblpbl," came from Clievan's fat wiggly tongue.

"How do you get here by accident? I thought the portals were activated intentionally."

"They are. My kind hit a rapid growth spurt around twenty-five years. Before then, we start out much smaller. When I was ten or so I was playing in a meadow along-side a well-travelled path. I saw a man with a white beard wearing a long jacket and white hat. I didn't know it was a man at the time, I had never seen one before. He looked close enough to my people that I wasn't afraid. Out of curiosity and I also thought it would be fun, I decided to follow him. I stalked him maybe thirty minutes before he stooped beside a stone in the ground. I crept up behind him. I had an insatiable curiosity to touch his shoes - I had never seen clothing on feet before. I still remember the feeling of the leather on my fingers. I then fell down very woozy and never saw him again. When I gathered myself, I stood in a foreign land. I haven't been able to figure out how to work the stone until today. When I help you get the Eye, maybe we can figure out how to get me home," he said.

"So that's why you're here?"

"Yep."

"And why you stay close to Seth? Because you've

been hoping to stumble upon a way to go home?"

"Which we did."

"I suppose we did. Sure thing. I'll help you get home if I can. How long have you been here?"

"Close to two hundred of your Earth years."

"Dang! Two hundred years? We must seem insignificant to you with our short life spans."

"It hasn't been all fun and games. Try being alone for two hundred years. Try being the only one of your kind for that long. It can get pretty depressing."

"I suppose you're right. Most of us go insane after just a few months without human interaction, and there are billions of us here."

"Yeah, you *are* a depressing species," Clievan said with a laugh. "You worry about all sorts of ridiculous things that might not ever happen."

After a short pause Nick said uneasily, "So, um, we'll be out here alone for a while. You were just kidding back at the apartment when you asked Seth if you could eat me. Right?"

"What did Alex pack us for the trip?"

Looking into the satchel, he said, "A loaf of bread, pancake looking things, a couple bags of what looks like couscous, and a few sausages."

"The sausages saved you this time," Clievan said giving Nick a mischievous grin.

"Just kidding," Clievan continued. "People taste horrible," he said as he trotted his camel forward with a big smile leaving Nick time to consider the comment on his own.

After riding for several hours under a sweltering sun, they stopped to rest beneath a crisp clear night sky.

Before him stood a wall of knives. The massive dog appeared in the window. Flakes of rotting flesh flopped on its forehead as it quickly turned. A foaming mouth of blood opened to reveal three rows of razor-sharp teeth. The room shook. A black bladed knife with an emerald green handle fell to the floor. Just as the beast hurled itself to end Nick's existence, he awoke in a cold sweat.

Nick opened his eyes to a deep orange horizon fading lighter into darkness.

It'll be daylight soon. Where's Clievan?

He started a small fire, then placed water in a tin cup onto a rock next to the flame hoping for some tea in the chilly morning.

Several minutes later, sipping the warm tea, he watched the sun sneak up in the distance, setting the campsite ablaze in oranges and reds.

He took in several deep breaths, giving thanks for the special moment.

Suddenly, sand exploded across the fire sending Nick toppling backward.

"Good morning!" yelled Clievan laughing hysterically.

"What is wrong with you!" screamed Nick picking himself up off the sand.

Clievan continued laughing.

"Look, you made me spill my tea," he said in a lower voice and more relaxed.

"Braaahhahahahah!" Clievan replied with more intensity.

"Yeah. Very funny. Keep laughing clown. Let's get going."

Clievan calmed his laughter enough to ask, "You got any more of those sausages?"

Nick shook his head in exasperation, then threw at Clievan the satchel of food.

They rode in the blistering hot morning for three hours before stopping at the edge of a quiet, sandy village. A small boy watched intently as one man dismounted, then held two camels steady.

"Ana Brahim," a burly man said surprising Nick from the opposite side.

He took the reins, then walked away without saying another word.

"You still there Clievan?"

"Yeah," he replied but didn't show himself.

"The building displayed on the stone at the alter should be just up that street and to the left."

"I know the way but can't walk down the street," said Clievan. "They'll see my prints. I'll find another way and meet you there."

"Okay. But make sure you're careful not to be noticed. This is no joke. We can't fool around here. You understand me? Clievan? Are you there?"

"Argg!" Nick said under his breath.

He turned up the street and met only Clievan's floating head.

"Ahhhh!" screamed Nick.

"I hear ya, Boss," Clievan said. "But you should really be quieter," showing a crafty smile as he faded away.

After a minute passed, he said again, "Clievan? Are you still here?"

He moved his arms around searching to be sure he had really left.

"That guy's gonna get us killed," he said to himself as he walked up the empty street.

Nick neared the intersection where he saw the girl in the dream, she was nowhere in sight. He turned down the perpendicular street to where she pointed. The street ended in a T intersection, just like in the dream. A building lay directly across the junction. Several men loitered outside and along the streets.

It seems unusually quiet. I can't shake the feeling I have a thousand eyes on me, he said walking alone. *Where the hell is Cilevan? Does he even know where he's going?*

Nick continued down the street, toward the building. Three men watched him closely as he passed.

A muscular middle eastern man stepped in front of Nick with a hand raised, then said in a friendly but seriously deep voice, "You can go no further Mr. Hampton." The other two men were now standing behind him. "What you seek cannot leave this place."

The man had the shield tattoo just like in his dream.

Two additional men stood at the entrance to the building.

"How do you know my name?"

"Come with me Mr. Hampton. I will ensure your safe passage back to the U.S."

"I'm not looking for trouble. I just need to get –
" The man nodded, then one of the guys behind struck Nick in the back of the head knocking him unconscious.

Carry on

Trey awoke to flashes of colorful light pulsing in his eyes. A playful group of fairies sang and danced as their magnificence reflected off smoothed gemstones donning the walls of the Keeper's lair. As he rose, a tiny roar of cheering and clapping came from the minuscule winged crowd.

Sensing no danger and better yet, no mind probes, he pushed himself off the ground.

What happened? Sparky! Sparky. He became instantly sad, laid back down and closed his eyes. He tried to fight back tears, but a few escaped.

He opened his eyes to a beautiful yellow bodied fairy kissing him on the nose.

"Coméllula? Is that you?"

The fairy nodded with great excitement.

He wiped his eyes dry.

"Are you going to change into a creepy black creature and eat my ears?"

She frowned, then shook her head no.

Trey projected into her mind, "Tell me what happened?"

The tiny girl's face lit up. She opened her mouth in a huge smile while clapping her hands, then said in a lovely mousy voice as if she were singing a hymn, "You speak Dandrelierdenish?"

"No. But I suppose telepathy shares a common language."

"Ah ha! What a joy!"

Trey smiled at her excitement.

"I don't know what happened. The Keeper was in control of our minds. We only received glimpses of the real world. It was like being in prison beneath an ocean of despair. I remember you passing with Simon through the forest and hating you for it. Jealousy and envy for not being touched by his evil magic enraged me." She looked down shamefully and said, "I'm sorry."

"It's okay. You weren't you. Tell me what happened next."

"I just came to. No more ocean, no more anger or jealousy. We all awoke. Wondering what happened we carefully approached the lair. We found you here on the ground with small flames alight on charred parts of your body. You were," she looked away morosely. "You were not alive. We were tremendously sad for you but ecstatic we were free!" She received approving nods from her glittery companions.

"Not alive! What? Charred?" he said in alarm briskly checking his body for injury. "What do you mean not alive! Nothing seems to be wrong with me. I actually feel great!"

"It's okay. We fixed you," a blue one said in a chirpy voice with a big smile.

"I see that, and I thank you tremendously! Maybe I just need a minute."

Trey laid back down to take in the disturbing update.

"We also fixed your friend, but he was much harder considering we don't know what he is. It took a little while. We didn't think it would work."

Just as she finished, vibrant electricity popped on Trey's stomach.

"Sparky!" he said just as the little guy appeared.

"Sparky! You're alive! I'm so happy you're alive!"

He popped and snapped and snapped and popped. He bounced around sending tiny bolts of harmless electricity in wavy arcs. Sparky then rambled up Trey's torso and rubbed his furry body on his face. Trey stroked his back, elated to have his friend back.

"Thank you for what you've done for us. I am forever in your debt," Trey said solemnly while sitting up. He seemed to have a new source of energy now that the gloomy sadness was gone.

"Don't be silly! We're the ones in *your* debt. You freed us from centuries of torment. You will always be welcome in our loving forest!"

She kissed his cheek throwing off colorful sparks then said, "I hope you like the gifts. They were surprisingly easy to grant. We found you to have a penchant for magic." The others kissed him likewise, then joined Coméllula as they zipped from the lair.

"Gifts? What's she talking about?" he said looking at Sparky who was now on his shoulder.

Sparky popped and whistled.

Trey replied, "I know. They certainly were nice helping us out."

He sparked whistled and popped.

"What do you mean I don't understand?"

"Whistle, pop."

"You aren't making any sense, Sparky. What do you mean I can't understand that I understand?"

Sparky popped excitedly.

"Wait! I understand you! How can I understand what you're saying?" He grasped the little critter and raised him to eye level.

"Whistle. Pop," he said with big excited eyes.

"Yeah! That must be a gift she gave me! The ability to understand you! Ha! I'm so glad to have you back. I'm sorry I sucked at protecting you."

He whistled in return with a sympathetic expression.

"No. It's not ok. I promise I won't let it happen again."

"Pop. Pop," he said with downturned eyes.

"I know I've promised that already. I mean it this time. Now I have a better idea of what we're up against. I'll be more prepared next time."

"Spark. Pop."

"Whatever, buddy. I'm just glad you're alive."

Trey stood with Sparky on his shoulder. They regarded the large snake piled in smoldering lumps. The remaining portion of its charred head held a lifeless eye staring shockingly at Trey. Large swaths of the demon completely disintegrated.

Sparky and Trey shared a look.

"Simon!" He was nowhere to be found.

The sword lay on the ground separated from the joined disk and stone. He picked up the sword and sheathed it. He then lifted the completed disk and stone which sent a river of energy through him.

"Whoa that was intense."

He pocketed the stone and disk then said, "Sparky. Let's not get these pieces together again. Ever."

"Pop! Spark. Whistle!" he said in agreement.

After taking a few steps he stumbled to the ground, then sat for a minute.

I want to see Mom. I want to see my friends. I just want to leave this nightmare.

For just a moment he cried. Sparky consoled him by cuddling against his neck.

Trey gathered himself and once more regarded the lifeless demon.

"What's that?" he said thoughtlessly out loud.

He walked cautiously close to the remains. He removed the sword with one hand then gently poked at a protruding object within the body. It was stuck. The melted skin hardened around it like superglue. Trey forced the sword under the object, then carefully edged it out.

"It's a bag."

Using his finger and thumb, careful not to touch any part of the demon, he opened the bag and poured its contents onto the stone floor. With a light clank, a flat object that looked like animated red clouds rested in front of him.

"I've seen that shape before, Sparky. But where?"

Sparky replied with a soft whistle and curious look.

The clouds swirled around the shape like a trapped mouse in a maze, but no housing could be discerned. It looked like they were constantly choosing to form and stay in the shape. He bumped it with the tip of the sword. It moved as if he tapped a coin or other light metallic object.

"But what's that shape?"

He looked at it a moment longer then it hit him.

"No. It can't be. It can't be."

He pulled the torn paper from his pocket and said, "It's the same. Simon said he escaped. This must be how."

"Pop. Pop. Spark."

"I think it's a key to the Etherios."

Sparky responded with a high to low to high whistle.

"You're right. We should leave it. But where? We can't let chance decide who walks in here next to discover it. No one knows I'm here. No one will know I have it. Maybe I can hide it later where no one will find it."

"Pop. Snap."

"No. The centaurs are too chicken. They'll give it up to protect themselves. There's a chance no one even knows he had it. I'm sure it'll be safe with me."

He brushed it back into the bag with the sword, cinched it up, then scraped from the bag the remainder of the Keeper. He placed the bag in a zipped pocket then walked to a protruding stone embedded in the floor.

"Before we go, Sparky. I want you to know how much I appreciate what you did for us back in China as well as what you did here. You're very brave – and really awesome with that electric zappy thing you do. I'm happy I found you."

"Pop! Whistle!"

"Ha, ha. Okay. You found me." He embraced his blue friend affectionately before continuing. "This must be the portal. We need to warn the others. We must save Mr. H. Commerand *can't* get the eye. We have a lot to do and not much time to do it. Are you ready?"

"Whistle," Sparky agreed before he popped away.

"She said to concentrate on where I want to go. Island in the middle of the salt lake. Island in the middle of the salt lake. Island in the middle of the salt lake."

He held the image in his mind, then shoved the sword into the stone.

Confirmation

"Lyza ran through the Keeper's Burrow and knelt before burnt remains of the corpulent snake. She said with wide unbelieving eyes, "The prophecy is true."

She bent her key into a particular shape and disappeared with a touch to the portal.

Enter the Protector's Realm

Stumbling but not falling over, Trey raised his head, feeling a warm breeze on his cheeks.

"I did it! I actually made it to the island! Woo Hoo!"

Whoosh, Whoosh, Whoosh came from behind. He swiftly turned raising the sword to end whatever was approaching.

"Whoa! Whoa, Trey! It's me!"

"Seth!" Trey said excitedly. "I'm so glad you're here! I have so much to tell you! There was this crazy bug in a beautiful place then the centaurs wouldn't let me leave and sparky I thought he was dead but then he was alive then he died again then I died and then the fairies brought both of us back and now I'm here and now we have to save Nick and warn the others! Commerand is coming for the eye! We have to get to it before he does!"

"Whoa, hold on a minute. What? What are you saying?"

Trey took a deep breath to calm down. "Nick's in trouble and the eye, it's how Commerand intends to free Khaitu."

"Right. The eye. But there's no one to tell. Alex is back dealing with Jessie, Lyza went after you and Nick took Clievan to secure the eye. There's nothing for us to do."

"Really? Nick and Clievan? But they don't know what danger they are in. Call him. Tell him Commerand is coming."

Seth dialed his phone. "Voicemail."

We have to go to them!" Trey said emphatically. "Do you know how to get there?"

"Yeah. I was at the altar when Nick discovered the secret location. I can drive us near the border, then we'll fly the rest of the way."

"Fly? You can fly us that far?"

"Carrying you? No problem."

Seth stopped the car after an hour of driving a west northwestern course.

"Have everything you need?" asked Seth.

Trey wore the sword on his back, then patted the completed disk in his pocket, the pack of potions on his belt and the Etherios key and gold coin in another pocket. "Yep. I'm ready."

Seth attached a crude harness to Trey and up they went. The land with sporadic vegetation on which they drove from the oasis gave way to an expansive sea of sand. Trey pointed out several tips of well-worn

Trey Roberts and the Ancient Relics

buttes as Seth flew them low over miles of wavy sand ridgelines. The peaceful flight came to an end when Seth shouted, "We have to go higher!"

Trey gave him a nod, then they swiftly increased altitude with several beats of his wings. Seth made a series of calculated dives, then soared higher and higher after each dive.

"We're almost there," Seth said. "Get ready. We have to come down fast to avoid detection."

"What?" Trey said with loud wind rushing past his ears. "The fat dumb cow has avid protection?"

"OK. Let's go!" Seth said.

"What did you saaaaaaaaahhhhhhhhhh!" screamed Trey as Seth folded his wings, diving directly toward the village.

Trey could only look away the few times he attempted to open his eyes – the force of the wind was too great to meet head on. Tears briefly streamed down his face before whipped away. His clothes flapped. His heart raced. After he adjusted to the fall, the rest was pure exhilaration...until the landing.

Seth opened his massive wings at the last second, stopping them almost instantly before resting peacefully in a deserted side street.

"I don't think anyone saw us."

"I think my stomach nearly exited my nose," replied Trey holding his ribs.

Seth released the harness. Trey fell to the ground exhausted from excitement.

"Oh my god that was so fun! Whooo! You have *got* to come home with me! You're amazing. I wish I had wings like that."

"I'm glad you enjoyed it, but we have to move

just in case someone saw us."

Trey rose and took a few steps.

"Ahhhhh!" Trey screamed falling backwards on the sandy street as Clievan appeared in front of them.

Speaking mainly to Seth he said, "Nick's been captured by the Order. He is in a building just up the street. I can get in, but I can't get him out without causing trouble."

"The Order," Seth said roughly. "The Phoenix must have sent them. He'll be safe with them."

"No. He's not safe," Trey butted in. "We have to get the eye, get Nick and get out of here before Commerand shows up. If we're also captured, Commerand is sure to get the eye," continued Trey from the ground. "Did Nick tell you anything about how to get it?"

"Sort of," Clievan replied. "He told me about this dream he had when we were in the desert. There was a man with a key and a woman looking like she is guarding a door. Inside that door was a chest with a big keyhole. Oh yeah! Above that keyhole floated the eye."

"Ok. That sounds like pieces of the puzzle. What about the Protector?" asked Trey.

"He said there was this big dog by a window," replied Clievan.

"Was there anything else? Any details about the dog or the room? What happened in the dream?"

"I don't remember much else. There was a dog. I know that. The room was small, and it had...ummm... Yes! It had knives on the wall. Many knives. Knives. Knives. What did he say about the knives? Oh yeah. He said something about a green handled knife. Or was it red? No. Definitely green. Green with a black blade."

"Anything else?"

"No. I think that was it. We must get going,"
Clievan urged, then began stalking up the sandy street.
He turned to them and asked, "You bring any snacks
with you?"

"How can you eat at a time like this?" Trey
responded.

Clievan patted his narrow chest and said, "You
don't get a body like this by skipping meals."

"Actually, you do," replied Seth.

Trey and Seth chuckled.

"Seriously though. You have anything to eat?"

Clievan walked a few paces ahead of Seth and
Trey, disgruntled at the lack of snacks.

"It's all clear. Let's keep moving," said Clievan
as he guided them toward the small building at the end
of the street.

He led them down several back alleys passing a
woman scrubbing laundry. When they reached the final
street Clievan said, "There are three guards. I'll distract
them while you two get inside."

"How will we know?" Trey asked but received
no response.

Clievan crawled onto the side of the building
heading toward the guards, then disappeared.

"I didn't know he could do that. He can climb
on things *and* disappear?" Trey asked quietly.

"Yes. Clievan is an amazing...whatever he is."

Moments later, one of the guards was propelled
several feet away from the door. He then flew several
more feet sprawling painfully in the road. The
remaining men rushed to his assistance. Seth and Trey
bolted for the door.

Pop, Pop. Sparky briefly appeared on Trey's shoulder before flickering away.

"What do you mean you can't go in?" Trey whispered as he looked around for Sparky.

"What'd you say?" Seth said without looking back. He then entered the building.

"Oh. Nothing," Trey replied. Trey then followed Seth into the building.

Just as the man regained his footing, Clievan tossed him one more time – barely avoiding a collision with the oncoming assistance.

The confused guards never noticed the footprints casually walking into the building.

The room was empty. No furniture, no windows, no doors, nothing. Even the door in which they entered disappeared.

"Are you sure this is the place?" asked Clievan.

"It must be. Why else would they be guarding it," said Seth curtly.

"There must be something here," said Trey as he dropped the sword onto the bare floor. Its disappearance went unnoticed by the trio. "It's unbearably hot in here," he continued as he wiped beads of sweat from his forehead.

"There's nothing here! Face it you were wrong," said Clievan in a deep disturbing tone that took Trey off guard.

"Easy buddy. No reason to get so angry," Trey flatly responded.

"Look at that, a butterfly," said Seth wandering off toward the corner of the room. His human disguise faded into a cat-like form.

"Seth! What the hell's wrong with you! Get

back here!" shouted Clievan.

"What are you anyway?" asked Trey. "And what's the deal with those balloon fingers? Geesh!"

Clievan's brow furrowed, his face reddened. "You punk kid! How dare you speak to me that way! Take that smartass attitude back to your babysitter!"

"Hey Trey! Let's get ice cream after this!" Seth joyfully hollered as he wandered aimlessly around the room.

"Ice cream would be wonderful! Great idea!" exclaimed Trey clapping his hands like a toddler at a birthday magic show.

"Seth! Get over here! Now!" Clievan yelled again before storming toward the winged feline.

Trey sat on the floor. A ball and set of jacks appeared in front of him. "Ah, Jacks! I didn't know this game still existed." He bounced the ball gathering a few jacks. He did it again but deflected the ball across the floor.

He casually glanced up at a pale dark-haired woman staring with colorless eyes. She wore a long plain green dress with full sleeves that cinched at the wrists with neat white ruffles protruding over her hands. He ignored her presence, grabbed the ball, then went back to his game. A puddle of salty liquid formed from the drops of his flushed face.

After several rounds of jacks, Trey stood watching a large white cat with golden tipped dragon wings fly around the room and a weird looking short man with amphibian hands hanging from the ceiling. The jacks disappeared from the floor.

"That's strange. Do cats usually have wings?"

He walked excitedly over to Seth and asked, "Do you want to play a game with me?"

"Yes!" Seth replied enthusiastically then landed next to Trey.

"The object of the game is to get the little man off the ceiling. Lift me up and I'll tickle him until he falls."

"Yes! Yes! That will be fun!" replied Seth.

He lifted Trey toward Clievan.

"Are you ticklish?" Trey asked Clievan.

"No! But you are!" Clievan replied laughing hysterically as he reached down accosting Trey's ribs with fat sticky fingers.

Trey squiggled and squirmed until Seth dropped him to his feet.

"You got me you sneaky gecko-man!" Trey said while everyone laughed.

Trey skipped several steps then spun in the room paying no attention to the staring woman. He continued to spin. Laughing, spinning, laughing until he fell into a heap unable to catch his breath.

The laughter subsided. "What's this in my pocket?" he said curiously. Awareness crept into his consciousness while his elated smile faded.

He clutched the disk and the image of the trim bearded man appeared, instantly bringing brief clarity to the situation.

"This is the distraction spell. I have to shut it out."

He burst into laughter and ran around the room, dodging Seth and Clievan as if he were running for a touchdown – spinning and stiff-arming imaginary opponents.

He fell to his knees, then looked up at the woman who continued to stare intensely.

I must shut her out! He willed his mind to obey.

He remembered Simon and the Keeper. He launched in the air onto his feet. And then jumped again – and then again.

"Hahahaha! Whoo hoo!" he said as he jumped up and down as if on a trampoline looking like a psychotic monkey with his arms flailing around his head.

"No! This is not real!" he shouted steadying himself.

He began to fade away again. His mind drifted. His had grasped an object in a different pocket. He removed a bag. He twirled it on his finger for a few seconds before opening it. He turned it over, releasing the object from its dark encasement. A crimson cloud in the shape of a cyclone fell onto his hand.

He disappeared.

The Etherios

"You do not belong here," said a voice in the darkness.

"I can't see. Where am I?" Trey said with full clarity.

"Somewhere between all worlds."

He sensed he had no body as if he were floating in a dream. But this was no dream and he felt no fear.

"I'm sorry to be ignorant, but can you please tell me where *my* world is?"

"Maybe Ragnistant was correct. You are intelligent but not so bright."

"I certainly do feel that way. Who's Ragnistant again?"

"Yes. Ragnistant. I thank you for sending his spirit back to me. It was an unfortunate mess when he escaped."

"You mean the Keeper?"

"Certainly."

"I'm in the Etherios?"

"Certainly. But didn't you already know?"

"Yeah. I think I did."

"Why can't I see?"

"Human eyes can't perceive this dimension. Only when you join us in spirit form can you realize this realm."

"But I can feel it."

"Can you?" the voice replied unimpressed.

"Yes."

Trey gradually felt things in greater detail. He felt he was in a vast chamber, bordered by a protective field made of light which aroused all senses other than vision. He suspected what existed outside the field was danger and death. He sensed the size and shape of the entity – human size with similar features but somehow formless as if it were loosely held together in a familiar energetic silhouette. He wondered how much he should share with the entity.

"Who are you?" Trey asked.

"That is none of your concern."

"How did I get here?"

"You used Ragnistant's key."

"I don't remember. I was in a room, then I was here."

"You were in a protector's realm. The key shouldn't have worked. No magic is allowed other than that which was created in the sealed realm – and the key was created here."

"Yet, here I am."

"Certainly, you are."

He felt a closeness – like the bond a mother has with her unborn child. Not with this entity – someone else, someone he knew was here – somewhere.

"My grandfather is here, isn't he?"

"Certainly."

"Can I see him?"

"No."

"Why?"

"He doesn't want to see you?"

"He knows I'm here?"

"Certainly. Everything here knows you are here. We are all connected. You have caused quite a commotion."

"I feel it – the connectedness."

"Certainly. The longer you stay the more connected you become, until you become part of us."

"Then I can't leave? I can't be separated?"

"Certainly."

Trey felt the connection growing and knew the entity was right. He could not stay here too much longer.

"Grandpa can't be separated now, can he? He's been here too long?"

"Certainly."

"Why won't he see me?"

"Your grandpa, as you call him, is here for a reason. He cannot be disturbed."

"Disturbed? What could he possibly be doing here that I could disturb?"

"You wouldn't understand."

Trey felt a greater sense of his grandfather. He almost knew where he was as if he could reach out and touch him.

"If I can't see him, then tell me how to get back."

"I cannot."

Trey perceived the area beyond the light barrier

containing galaxy like swirling forms confining various entities within each. He took a chance to gather more information. "Outside of this room, all worlds exist?"

"Certainly."

"So, it isn't a place of spirits and demons. It's the place of everything."

"Naturally."

"This key enabled, Ragnistant to travel throughout the Etherios and eventually to Airhame? How did he get it?"

"You already know the answer."

"Khaitu helped him acquire it."

"Certainly. Containing everything, the Etherios also restrains evil spirits and demons eager to set chaos loose throughout the multiverse. Through Khaitu, they can succeed."

Trey was now certain he could locate his grandfather. His connection to the Etherios continued to broaden his consciousness throughout its expanse.

"I must go, before I'm unable to leave."

"That is an uncertainty. We cannot allow you to leave with the key and without the key you cannot leave."

At that moment is when Trey realized the entity was intentionally entertaining his questions to trap him in the Etherios.

"I've been faced with this predicament before. A friend helped me escape then just as one will help me now."

He sensed the key in his non-existent palm. He sensed his grandpa one last time then said, "I am not staying – and I can see you."

Colors collided in his perception. He felt himself move and not move at the same time as if the

Etherios swirled about like a globe at his fingers. Feelings of confidence were replaced with calmness as his consciousness spun. Feelings of sadness were replaced with love.

"Here!" Trey thought.

He propelled himself through brightly lit clouds of gas and stars as he plunged into his grandfather's ethereal domain. Everything stopped. Inescapable darkness remained. A dim distant light slowly grew brighter. It became larger as it approached. It morphed into various shapes: first a floating orb then a majestic flashing falcon followed by something bear-like running on all fours then it slowed and raised onto its hind legs before settling in front of him in the form of a fit lively elderly man in a white panama hat.

"Grandpa!"

"Trey. How good it is do see you." He said in a Cajun accent – maintaining a small space between the two.

"Why are you here? The Keeper! The stone! How could you do that? What – " he said anxiously before Grandpa calmly interrupted.

"Trey. Calm." Grandpa said as he waved a palm-faced hand in a lowered arc.

Trey quieted as he felt at ease. His questions faded as they became less important.

"You ave many question that can no be answered now. I will dell you what you need do know before we run out of time. Logos will not be far behind. I am ere of my own choosing. I am now part of dis place, you cannot release me."

"I didn't say that's why I – "

"Hush, boy. You mus listen. My friend, Don, unintentionally ported himself here. The only one I knew dat could help was Ragnistant. I made a deal wit him to free Don. For dat I was to acquire the stone and remain here in his place. Ragnistant kept his word but didn't return Don to his world."

"Why didn't he do what he promised?"

"Ragnistant is a demon. No demon can be trusted. He thought it was entertaining to send him elsewhere."

"Where's Don now? He's the dad of someone I know."

"He is in a place called the Highlands. Is not so bad dere I hear, however, plenty of peril still exists. He can help you if you can find him. But I'm afraid you don' have enough time. Commerand is riding swiftly toward the Oasis."

"What is the shape? The shape of the key to the Highlands?"

He regarded Trey proudly.

"You are a brave boy. It's an M." He made the shape with his forefingers and thumbs. "It has outstretched ends and de center bend is about 'alfway to da bottom."

"I'll bring him home."

"I know you will try." He looked away briefly then back as if the next words were laborious to say. "You mus' know, Khaitu will be freed."

"No! I can't let that happen!"

"Dere may be nothing you can do. It has been prophesized."

"You say that as if it has already happened."

"Time is not as you perceive it. Even in dis place, time doesn't exist."

"I don't understand. Does that mean I can't change what happens in the future?"

"You will understand soon enough. The future is malleable which means you may ave some impact on minor instances."

"What if I impact many minor instances that together have a great impact?"

"You are a smart boy. Now shut up. You mu's know, one among your group you can trust above all others. Ano'da will deceive you. I do not know which. Hopefully, you will determine who is who before it happens. Trust your intuition, it will not fail you. You *are* de chosen one. I love you. I hope we don' meet again. Do not come back to dis place. You mus' go now! Turn the key in your palm! Logos is coming! Go, Trey! Before is too late!"

Trey moved in for a hug, but Grandpa raised a hand that stopped him.

"We must not interlace our energetic essence."

"Oh. Okay." Trey said, dismayed. "What do you mean? I don't understand this whole prophesy thing. What is it that I will do?"

"But you already know," Grandpa replied in a calm less Cajun-sounding manner – unlike his urgency before the attempted embrace.

Trey barely sensed the love that guided him here.

"I'll stop Khaitu?"

"Certainly."

"But you just said he would be freed. How can I stop him if I've already failed?"

"You already know the answer to that question. We must be moving on now. Come this way." Grandpa turned slightly issuing a hand in the direction for Trey to travel.

"But Grandpa. There's so much I don't know."

Trey looked around, slightly confused. "Something has changed. Is this the way I get home? You said to use the key?"

"Yes. Home is this way."

Trey felt no Love as he did when he arrived. He now felt anxious and fearful. Grandpa returned to him but now Trey could see the imperceptible form from before.

"Logos! Where's Grandpa?"

"My, my. Aren't you a quick learner. As I said before, we are all connected."

Logos raised his arms then swiftly swung them as if chasing a curve ball – propelling Trey through the Etherios. Lights and galaxies blurred his peripherals. A rapidly approaching cluster of gas and multi-colored light loomed ahead – or more precisely, Trey rapidly approached his intended prison. He felt Logos pushing him.

Gaining his wits in the fast-moving scenario he said, "Not today, Pal!"

He turned the key in his palm then crashed onto a hard surface like Travis Pastrana missing a landing. He rolled into a lump against a firm colorless wall.

The Eye of Kartho

Trey laid motionless for several seconds before he realized where he was. His mind had already mostly left him. Just before he lost it completely, he stood, sweating profusely. He closed his eyes, then cleared his mind of all obstructions and invasive illusions. He cleared his mind of Grandpa and Logos. He cleared his mind of his future and impending doom. He opened his eyes, walked forward, then stared directly back at the woman. Her eyes faded to a bright green, then a door appeared behind her.

He looked back at the other two realizing they were still caught in the spell.

"I have to do this on my own, and quick before they heat to death."

After taking several steps through the doorway he turned to find the woman staring at him with colorless eyes. "I guess I'll have to continue blocking her," he said somberly.

A grey-haired man with a long beard sat behind a desk in the diminutive room. On the desk sat twenty-four blank tiles.

"Do you accept the challenge?" asked the man in a cold, ghostly voice that spiked the hairs on the back of Trey's neck.

Trey paused a moment to look around then asked, "What is the challenge?"

"Do you accept the challenge?" the man said in the exact same tone as before.

"What are the rules? What am I trying to do?" he asked more urgently.

"Do you accept the challenge?"

Trey hung his head, wishing he would wake up and end this ludicrous dream.

"This must be the puzzle. I suppose I am to solve it before moving on. This should be easy. I'm good at mental challenges."

"Can I at least have some ice cream before beginning?"

"Do you accept the challenge?"

"Yes," he answered hesitantly. "I accept the challenge."

"You have five minutes to complete the challenge."

The man sat back in the chair, then closed his eyes.

"What happens after five minutes?"

No response.

"Hey old man! What happens after five minutes?"

The man didn't move.

"Thank you for being so helpful," Trey said

sarcastically.

The tiles came to life, moving around in geometric patterns before resting in a square with one piece missing in the fifteenth position.

Trey checked his watch.

"I see. It's a 5 x 5 sliding puzzle. But the tile images keep changing. How can I possibly solve this puzzle?"

He took a few seconds to watch the tiles, hoping to find a pattern.

"That tile changed from a green eye with long lashes to a brown eye with a narrow pupil. That one changed from a soft looking paw to a cloven hoof. That one changed from a wing to a spiked shoulder. I think I understand. The tiles represent the same piece in the puzzle, but the image constantly changes to make it tougher. This shouldn't be too hard now that I figured that part out."

Trey began shifting pieces – working from the top left corner to the bottom right.

He checked his watch. "A little over three minutes left. Plenty of time."

He sang, rather enjoying the task, "This goes heeere. Move that one theeeree. Slide this one baaack and that one forwarrrrd."

Smiling, he matched tiles of blue wings to tiles of bulky arms to tiles of snake bodies.

I have two minutes left.

He moved a tile into place then suddenly froze. The joy of the activity sank from his face. The portion of the completed puzzle began to change one image at a time rather than random images as before. An image of a four-legged winged creature with a massive beak changed to a red and white zombie dog with rows of jagged bloody teeth changed to a hulking one horned ogre holding a large club changed to a six-eyed serpent with dripping fangs.

The images continued to cycle.

"The Protector. I must choose the form of the Protector. You have *got* to be joking!"

He checked his watch. *I only have one minute left.*

Trey hurriedly continued to solve the puzzle.

Twenty *seconds.*

"All that is left is to slide this last piece and the puzzle will be complete. Clievan said Nick mentioned the dog. It's the scariest looking one of them all. I think I'd rather take on the ogre. He looks slow and stupid. Why the dog? It does *not* look like the best option. I already beat a big snake. I don't think I want to do that again, but maybe."

Ten seconds.

The images continued to change.

Five seconds.

"Arggggg! Fine!" he said as he timed the final slide to match the image of the gruesome dog with a second or two to spare.

The old man's eyes abruptly opened with an empty gaze. The back of the room expanded into a spacious arena circumferenced by large, crumbly stone brick walls. The bricks of different sizes were colored grey and black. They seemed to be merely stacked upon each other haphazardly until a solid wall formed. Torches provided dim but consistent flickering light which produced shaky shadows throughout. Only blackness formed the ceiling.

An eerie wind blew.

The old man fell off the chair to his knees. He painfully arched his back. His torso elongated. His head grew large as his nose projected outward with his mouth, forming a snout. Serrated teeth jutted from emancipated jaws. Clothes withered away as thick, blood-red fur grew from thin, pallid skin. Hands and feet twisted into white paws full of long sharp claws. Once complete its head reached high into the air and it roared – shaking the floor under Trey's feet. A large ferocious beast of a dog stood before him.

Then it did what freaked Trey out the most, it began decomposing. The fur thinned and chunked off sporadically, blood dripping hunks slopped to the ground as it walked, large open scabs appeared across its face.

Standing as tall as an elephant, it released a thunderous howl.

"I think I made a big mistake," Trey gasped.

Walking horizontally past the desk the Protector stared at its opponent. Ears cocked, blood-splattered white tail alert, menacing snarl exposed enormous fangs.

Trey stood motionless on the other side of the desk.

A flash of light shot across his eye reflected off something dangling from the collar made of scabby skin. The beast continued to move into position. The metallic piece on the collar continued to mirror firelight into his eyes, breaking all concentration.

The object shifted beneath a thick slab of rotting flesh before Trey could get a better look.

Trey eased past the desk into the sizable room.

Suddenly, hundreds of sharp objects fell from above as he entered the arena. He dove for safety under a ledge – several fatal strikes missed by inches.

"Knives from the sky! You couldn't remember knives falling from the sky!" he shouted at Clievan.

He assessed several minor lacerations and determined he was in good shape. He wrapped the only bad one on his leg with material from his shirt.

The dog, seemingly uninterested in progressing rapidly, approached with care and stepped gracefully around the fallen blades. It somehow avoided the knife barrage.

"Knives, knives. What did he say about knives? Green handle! I'm looking for one with a green handle and black blade."

Trey eyed the great dog, which continued stalking. "Back home, the neighbor's dog would always chase me if I ran. Maybe if I casually walk and stay out of sight, I can find the knife without interference."

Trey stooped, then slowly made his way around the perimeter of the room. The dog maintained a bloody eye on him and matched his direction. Trey turned, then swept another section of the room with the dog seeming to quicken its pace. Trey settled down watching closely. Looking around the room, he tried to see as much knife detail as possible but couldn't make out many near the continuously progressing animal.

I'll have to let him get closer to have a chance to search that area.

He waited. The dog tirelessly approached. Bloody drool hung from scaly lips. He was now close enough for Trey to view rows of grey and black teeth.

"It's definitely a locket tied to a rotting skin collar ...and it has a keyhole! I don't have any idea how

I'll find a key in this shadowy place or how I'm expected to get it into that locket. But dang-it, it's a keyhole!"

He moved to the left as the dog became uncomfortably close from the right. Careful not to quicken his pace but to remain just ahead of the monster. He searched the new area but found no green handled knife or key for that matter.

"It must have fallen in the center. I'll get eaten alive if I get that close."

The dog continued a persistent pursuit.

Trey noticed several places along the wall where knives should have been but weren't. He looked up and found ledges jutting out over the area.

I wonder if some fell up there. I could do a climb-up to reach those ledges. But I would need a running start. I'm not sure how my furry friend would take to that. The benefit, though, is that I may be out of reach if he gets frisky. I think it's worth the risk. I can walk toward the center of the room looking the best I can, then at just the right moment I'll dart toward the far-left wall, hopefully avoiding any unwelcome interactions with mister lively.

Trey gathered all the courage he could muster, then began walking the perimeter toward the Protector. Trey turned right toward the center of the room. The Protector matched his movements on an intercept route from the left.

"None of these have a green handle. Dang!"

Trey took another few steps as the beast neared. Just as he could feel its hot breath, Trey took one more step then turned on his right foot, then darted past the dog toward the left wall. The Protector lunged with a gaping mouth, barely missing Trey's foot. The miss gave Trey the time he needed to reach the wall. He jumped, planted a foot on the wall and boosted himself onto the ledge to the left.

"Ha Ha! Didn't expect ole Trey the wall climbing master to take you on did ya!" he said proud of his athleticism.

The beast lunged and snapped just above the ledge causing Trey to fall backward in panic.

He pushed himself against the wall and said, "That was too close," as he wiped sweat from his forehead.

The ledge provided safety, but not much. The Protector released an unrelenting burst of deafening barks as it desperately tried to reach Trey on the ledge. It jumped and barked, barked and jumped. Bloody slobber slung everywhere.

No green handled knife here he thought trying to shut out the booming noise.

Claws frantically scratched the walls flinging hunks of debris several feet in every direction.

"I need to move before he rips this ledge down!"

Trey ran to the left, jumped off the ledge, then tic tac'd off the wall onto the next ledge. The dog jumped just behind him, snapping at his feet.

"No green handled knife here either. I can't think with all that infuriating barking!" he screamed holding his ears.

He tic tac'd once again to the next ledge but this time the beast anticipated the move, nearly chomping him in midair. His nose bumped Trey which sent him sprawling over the ledge. He barely grabbed on with one hand and quickly climbed onto the ledge just as the mighty dog snapped again missing him by less than an inch. It resumed its inexorable barking.

"There it is! I can't believe it! It actually exists!"

he said elated.

He picked up the knife which was jammed into the stone ledge. He examined the details and was amazed at what he found.

"There's an image of a key on the blade! This must be the key to the locket!"

His enthusiasm was short-lived as the thought of how to proceed weighed on him.

"Now, how do I get it in there?" he said out loud.

His head pounded from the animal's sharp barks. He held his hands to his ears which seemed to do nothing to suppress the sound.

Another foolish idea popped in his mind as the dog continued to leap beneath him, snapping just over the ledge, barking ear-piercing barks and scraping chunks of stone away from the ledge causing it to become less steady by the second.

"This is a very bad idea," he said just before he hurled himself off the ledge toward the massive beast.

Escape

Just as the Protector set its front paws on the floor, Trey landed on the back of its thick neck, grabbed the collar with one hand, then sliced it off with the blade in the other mid-stride. He took two more steps down its back before turning a 180 flip off the rear end of the beast. He landed on the floor falling to his butt with the knife securely in the locket.

The Protector howled in defeat then, before Trey's astonished and exhausted eyes, instantly turned into an aged wooden chest with a golden keyhole. It opened revealing a brightly shining palm sized geode. Trey shielded his eyes from the blinding light as he approached. He looked around, careful about traps but found none. He removed the Eye of Kartho and held it in his hand for a moment. A moment which illuminated his life experiences. A moment of triumph in a string of unbelievable circumstances a thirteen-year-old nobody from normal-town USA could only imagine.

He then placed it in a buttoned pocket extinguishing its magnificent radiance, returning him to an empty room with a confused flying cat and a small man with large digits.

Seth and Clievan fell to the floor in exhaustion. After a few seconds a cool breeze gushed through the enclosed room. Seth resumed his human disguise.

"Seth! Clievan! You guys are still alive!"

"Trey?" said Seth shaking his head. "I'm so glad you made it. What happened? I remember entering this room and then we...we had a fight? I remember someone yelling at me."

"Good to see you again, bud. Did you get it?" asked Clievan eagerly.

"Yeah! I got it! It was so wild. I could have used you Clievan. I had to jump up a wall!"

"A wall? No Way!" He paused a second then said, "Maybe *I* should hold on to it. We can put it here in my buttoned pocket. Plus, if something happens, my grip is significantly better than yours," Clievan said hopefully.

Trey looked at Clievan with a cautious eye then said, "It's safe in my zippered pocket. Thanks for offering," Trey concluded as he noticed Clievan fade into a disappointed demeanor.

Trey then told the story of what happened with Seth and Clievan staring in disbelief.

"That's an amazing feat you just accomplished. Few others would have been able to complete it. I mean look at us, we barely made it through the front door," said Clievan.

"Yeah. You saved our lives. I am grateful for you," said Seth hugging Trey tightly. Clievan joined in.

"You guys are squeezing my guts out," Trey wheezed.

Seth chuckled, then said, "Now, let's go get Nick!"

Trey grabbed the sword from the floor, sheathed it then stepped through the rematerialized door onto the façade. Two crusty roggletts, waiting in ambush, secured him to the ground. Seth rushed out tackling one freeing Trey enough to escape. Clievan disappeared so he could move out of the building unnoticed.

Stumbling into the street, Trey and Seth became surrounded by dozens of hooded creatures. Several men lay in the street either unconscious or killed along with many roggletts that were clearly dead.

A tall man in a black cloak approached steadily – effortlessly – as if floating inches from the ground like an unchained wraith pursuing its next soul. The cloak drug the sand like the tail of a dragon stalking a hapless victim – seeming to move independently from its wearer. Dark rings encircled forebodingly black eyes that no light could penetrate. A long skinny nose protruded from a gaunt, pallid face etched with lifeless scaly skin. Raised before him in his right hand donned with various rings was a shiny, black, shoulder high staff topped with a small dark blue crystal sphere – his other hidden deep in the cloak. He wore no facial expression as he neared. Three roggletts followed pulling Nick along with them.

"Mr. H! Are you ok?"

"I'm fine Trey. Don't give them anything!" Nick said before taking a blow to the back of the head.

Trey was scared, petrified. Intense horror overcame him. Disillusionment and despair filled his soul, as if he were in a pit of mud, sinking ever deeper. He hoped for death – which was surely to come effortlessly.

"Wallace Roberts – the third," Commerand said in a college professor sort of way. "How nice it is to finally meet you."

Trey's stomach churned. He felt as if he would pass out.

Seth quickly snatched Trey into the air. Commerand waived the staff. White clouds swirled in the once solid blue sphere, bringing them crashing to the ground – ending the feeble attempt at escape.

"I sensed you were somehow – disguised," Commerand directed toward Seth. "I thought your kind were only interested in helping yourselves," he continued intriguingly. "What is it the boy has that you desire?" Commerand said staring deeply at Seth – slowly circling the tip of the cloudy staff.

"Nothing I want nothing from him," Seth said holding the sides of his head. "ARRGGG! I-don't-want-anything-from-hiiim! AGGGGG!" Seth screamed in pain as he rolled back and forth on the ground.

"Leave him alone!" yelled Trey, who had found his wits now that Commerand's focus was elsewhere.

Commerand turned slowly continuing to hold Seth who wretched in pain with each movement of the staff. "What is it you have that he wants?"

"Go to hell!" Trey screamed.

Commerand swiftly became face to face with

Trey, revealing deathly eyes and pale decaying skin. Green puss oozed from an open sore on his cheek.

Staring deep into Trey's eyes as if he could harass his very soul, Commerand whispered with putrid hot breath and a scowl, "What do you know of heeell, boy?" Trey again became petrified with fear as Commerand continued, "Can't you see? I am already there."

Commerand glanced over Trey's shoulder, then said, "Andressen's sword! My lord will be very pleased to have it back at his side. It seems as if *you* are now it's protector. Unfortunately for you, you cannot give it to me like you will the eye. This, dear boy, looks like the end of our pleasantries."

The rotting sorcerer floated backward and raised the magical staff releasing Seth from its grip. He then waved it slamming Trey face first onto the road. He then flipped him onto his back like a short order cook would flip a pancake – Trey bounced with an audible OOOOFF! Trey tried to move but couldn't, the force from the staff kept him pinned. Commerand then raised the pinky from the staff which unzipped a pocket and slowly fished out the eye. The eye rose for all to see. The brilliant light emanating from the artifact forced all but Commerand to shield their eyes.

"Finally, the time has come. The great king will be free. He will ravage you all and this god forsaken planet. You will beg for forgiveness but will find none."

An engine from above roared to life as a plane nearly landed on the party. It descended onto the road. Sparky popped onto the scene blasting a grenade of electricity onto Commerand and nearby rogglets. Lyza hung out the door raining bullets from a submachine gun onto the crowd – scattering everyone. The eye fell onto the sandy road as Commerand was forced to defend himself.

Sparky popped to Trey – his bright loving eyes begged for approval. "Thanks buddy! I wondered when you'd show up!" His kitten mouth smiled, he released a joyful set of sparks then popped away.

Clievan rushed the roggletts freeing Nick. He then ran to help Trey and at the same time secured the eye in his massive grip. He received an approving nod from Trey just as Seth grabbed Trey lifting him above the commotion and out of Commerand's range. Clievan seized Nick then hauled him in the direction of the plane.

"Get them!" Commerand commanded.

Dozens of roggletts closely pursued.

"Look at Clievan go! Dang he's fast!" said Trey from above.

Lyza was in the door of the plane just outside of town ushering them to hurry. She leveled precise shots onto the trailing horde. Noting their pace, she yelled to Assauf, "Go! Go! Go!"

The plane began a slow acceleration just as Clievan arrived. He threw Nick through the door. Shortly after, Seth crashed in with Trey braced in his arms and invisible folded wings. The pilot fully accelerated lifting the group to safety.

"Holy crap that was good timing!" said Seth.

"We were trying to be quiet on the landing but saw you in trouble. Thought you could use a distraction," said Lyza.

"Yeah! That worked great!" said Trey. "How's Nick?"

"He looks pretty beat up but nothing major," she said. "What were you guys doing there?"

"Initially rescuing Nick but also trying to keep Commerand from getting the eye."

"The eye? How did you know he was there for the eye?"

"The Keeper told me. He also told me that Nick was gonna die." Trey kept quiet about the demon key.

"He said all of that? You are very clever to get information out of The Keeper. Were you successful? Did you get the eye?"

Trey hesitated. He looked worriedly at Seth who nodded assuredly in return.

She repeated more directly, "Did you get it, Trey?"

"Yeah. Yeah I got it." Trey felt as if he had been defeated. He remembered what Grandpa said about one of these people will deceive him. What if it was her? She saved them but he didn't trust her.

"Clievan and Seth helped you?"

"Well. Sort of," Trey replied.

"No, your hi...." She cut fierce eyes at Seth, stopping him mid-sentence. He paused, momentarily startled then continued, "We didn't make it past the spell," said Seth.

"So, you did it by yourself? That's amazing!" she said refocusing her attention on Trey.

"Where are we going now?" asked Trey.

"You're going home. I'll relocate the eye, then put the word out that you no longer have it. You should be safe while Commerand expends his resources trying to find it. The sword you will have to keep. You must either keep it on you or hide it carefully. The spell only works if it is on you. Otherwise, anyone can pick it up just as Seth did in the Sea Troll cave."

"Why can't I just hide it, then tell you where it is?"

"Like with the disk, it doesn't work that way. I can't possess the sword. Plus, you were able to wield it. You are now its protector."

"No. I'm not. I wouldn't be here If it hadn't been for the Dandrelierdens."

"The Dandrelierdens? They helped you?"

"Yeah. This really pretty one was there in the forest, but she wasn't pretty then. She was there when I woke. She said they had to bring me back to life, but I didn't ask how. I was pretty freaked out."

"I bet you were. I'm glad you're alive. Nevertheless, you must keep it safe and do not bring the pieces together again. The fairies won't be there for you next time." she said.

"Trust me. I'll never do that again."

Nick awoke saying, "Where are we?"

"In a plane," said Lyza.

"You again? How'd you get here? How did we get on this plane? Are you holding my hand?"

"I...I was just checking to make sure you were ok," she said abruptly letting his hand go.

"I suppose I owe you a thank you," he said to her softly.

"You're welcome," she replied with a bright smile.

He looked around, then said, "I owe all of you a thank you. I was in a real bad spot back there."

"No problem," Seth replied. "Another day another danger."

Nick turned to Trey, "Hey Trey. Did you get it?"

"Yeah," he replied proudly.

"How?"

"The distraction spell was first. Seth and Clievan nearly offed themselves under that one."

"And the old man?"

"He became the Protector after I completed the puzzle."

"And the dog?"

"Big and gruesome."

"Uhhhgg. I'm sorry you had to face it. I want to hear the whole story when we get home."

"You all did an amazing thing today and no one even got seriously hurt," Lyza proclaimed.

"What are you talking about?" Trey objected.

"Well, no one was permanently seriously injured," she said with a smile.

"Had it not been for Clievan, we wouldn't have been successful," said Trey. "Hey. Where is he anyway? Clievan! You can appear now," Trey said to the air.

Nothing happened.

"Clievan? Are you here?"

Lyza looked worriedly at Seth then back to Trey.

"Trey. I don't think he's here," Lyza said calmly.

"No! He has to be here! Clievan! Where are you! Come out now!" he called out frantically.

"Trey," Seth said putting a hand on Trey's shoulder trying to calm him down. "I don't think he made it on the plane." He looked at Lyza then Nick then back to Trey. "It's ok. He's a big boy. He can take care of himself. As you know, he can stay hidden well."

"No!" Trey yelled at Seth. "That's not it! Clievan! Stop playing around! Show yourself!"

"What do you mean? Just calm down will you. Tell us what's wrong," Nick said.

"What I'm trying to say-" Trey said panicked.

"Clievan has to be here!" They all looked at each other while Trey stared out the window of the plane. "He has to be here because he...he has the eye." Trey nearly broke down in tears afterward.

"Oh no!" was all Lyza could say.

Rescuing Don Smith

"We have to go back," Trey said.

"There's no time," Lyza replied vacantly. "Plus, there's no way we can stand against Commerand.

"But we have to get the eye back."

"Yes, we do, but for now we need to get you and Nick home. Let me worry about retrieving the eye."

"But Clievan probably already gave it to him. Commerand could be freeing Khaitu right now! How can you be so cold about it?"

"There's no evidence linking Clievan to Commerand. I think he has his own motivations for wanting the eye," Lyza replied.

"She's right," Seth added. "Clievan is sneaky and not always trustworthy, but he wouldn't do anything to risk Commerand gaining the eye."

"But why? Why would he take it? Why would he do that to me – to us?"

"I don't know," Seth replied.

"We're just gonna let him run off with it?"

Lyza looked at him with confidence, "He may be the best hiding spot we have – always on the move and with the ability to become invisible. Don't get me wrong, we have to get it back, but I think for now it's safe."

"Assuming he escapes Commerand in the desert," Trey said doubtfully.

"If you didn't notice, Clievan has some rather peculiar characteristics," Seth said. "He is adapted well for the desert climate. He has a great chance to avoid Commerand and his cronies. They'll never follow him into the deathly depths of the Great Sand Sea."

"Whatever you say. Let's just get me home so I can forget about all of this."

"I know you're upset but there's nothing we can do now," Lyza said trying to comfort the distraught boy.

"I just can't believe after all I did, I lose it due to one bad decision. Argg!" He slammed his fists onto the wall of the plane. "I knew I should've made him give it to me in the fight. I trusted him."

"We all did," Seth added.

The plane landed on a desolate road in southern Egypt.

They jumped out of the plane and Trey said to Seth, "I'll miss you. Will I see you again?"

"Of course," said Seth, unsure of the truth of the response. "Lyza will keep me updated, won't you?"

"Sure," she said.

Trey hugged Seth, who stayed by the car while Trey, Lyza and Nick trekked into the desert.

She led them to the portal she and Trey

previously used to arrive a day ago.

Lyza removed the key from her locket, then formed a star attached to the shape of an "L". Nick's eyes widened at the sight of the key.

"No," Trey said lightly.

"What do you mean no?" replied Lyza looking at him with concern.

"No," he said firmly. There's more. I – "

"What is it, Trey. You can tell me."

"I know where Don and Grandpa are."

Her heart sank. Her eyes told a graphic story of her exploding emotions. It was an expression Trey was happy to see – shock along with elation and hope.

"What do you mean, you know where they are?" She was nearly crying. It looked as if she wouldn't be able to contain herself long.

"I know where they are."

"But how?"

"When I was with the Keeper, I found – I mean he told me where they were."

"You found or he told you?"

"He told me. He told me Don was in a place called the Highlands."

"And Patrick?"

Trey looked down searching for words in the sand.

"And your grandfather? Where is he? Tell me, Trey!" she said with tears streaming down her face.

"The Etherios," he said sadly. "He's in the Etherios."

"No!" she cried. "No. No. No. No. NO! That can't be! He couldn't possibly get to the Etherios on his own."

"The Keeper sent him there in return for Don."

She fell to a knee and wept.

She sniffed, "How did Don get to the Etherios?"

"He said by accident."

"No one gets to the Etherios by accident," she replied with a sniff. Her deep blue eyes streaked with thin red lines ate into him like a coyote on a carcass.

"That's what he said."

"I know Trey." She sniffed back tears. "It's not your fault. Let's get you home," she said regaining her feet and wiping away wetness from swollen eyes.

"No. I want to bring Don home."

"That's brave of you, but he may be safer at Highlands."

"If there's one thing I learned over the past couple days is that no one is safe anywhere. Plus, he's been gone a long time. I'm sure his family wants to see him."

"Let's get you home and then I'll go get him."

"No, Lyza. It's something I have to do."

She looked at him a moment then understood his unwavering stance. She looked at Nick and with a cunning smile she said, "Ok. What do you think, Nick? What to go to Highlands to get Don Smith?"

"Do you mean Don Smith, as in your school mate Donald Smith's father?"

"Yeah. I found him."

"Of course! Let's go get him!" He walked off in the direction they came.

"Nick! Back this way!" Trey hollered.

"But the car is this way." Nick confusingly replied. He stood in the sand looking at them looking at him.

"It's this way, Nick," Lyza said alluringly.

After Nick made his way back, Lyza said, "Hold onto me guys."

"It's an M," Trey said.

She turned and with a furrowed brow said, "The Keeper told you that too? He told you where to find him *and* how to get there?"

"Uh. Yeah. I was, um, very persuasive?"

"You're not telling me the whole story are you?"

"A lot happened. I don't remember some of it," he stammered.

"When this is all over," she said to him in a serious but playful manner, "we're going to have a sit down to discuss these details you keep forgetting."

He looked at her without a further comment.

She folded the key into and M. Trey and Nick each held a shoulder. Nick offered Trey a concerned look as she touched the key to the stone.

Whomp, Whomp Whomp

Nick rolled on the ground, lurching to not vomit while Trey and Lyza stood watching.

"You're porting nicely," she said to Trey.

"I'm getting the hang of it," he said smiling.

"You'll feel better in a few minutes," Trey said to Nick.

"Ooooohhhhh, that is *not* fun," Nick said as he raised to a knee looking up at Lyza. He was pale and looked squeamish.

Trey shivered, "It's cold here. I should have packed a jacket." He looked at each but drew no laughs. He then looked out over a livestock filled pasture onto a sparkling lake below which was overshadowed by a formidable mountain. Piles of rock decorated the grassy land in irregular intervals. Near the lake on a raised hill sat a small farmhouse, which was more like a hut – a farmhut, with smoke protruding from a brick chimney.

They hiked through the pasture, passed through a wooden fence bordering a plot of colorful vegetables, walked along a stone pathway then ducked to avoid a hanging plant to reach the only door. It opened just as Nick began to knock. A tall, thin man emerged through the doorway.

"I thought you'd never come," Don said as he rushed past Nick to hug Lyza.

He was easily six and a half feet tall, so he turned his head to keep his chest-long beard out of her face.

She pulled away from the embrace and said, "Don. You're so – skinny." She tried to think of a better word but failed.

He looked anxiously into the air then said, "You shouldn't have come. Hurry inside before she sees you."

He rushed them into the farmhut and carefully closed the door after taking one last peek. He then proceeded to pull all the drapes shut on the interior windows.

He returned to Lyza and said while grabbing his midsection with two large over-burdened hands, "You like? Not the portly Don you used to know, huh? I've worked hard for what I have. I had to scavenge the first few months." He gazed into the fire and recalled a vivid memory, "There were a few days I thought I wouldn't make it." He looked back at his longtime friend, ran his fingers through bushy black hair then said, "I built this place with wood from the forest using tools I crafted from stones found nearby. I wanted to make sure you could find me, so I didn't stray too far from the portal up on the hill."

"It's really amazing," she replied thoughtfully. "I'm so sorry you had to go through this."

"It's okay."

Nick butted into the pleasant conversation, "You said we were in danger."

"Yeah," Trey added. "You said before she sees us. What did you mean? What sort of danger are we in?"

Don shot them all a foreboding look. He said, "You should all sit down."

Don took a seat in a wooden chair that resembled a recliner, the other three sat on a cloth covered wooden sofa.

"Shortly after I built this place and set up the farm, on an ordinary cloudy day while attending sheep, something came through the portal." He looked at them gravely.

"What was it, Don?" Lyza asked seriously.

"A dragon," he said sitting back in the chair.

"No way!" Trey said excitedly.

"A dragon? Seriously?" Nick remarked clearly not believing the remark.

"Her name is Tanarkin the Green. She was sent by Ragnistant to ensure I stay here – forever. I'm responsible for keeping up this farm for her subsistence."

"So, you're her slave?" Trey asked as nicely as he could.

"Yeah. I guess so," he replied sadly. "She lives in the mountain so she can easily oversee my activities. I'm sure she knows you're here."

"Why would she let us pass without restriction?"

Nick asked still not believing the story but playing along for the sake of the group.

Don regarded them all individually then said, "Now there are four prisoners rather than one."

"No way! I'm not staying here any longer," Trey said as he jumped from the couch. "Get your stuff and let's go now!"

Don rose to meet him, "It's not that easy. She won't just let us leave. We have to develop a plan."

"Fine," Trey finished then sat back down.

"How did you find me, anyway?"

Lyza answered, "Trey. Trey found out where you were. By the way Trey, meet my good friend Don Smith. Don Smith, Trey Roberts."

Just before Trey could take his outstretched hand, a loud popping sound startled the group. *Pop, Snap, Pop* followed by a long high-pitched whistle. Bolts of electricity arced from Trey to Don.

Sparky appeared on Don's shoulder. "Tessie! You made it! I was so worried about you!"

He grasped the blue creature Trey named Sparky. He vigorously rubbed it sending shooting sparks all about. He pressed Tessie to his face. Tessie nuzzled him affectionately in return.

"Tessie?" Trey asked dismayed.

"Yeah! Tessie. She's been with me for many years. I thought I lost her in the... Oh. That means – " he looked at Lyza with fearful eyes.

"I know about the portal in China, Don," Lyza interrupted. It's ok. No one's blaming you for anything."

"You know? But how?"

"The Phoenix led us there. It was a mess."

"I – I'm sorry. I didn't know. I was having these

dreams. I thought it was Master Olerand. He said to keep it quiet, that I couldn't trust anyone."

"It's okay. We've squared all that away."

"I tried to smash it before I –. It wasn't supposed to send me there. I didn't have the eye. Commerand attacked so quickly. I think he has the ability to open portals."

"There's been lots of weird stuff happening lately," she comforted as she looked into his dark brown eyes. "If he can open portals without the eye, then we may be in more trouble than we thought."

He hugged her once more then turned to Nick and Trey. "It's my pleasure to meet you both." He extended a hand to Nick first then addressed Trey. "I don't know how you did it. Ampers are very wary of strangers. You're lucky to be alive. I thank you for keeping Tessie safe."

"It's been awesome getting to know him, er, I mean her."

Don said to the group, "Cup of tea, anyone? I grow it in the garden there. It's bitter but it beats no tea."

"Is it hot?" Trey asked. "I'll have some if it's hot."

He brought them all a cup then retook his seat in the recliner.

Trey cupped his hands around the hand-crafted wooden cup and held it close to his face.

Lyza placed a hand on Don's knee and said, "Don, it's been so long. Have you been here this whole time?"

"No. I was somewhere else before, but somehow I ended up here," he replied then sipped his tea.

"The Etherios. You were in the Etherios."

"Of course. No wonder I couldn't figure it out."

"It didn't seem like I was there for very long. But I think time works differently there."

"Trey said the Keeper made a deal with Patrick to free you."

"Patrick wouldn't do that. He knows not to make deals with that demon."

"Believe it."

"What kind of deal? Where's Patrick?"

Lyza looked at Trey.

"No! Don't tell me." He looked at Trey then back to Lyza. Her eyes answered his question. "He took my place didn't he? That arrogant Cajun took my place. Why?"

"We don't know. Much has happened since you were gone. The Keeper is dead and Commerand nearly acquired the eye."

"He actually might have the eye," Trey countered.

"Dead? How's that possible?"

Lyza again looked at Trey.

"No. Really? Him?" Don replied looking starstruck at Trey. "That must be how he befriended Tessie."

"I didn't believe it until I saw the Keeper. No one else can wield the sword," continued Lyza.

"I already told you. I can't wield the sword without burning up," Trey blurted but drew no attention from the two.

"There've been some discrepancies, but the prophecy is generally holding true," said Lyza.

"Where is the eye now?"

"We don't know."

"That's not good."

"I think it's ok for now," Lyza continued. "Don. We're here for you. Come home with us."

"Home," he said as he settled back into the chair. He stared into the fire. "It's been so long. I assumed I would be here for the rest of my days."

"It's time for you to leave this place. It's time to get back to Clara and Donald."

Don continued to gaze distantly. "Little Don. He must be so big now."

"Yeah. Tell me about it," said Trey.

"He is. He and Trey are friends. Trey is the reason we're here. Little Don needs you," said Lyza.

Don cast his attention to Trey. "You're his friend? Does he talk about me?"

"Well, not exactly. Donald and I know each other but we aren't really friends. We don't talk much."

Don rose and walked to the window. He peeked through a crack to look over the pasture at dog-sized black-wooled sheep-like animals huddled around a trough. "What if they don't want me back? What if they reject me?"

Trey stood and replied confidently to Don's back, "Those are if's that haven't happened. Don't be afraid of things that don't exist. You're here. You're alive. They're at home wishing for you to return. Come with us. Go home to them."

Don braced himself against the windowsill and looked down. "I don't know. I've made such a mess."

"That's ridiculous. There's nothing you can do to make you unwanted at home," replied Trey.

Don turned and in a quiet scream directed at Trey he replied, "What do you know? You don't know what it feels like to leave your wife and child alone to fend for themselves without the smallest goodbye."

Rescuing Don Smith

Trey leaned back at the blast from Don then walked several paces closer looking him square in the eyes. He handed him the picture of him and his son from the office. Don took it then held his hand over his mouth as his eyes widened.

Trey's voice was calm with a hint of disdain. "You're right. I don't know how that feels." He regarded Lyza who shared an approving nod. "But I do know that if *my* father, who left *my* mom and I in a similar situation were to decide to come home, I would welcome him. I would hug him. I would be thankful he was there. I'd be plenty mad and demand explanations and apologies, but I would want him home – I want him home." He lowered his head and attempted to wipe away the sadness. Don stepped in and held him. "I want him home," Trey said in a whisper into Don's chest. Lyza and Nick joined in the embrace. "I want him home," Trey whimpered.

Don looked at the image of Donald again and said, "Ok. I'll go home."

"If we're leaving, we should go now," Lyza said pulling away from the cluster.

"Agreed," replied Don. "But first, we have to figure out how to avoid Tanny."

"Tanny?" Trey questioned.

"The dragon," Nick replied dryly.

Tanarkin The Green

"Tell us about Tanarkin," Lyza said to Don.

"Tanny? She's green like a forest with a grey underbelly. Considering she's the only dragon I know, she seems really reasonable – almost friendly at times. I often get the sense she's reluctant about her purpose, like she resents Ragnistant for forcing her to be here."

"That's good. Maybe we can use it somehow," Lyza added.

"No. There's no talking to her. I think communicating with us is beneath her. She's never spoken to me, just threats and a lot of molten fire warnings when I do something wrong."

"Plus," Lyza added, "if by some reason we can get a few words out, those words would have to be projected powerfully and have a specific purpose that is meaningful to her."

"So, talking her into letting us go is out," Nick commented drawing an eye from Lyza. "Does she have any patterns? You know, anything predictable?" he continued.

"She comes down sporadically. As long as I keep up the herds, we hardly ever see each other. I sometimes hear her outside when she feeds but other than that she stays in the mountain."

Trey peeked through the window and said, "How do you know she knows we're here? Maybe she just trained you to think that way. Maybe we can just walk up the hill and port out of here without her knowing,"

"No way!" Don replied quickly. "I wouldn't try that. Once, several months ago, I casually walked to the portal. I had no intention to use it, heck I don't have the means to use it. However, once I neared the stone, she swooped down and blasted an awful ring of fire around me separating me from the portal. She hovered a few seconds overhead to ensure her warning was received before flying back to the mountain. That was just a random day."

"That's how you know she's watching," Nick stated.

Don returned a confirming glance.

"But Ragnistant's dead. I killed him. Won't she let us go if I tell her? She doesn't have to talk back," Trey refuted.

"No, Trey," Lyza replied. "Once dragons agree to something, nothing can keep them from seeing it through. If she agreed to watch over Don until the end of his days, that is what she'll do – regardless of Ragnistant's fate."

Trey's eyes twitched, his mind whirred. He looked distantly then said, "Would she yield to a more powerful entity?"

"What are you getting at, Trey?" Lyza asked.

"What if we could convince her that there's a more powerful entity that demanded her to release her duty to Ragnistant?"

"You mean scare her into submission?" Don replied. "Don't be silly. She's a *dragon*," he said putting great emphasis on the word dragon as if Trey was misinformed as to what they were discussing. "Nothing will *scare* her."

"Yeah, I'm with Don," Lyza replied. "I don't think it's possible to intimidate a dragon. Even if it were possible, we don't have one of those entities handy."

"I guess you're right," Trey said as if he didn't hear her full explanation. "I need to lay down. Can I use your bed?"

"Sure, Trey. It's on the other side of that curtain," Don replied.

Trey walked into the room which held a long skinny bed and a single window. He sat on the edge of the bed, waived to the group then closed the curtain. The group continued to discuss ways to escape.

Trey removed the sword from his back and laid it upon the bed. He then removed the disk with completed stone and set it on the bed apart from the sword. He caressed the pouch he received from Lyza outside Jessie's front gate as he stared at the disassembled weapon.

He spoke softly to himself, "Had I not brought us here, we wouldn't be in this mess. They didn't have to come. I could have ported on my own. Then they would be safe. I'm so stupid. This whole week has been a big stupid mess – and all for nothing. I failed to get the eye, I failed to rescue Don, I couldn't even hold Sarah's hand and now we're stuck in this tiny house with a crazy dragon threatening to incinerate us. There's really only one option that has a chance to work. I have to be brave. I have to be bold. I have to kill the dragon."

~~

"I don't think we can outrun her," Don replied to Lyza. "It's just too far. I should have built the house closer."

"Could we create some sort of diversion? We could set something on fire, like this house, that would distract her and possibly block her vision of our escape," Nick suggested.

"That could work," Lyza said. "If we created enough of a smoke screen, she might be delayed enough for us to reach the portal."

"We'd only have the one chance. After that we'd be sitting ducks," Don added.

"Maybe we can just wait her out until she makes a mistake or an opportunity presents itself." Nick suggested.

"I've been here four years. I think she has more patience than all of us put together."

"What was that!" Nick exclaimed as he reflexively crouched to avoid a loud screech above his head. The farm hut shuddered violently.

"Tanny!" Don said alarmed. "She never comes this close to the house. What drew her from her roost?"

"Trey!" Lyza screamed. She jumped from the couch, darted through the curtain to find an empty bed, two empty glass bottles and an open window. She grasped the bottles and said, "Trey! No!" She hurled herself through the window in time to see a massive green dragon descend upon the helpless child.

~~

Trey hurdled stones and avoided piles of manure as he ran through the pasture – he periodically looked over his shoulder for trouble. He lost his breath twice while scurrying up the hill causing him to slow his pace.

He nearly made it to the top when the dragon's call detonated across the farm. It was loud and thunderous – like the roar of a mutant lizard in a movie he watched with Marcus a year or so ago. He winced at the pain in his ears as his knees buckled from dread. He almost fell but found solid footing and continued. After a few more steps while panting rapidly, he prepared himself for the uncertainty to befall him.

He held the sword in his right hand, the disk in the left at his side. He knelt as he said to himself as if in prayer, "You can do this Trey. Strong and bold. Show no fear. You can do hard things." He studied the ground around his front foot and said, "I hope this works." He courageously rose to face the rapidly approaching nightmare.

Lyza said as the others joined her next to the house, "Oh my, Trey. What are you doing?"
"You have to stop him!" Nick screamed at Lyza.

"We're too far away!" she panicked. "She's already on top of him."

The dragon swooped low over Trey – nearly bashing him with a thick foot covered in greyish brown roots that jutted out into long sharp claws. As she turned in the sky, sunlight reflected off green leaf shaped scales. She screeched loudly through massive jaws housing a row of straight jagged teeth. Trey held his ground without taking a stabilizing step. He gripped the sword straight and strong. His front foot quivered but he remained steady.

"We have to do something!" Nick yelled.
They watched in horror as the graceful dragon swooped in again, lower this time, then hovered above. She attacked with a solid stream of molten fire.
"No!" Nick screamed as the deathly breath engulfed the child.
Lyza saw Trey briefly raise the sword. She pushed away the thought of how weak the defense looked against such a powerful creature. She stared wide eyed at the wall of fire on the hill – speechless at the loss of the teenage hero.
As the blaze quickly died down, Trey remained standing in a circle of charred earth.
"That's the same thing she did to me!" Don exclaimed with a big smile and a chuckle.
Lyza hit him stiffly in the chest as an indication to stop making light of the situation.
"He's still alive!" Nick yelled. "He's still alive! Hey! Over here! Come fight us! Hey!" He flailed his arms and jumped around in a poor attempt at a distraction.

Tanarkin remained undeterred.

She screeched much louder than any time before. Trey sensed she was finished with idle threats.

Still hovering above, she dipped her head as if to strike. He leaned forward and yelled with his mightiest voice, "Tanarkin! I command you to stop!" Trey hoped the sound of a tiny bottle crushing beneath his foot didn't give away his secret.

She pulled back from the attack, as if agreeing to Trey's command.

He spoke directly to her mind. "I am Wallace Patrick Roberts the third. I slayed Ragnistant. Your purpose here is no longer required. You are free to go."

She beat massive wings the color of autumn leaves before diving toward Trey. She pulled back to land gently outside the burned circle. She towered over Trey's miniscule frame.

He sensed curiosity and purpose. "I wield Andressen's Sword. You cannot stand against it. Yield!"

She replied to his mind in an elegant British voice, "How do you not *fear* me? You are just a boy. How could I possibly be commanded by a boy?"

"You can do as I say or you can die," he replied firmly. With a great amount of effort, he hoped she wouldn't detect his wavering confidence.

She pulled her head back, astonished at how Trey spoke to her. "You speak strongly for a mortal child and telepathic at that. Andressen's sword, indeed. However you, a simple human boy, cannot wield its power."

Trey wondered how much longer he could keep her talking but he couldn't think about that. His biggest concern at the moment was not becoming a dragon BBQ.

"You aren't listening!" he projected forcefully, hoping to buy more time.

"Our conversation is finished." She spread magnificent wings; a rumble gurgled up from deep within her throat. Heat emanated from her gullet. She arched her neck then blasted a violent beam of fire laced plasma directly at Trey.

Lyza screamed as the others stared in shock.

The dragon's torrent engulfed the small, heroic boy.

She took a breath revealing a burning mass twice as large where Trey once stood. She then pelted him again with another blazing barrage leaving a flaming shadow of Trey. She rose directly above and vomited a volcanic eruption onto the child below. Molten lava flowed all around and over the area where he once stood.

"Noooo!" Lyza screamed into the shoulder of Nick in a flurry of tears and anger. "He was just a boy! He was just a boy!" she continued crying violently. Nick held her tightly and shielded her from the dragon's destruction.

Tanarkin screeched then shot from the ground soared in a tight spiral then landed before her victim to inspect the results of her barrage. She then cowered as an imperceptible fiery image of Trey slowly rose into the air.

"Impossible!" she exclaimed wildly.

"Look!" Don shouted. He's still alive! I think."

Lyza gasped at the hill as the tiny flaming boy rose above the colossal beast.

She looked at the empty bottles in her hand and said with proud mama eyes, "You smart boy. You brave smart boy."

"How's he doing that?" Nick asked. Is he still alive? How can this be?"

"I don't know. He should be dead," Lyza replied.

"But he's not. At least not yet and that's good for all of us," Don added.

Lyza hit him again and gave him a sour face.

Trey's eyes burned diamond white. Flaming fire licked the sword as he angled it into an attack position. He settled the rise just above her lowered head.

"Denounce your duty to Ragnistant!" Trey commanded amid fire and flame. "Tanarkin the Green. You must yield or die!"

"What's he doing?" Don asked. "What did he say?"

"I don't know," Lyza replied. "But it doesn't look like she's happy about it nor does he have much longer on the potions.

Nick looked at her. "Did you say something about potions?"

"He took fireproof potions hoping he wouldn't burn." She shoved the empty bottles into his hand.

"The potions will keep him from dying?" Nick continued.

"He will die If the potions wear off before he separates the sword from the disk."

"I'm so confused. Sword?"

"We don't have time for this Nick," she said impatiently. "I'll try to explain it later."

"Look! He's coming down!" Don exclaimed.

They watched Trey slowly sink as the levitation potion wore off. The flame extinguished about halfway down. Trey collapsed then fell lifelessly the remaining distance onto the charred ground.

All three of the spectators gasped as they stood helplessly watching Tanarkin snatch Trey's body into her mouth then fly away.

"Noooooo!" screamed Lyza like a wailing banshee.

A Long Drive Home

"How could I let this happen? All I had to do was keep him safe!" Lyza cried into the thin damp air.

"He should never have been here," Nick said angrily. "Why'd you bring him!"

Don steadied Nick and said, "It's not her fault. We're all part of this. She did what she had to do to protect him."

"It wasn't enough," Nick said coldly.

She glanced at him with puffy eyes. Her red face streaked with tears.

"This is all bad," Don said urgently. "But we're still here. There's nothing we can do for Trey now. We should take this opportunity to escape."

"No! We can't leave him," Nick screamed.

"Nick. There's nothing we can do. The dragon." Don replied calmly.

"He's right," Lyza said distantly. "This is our only chance. I'll get you two home and then I'll come back for him on my own."

Nick looked at her for a long minute. "You think it's stupid – looking for Trey."

"No. I –"

"He was – " Nick teared up and continued, "like a son to me. His mom – " he made a stiff fist, held it to his chest and closed his eyes. "What do I say to her?" He opened his red streaked eyes and faced Lyza, "Don't tell me there's nothing we can do. I have to bring – " he said in a strained whisper. "I have to bring him home."

She embraced him then said into his broken eyes, "I'll bring him home. I promise."

He pulled away and looked deep into her blue eyes, "But you're no match for a dragon."

"He's right, Lyza." Don added. "Even you can't come back alone."

"I'll bring Seth. He'll help."

"You better get some of his cousins too," Nick said.

She looked at him curiously.

"He has plenty to spare," he added.

She couldn't hold back a single laugh. Then she cried again.

"We have to go if we're going," Don urged as he began walking toward the portal.

"You aren't taking anything?" Nick asked.

"I came here with nothing, so I'll leave the same."

"Ok. Let's go," she commanded.

They climbed the hill, each looking back periodically expecting Tanarkin to appear at any moment. They arrived undisturbed at the stone. Lyza formed the key and seconds later they stood in the forest next to the old well.

Lyza remained standing. Nick and Don were on their knees.

"I've never gotten – ugghh – used to that," Don said nearly barfing in the grass.

"It's been a long time. You'll get it back," Lyza said as she comforted him with a light hand on his back. He rose and turned to her as she continued, "I'm so happy you're alive. I'm sorry it took us so long to find you."

"It's ok. You didn't know. I've been in anguish thinking I gave the keys to Khaitu's freedom to Commerand. I'm glad everything is still intact."

"It's not intact but I think we're still winning."

"You and I will catch up soon. Go home. Take all the time you need to make things right."

"Yes Ma'am," Don said with a big, nervous smile.

She hugged him tightly then turned to Nick.

"I have to find Seth and hurry back. Take the car to get home. Call me if you need me."

"I will. Let me know when you find Trey."

She looked down fighting back tears. "I will." Lyza held Nick's hands, kissed him on the cheek, then said looking deep into his eyes, "Bye Nick."

Nick seemed startled and didn't return the farewell.

She knelt at the stone then disappeared.

Test Results

Trey awoke dizzy. Shadows danced in his peripherals. He made several unsuccessful attempts to clear his vision.

"The fire tamer lives," said a calm, eerily familiar female British voice.

Trey's stomach plummeted upon recognition of the metallic voice. "Where am I."

"You are in my home."

A shiver engulfed him at the thought of being in a dragon's lair. However, it wasn't like in the movies he had seen. It was pleasant and felt peaceful. Also, no hint of a massive treasure.

His voice cracked when he said, "Why can't I see?"

"Your eyes haven't yet healed," she replied elegantly.

"What happened to my eyes?"

"They were badly burned."

He lowered his voice and said, "Oh. Yeah. That happened. What'd you do to me?" He swam a hand through cloudy water that stretched several meters to each side of the moderately lit cave, "What am I in? Is this some sort of pool?"

"Yes. The water induces your exemplary healing capabilities. You were badly burned from your ill-constructed plan. You nearly died. Tell me, wielder of Andressen's sword, do you descend from fairies?"

"Fairies? No. Why?"

"Anyone else would have perished from the injuries you sustained."

"But here I am,"

"Indeed, you are. I've only known fairies to possess such healing power."

Trey remembered Coméllula and what she said about the gifts then continued, "You didn't even care about the sword to begin with." Everything remained blurry but he was able to make out certain shapes, including the chatty green dragon resting peacefully next to him at the edge of the water.

"Yes. It is an insignificant weapon in the hands of anyone but Khaitu – including yourself. I would like to know how it came into your possession."

Trey laughed, "By accident. Like everything else that has happened – including you."

"Nothing, dear boy, happens by accident."

"Tell me again why I'm here? You tried to kill me remember, Tanarkin? Should I call you Tanarkin or Tanny?"

"I have grown fond of Tanny over the years. Don's incessant attempts to sway my favor with conversation didn't go unheard."

"Tanny it is."

"Killing you wasn't my intention. I had to test you."

"Test me? What if you killed me with your test?"

"Then you would have failed, of course."

"Of course," Trey repeated somberly.

"But why? Why did you have to test me?"

"I had to know if it were true. It has been foretold – Above the forest he will arise, the one from the line will become a savior of his forefathers, impervious to dragon's breath, resistant to death."

"What does that mean?"

"It means you had the sword and I had to test you. You didn't die so you must be the one."

Trey used his farce to continue his purpose. "My friends. Let them go," he said in a weak attempt at a manly voice.

"They're already gone."

A rush of relief surged through him. "Really? You let them pass through the portal?"

"As you said, my duties here are no longer required. Are you sure Ragnistant is dead?"

"Yes. Well. He's in the Etherios I, uh, was told, but the snake part of him is gone."

"Fire Tamer, you cannot lie to a dragon. I am aware of the potions and I know you have visited Logos."

"How do you know all of that?"

"I perceived it through our connection while you were healing. A connection we will now forever share."

"But I don't feel you like I did with Ragnistant."

"Thank you," she replied. Trey sensed pleasure in her words.

"Wait!" Trey said startled. "What do you mean

by forever share?"

"Once you make a mental connection with a dragon, that connection remains open through space and time."

"You mean we'll always be able to talk to each other, no matter where we are?"

"You are correct," she said cheerfully.

"That's just great," Trey said as he rolled his eyes and huffed a big sigh. He continued, "If you knew about the potions, why did you still help me. Wait, you yielded to me before I passed out. You didn't know about the potions until after."

"And my word is my bond."

"But you didn't have to save me. You could have let me die or," he gulped, "ate me."

The water rippled violently at the force of her hearty laughter. "I would never eat a helpless child." She leered with a playful eye, "But you were cooked just about right,"

"That's not funny," Trey replied. He shifted uncomfortably in the water then stood. His clothes were scorched rags. He rubbed a dark spot on his leg where his skin was burned. Trey's thoughts suddenly turned to himself, of spending the rest of his days with a vicious dragon.

She followed effortlessly as Trey moved through the lair.

"I suppose I will stay in Don's farm hut?" he said dismayed. "How do I get down there?"

"That would be fine, if that's what you choose. However, wouldn't going home be preferable?"

"Home!" Trey said excitedly. "You'll let me go home?"

She smiled in his mind, "Yes. And I'll take you

there."

"But how? We don't have a key."

She lowered a wing intending him to climb on. He hesitated. "Isn't there another way?"

"Yes," she said as she moved her massive head closer and opened her mouth wide.

Trey quickly said, "No thanks!" He then stepped onto the autumn colored tip of the great wing. Before hiking up he rubbed the wing surface in amazement. "Your scales are leaves." He rubbed leaf shaped scales the size of his head. They were hard and Trey thought, impenetrable to most weapons of which he was familiar. "They're beautiful." He then proceeded to slowly crawl along its length. He pulled toward her neck using dark green spines that trailed her from head to tail. He found a position at the base of her neck where the spines were smallest and more manageable than the human-sized ones on her back and neck.

She crawled to the opening high in the mountain. Trey shivered in the cold.

"Hold on tight," she said, just as she leaped from the edge.

Trey ducked low, holding onto a narrow spine with both hands.

The wind rushed through two tree-like antlers that split into four of haphazard shape. It blew down her neck at a hurricane's speed and pelted Trey with blistering force. He pressed his feet harder onto raised spines and held tighter, unsure if his grip would be sufficient to sustain the dive.

She spread her wings to level out over the tranquil lake. Trey softened his grip as the warm air and gravity eased his insecurity.

She made a wide, swooping turn then landed

gently at the stone on the hill. Trey observed the burnt crater created from their earlier battle. She lowered a wing prompting Trey to initiate a thrilling slide down onto the ground. She then rested a foot at the base of the portal. A grey root shaped claw grew from a large toe. It twisted into a familiar shape as it protruded outward.

Trey looked at her strangely then laid a hand on her wing. She pressed the shape to the portal sending them to the well in the forest.

Trey stood in the dark forest, holding the hand of a charming older woman. Her skin was pale in the moonlight – her tightly braided hair was the color of autumn leaves. She wore a flowing green dress with no shoes.

Trey felt oddly close to the woman, as if she were family or a dear friend. He stared longingly into golden yellow eyes.

"Shall we?" she asked as she pointed him toward a clearing just beyond the overgrown trail.

They walked quietly through the dense forest. She tenderly stroked soft fingers over several towering trunks as if thanking them for their majestic service.

When they entered the clearing, she faced Trey and took him by both hands. He looked curiously into her eyes. She then quickly spun him as if enthralled in a passionate Latin dance and tossed him high into the air as she transformed into the gargantuan dragon.

Trey screamed as he rose higher and higher until at the apex of his loft, he gently settled onto the base of Tanarkin's neck.

"Don't ever do that again! Please!"

She laughed as she darted toward the brightly lit city in the distance.

Reunion

A distant "Hey Jude," eeked from the speakers of Lyza's sports car. The two men sat quietly with their thoughts. Nick tossed around memories of Trey and how he would try to explain his disappearance to Janet, Trey's mother. Don thought only about meeting his family. About what they would say – about how angry Clara would be.

Don stared blankly out the passenger window, lost in a daze when he suddenly lurched forward then smashed into the passenger door as the car skidded to an abrupt halt in the middle of the deserted road. He stared out the smooth glass as his body petrified in fear. A huge glowing yellow eye peered into the tiny vehicle.

"Tanny! She's come for us! Go! Nick! Go! Go! Go!"

Nick stomped on the gas spinning the car around in a cloud of tire smoke. He immediately slammed on the brakes again when Tanny blocked their escape with a well-placed foot.

Nick jumped out of the car intending to run. He stopped when he heard a familiar voice call his name. "Trey? Is that you?"

"Mr. H!"

"Trey! Where are you?"

Trey came running around Tanny's enormous foot and nearly tackled Nick.

"Trey! We thought we lost you."

"I know. But I'm okay, thanks to Tanny."

"What? We watched her burn and eat you."

"No. She's good now. She actually saved my life. I'll explain later."

"I don't care how you're still alive I'm just glad you are." He hugged the boy again so hard Trey lost his breath.

"Mr. H! Mr. H! You're killing me!" Trey said jokingly.

"Sorry, son. I'm just happy you're safe. Can we go home now?"

Trey looked up at Tanny. She nodded in approval. He then said, "Yes! Let's go home!"

"Thank you, Fire Tamer," she projected to Trey.

"For what?"

"For setting me free and giving me another purpose."

"You're welcome."

"Just call out when you need me. I'll always be there," she said just before disappearing into the night. The wind from her wings nearly tossed he and Nick to the ground.

"I'm sure you will," he said staring into the darkness.

"I will what?" Nick asked.

"Oh. Nothing."

Nick and Trey joined Don in the car.

"You could have said bye to her," Trey said to Don. "She's really nice."

"No. I'm good. I've had enough of dragons for a while."

~~

"Hey. He's alive. Yeah. Hold on, I'll put you on speaker phone," Nick said.

"Hey Lyza."

"Trey! You're alive!"

"Yep."

"That's amazing! But how?"

"It's a long story."

"I bet it is. Another one that you will have to tell me soon."

Trey laughed at her insinuation of all the details he has left out up to this point.

She continued, "Your mom will be waiting for you when you get home. You should be safe for a while. I have people watching to help if Commerand should send anyone your way. But I wouldn't worry. His full attention will be on the eye."

"That means that he doesn't yet have it?"

"Right."

"What about Clievan? Have you found him?"

"No. But that's good. The longer he stays out of sight, the better off we'll all be. Seth is on his trail. We'll find him soon."

"But they came before looking for just the disk. Now I have all three pieces. Why wouldn't they be back soon?"

"That's exactly why he won't be after you now. He knows where it is and feels he can get it later. But for now, his mandate is to free Khaitu by securing the eye and the relics. Even if he got the eye tomorrow, it could be years, even decades before he finds all the relics. Plus, they weren't after the disk. You see, your grandfather left behind a book. The book holds the locations of the relics."

"So, they now have this book and can easily find the relics?" Trey said worriedly.

"No. I found it while you were sleeping. I hid it."

"Hid it? Why not destroy it?" asked Nick.

"The relics are what can bring him out of his prison, but they are also the only way to fully imprison him. He wasn't properly bound in the original ceremony. There's a possibility he can become free another way. He may even already be free. However, that is unlikely considering the effort they put forth to find the book. If he were to escape, we would need to quickly find the relics."

"I understand. So, me and my family are ok until Khaitu comes looking for the sword?"

"Yes. But if that happens, we have more to worry about than those annoying roggletts."

"Ok. Is there anything else I need to know?"

"No. I think that is it for now. I hope to see you guys again under better circumstances. And Trey! Good luck on your match this weekend."

"My match against Ridgeview! I completely forgot about that! Coach Rafiq will be furious with me for missing practice."

"You'll do fine. Take care of yourself...and Nick?"

"Yes? "Watch after that kid."

"I'm not taking my eyes off of him," he said, glancing at Trey.

"I know you won't."

"I'll see you all soon. Take care."

"Bye, Lyza," Trey, Nick and Don said nearly in unison.

Nick looked again at Trey in the rear-view mirror, "Let's get you back to your mom. I bet she's worried sick."

"But first, let's take Don home," Trey countered.

"That good with you?" Nick asked Don.

"Yeah. Let's do it," Don said nervously.

~~

Nick felt uncomfortable driving the fancy sports car through the rough apartment complex. A group of baggy-clothed teens huddled around a corner streetlight eyed them as they completed the right turn into block 306. He pulled the car into an empty spot fronting building C where Don's wife and son live. A repetitive beat echoed in the early night. Trey thought he could make out a few words.

Before the Maybach, I'd drive anythang
Buy my Range, make em go insane

Two men in their mid-twenties sat on the steps

to the building.

"You ready?" Nick said to Don.

"Which one is it again?"

"Stop procrastinating and go already," Trey said.

"Come with me, Trey."

Trey thought about Donald and the anger he expressed during the chase through the playground. "I – I don't know. I don't think I'll help much."

"It would make me feel better."

"Go on, Trey. It'll be ok," Nick said assuredly.

"Uh. O-kay," Trey said nervously. "I'll go. But don't be surprised when Donald isn't happy to see me."

"Same here," Don said. His heightened anxiety was stamped on his face. He looked like he was facing Tanny rather than his family.

"Let's go, Mr. Smith. We'll be ok."

When they exited the car one of the men on the steps said to Don, "That's a sweet ride, pops! Tell yo friend to let me take it for a spin." He then laughed and backhanded the other playfully on the chest.

The men politely moved aside to let Don and Trey into the building.

They climbed two flights of dimly lit stairs before arriving at C215.

Don stood in front of the doorway, took two deep breaths then turned to Trey, "Are you sure about this?"

"Just knock, Mr. Smith. We're here. You can't back out now."

He faced the door, took another deep breath, raised his hand and placed three knocks on the door.

A few seconds passed – then a minute.

"They aren't here. Let's go." Don turned toward the stairs just as a voice behind the door said, "Who's there?" It was Donald.

Don's face was white. He stood speechless. He didn't know what to expect but seemed caught off guard at the thought of meeting Little Don first - the son he unintentionally abandoned.

Trey urged Don to speak but Don said nothing.

"Who's there?" Donald repeated.

Trey looked again at Don who was frozen then said reluctantly, "It's me, Donald. It's Trey."

A series of locks turned. Donald said angrily as he opened the door, "Roberts! What the heck are you - "

Donald's angry face turned to shock. Don and his son stared at each other for a very brief moment not saying a word.

Donald's face then became red and angry. Trey thought he saw tears welling in his eyes just before Donald rushed to his father, gripping him tightly in a loving embrace.

"Dad! You came home! I knew you would! I knew you would come home," he repeated with his face planted in Don's narrow chest.

Don's eyes welled. A river of emotions flowed from his soul dampening his beard and draining onto Donald's head. He grasped the thick boy and said, "I'll never leave you again, Little Don."

"Donald, who is it?" said a woman's voice from inside.

Don looked up, "Clara."

The thin woman with hair askew stared through the doorway. Donald released his father so Don could reunite with his mother. They shared a long passionate kiss. She then hit him hard on the arm and slapped him in the face.

"I've missed you so much. Where've you been? Why'd you leave us? Where'd you go?" she said as she kissed him after each question.

"Let's go inside. I'll tell you all about it." He followed her hand in hand inside the small apartment.

Donald turned to Trey after watching his parent's reunion. "You did this? You brought my dad home?"

Trey began to speak but before he could utter a syllable, Donald hugged him. He hugged him in a pleasant loving and slightly painful manner.

"Thank you for finding my dad," he said still holding him tightly. He released Trey but kept his hands on each of Trey's shoulders. He spoke sincerely, "I'm sorry I've been so mean to you. I never told you, but I thought your dad had something to do with my dad's disappearance."

"Why would you think that?"

"They both left around the same time. Plus, my mom suspected he was cheating on her so she had someone follow him – a P.I. type guy. He found out that they both knew the same lady."

Trey's stomach fell. "The same lady?"

"Yeah. A tall dark-haired woman. My mom keeps the pictures in one of her drawers. There's only one of the three of them together. She thought your dad introduced her to mine and he ran off with her."

Trey's mind raced. He could barely keep up with the conversation. "Yeah. I guess I can see how you would think that," he said distantly. He pulled himself back to Donald. "And now I understand the rumors. You don't have to worry about her. She helped me find him."

"You know her too?"

"I've just met her this week. He didn't run off with her."

"That's good to know. I'll tell mom what you said. Thank you for bringing him home. Let's hang out next week. I'd like to try to make up for the past few years."

"I'd like that Donald. Now get back to your dad. He has lots of stories to share. Some of it might sound a little crazy but I promise, it's all true."

"Okay, Roberts. Whatever you say."

Donald smacked him with an open hand lightly on the shoulder then joined his mom and dad.

Trey stayed in the walkway a moment after Donald closed the door, reflecting on the beautiful reunification. He reflected on his new friend and how he wouldn't have to worry about getting into a fight at school or being tormented in history class. But mostly, he wondered how his father was involved in all of this and why he never told him any of it. He wondered if this was the reason he left. He wondered why Lyza lied to him about knowing his father.

Don suddenly emerged from the apartment. "I'm glad you're still here. I wanted to thank you again for finding me and encouraging me to come home. I was stupid for thinking those things back in Highlands."

Pop, Pop, Spark. Tessie appeared on Trey's shoulder.

"Hey, Tessie. Did you come to say goodbye?"

"Pop, Pop."

Trey scooped her into his hands then nuzzled her fur. Low voltage heated his cheek. "I'll miss you too.

"Snap, Whistle, Pop!"

"Of course, I'll see you again." He looked at Don, "Won't I?"

"Can you understand what she's saying?" Don said surprised.

"Yes."

"But how?"

"We can talk about that another day."

"Yes. Yes, you will see her again. Soon. We have lots to do."

"I have a soccer game this weekend. If you like soccer, you can bring her then."

Don smiled proudly, "I'd love to, Trey. We'll be there."

Trey snuggled Tessie one more time before she popped back to Don.

"Bye, Tessie."

She returned a pop and a low to high whistle.

"See you Saturday, Mr. Smith!"

"I'll see you Saturday!" Don replied as Trey turned toward the stairs.

Trey turned back and smiled.

Trey emerged from the apartment building to find Nick cutting up with the two men on the steps.

"Making new friends, Mr. H?"

"You know me. Trey, this is Lamar and Roderick."

"Nice to meet you two," Trey said extending a hand to each.

Lamar grabbed his hand twisted it into a chest bump (Trey caught on) they slapped palms then back hands, spun around then high fived.

"Right on! You're a cool dude, Trey."

Roderick did the hand slap then threw a hand

over his shoulder like he tossed something away combined with a *pshhh* sound with Trey in time.

Trey turned to Nick, "Can we get me home now?"

"Sure, Trey."

"Later guys!" Nick hollered as he opened the car door.

"Peace!" Lamar yelled while Roderick just gave a high wave.

Nick turned into Trey's drive, "You need me to come in?"

"No. I'm good. Thanks for asking. Later Mr. H!" Trey said as he jumped out. He tore into the house, aggressively hugged his mom who was standing in the kitchen with Aunt Kathy and said, "I'm so happy to see you!"

"I'm happy to see you too," she said with a confused look. "And what is this? A sword? Why on earth would you have a sword?"

"I hope you had a good time at Marcus' the last two nights," Kathy interrupted from the table.

Trey looked at Kathy with a questioning glance.

"Did you finish that project you two were working on?" Kathy continued.

Trey looked again at his mom then back to Kathy. "Uhh yeah, the project. It was a last-minute thing that we needed to finish up. The, uh, sword is part of it. I'm sorry I forgot to tell you," he said to his mom.

"I noticed you left your phone. I thought you'd come by to get it. You could have used his phone to text or something."

"I know mom. I'm sorry. We just got so caught

up in the, um," he fidgeted with his feet, "project. I'll do better next time."

"I know you will Sweet T. I hope you had a good day at school today. You can tell me about your project later," she said. She looked out the window, then said, "Is that Mr. Hampton in that fancy car? Ummm, mmm, that car looks good on him. It's about time they started paying teachers better."

"I don't understand what's going on, Aunt Kathy," Trey asked after his mom left the room.

"Lyza told me what happened so I took your mom to my house the night of the attack. We had some wine and she fell asleep. I sent a few people to the house that night to clean up before she awoke."

"Fell asleep or drugged?"

"I had to keep her safe. She wouldn't have believed the truth and would've been frightened about the house."

"They did a pretty good job. It was really messed up from what I remember," said Trey. "I learned a lot about grandpa today and a little about dad. What else do you know?"

"I think you know more than I at this point. But let's get together this weekend. I would love to catch up. It's late and you've had a rough time. Get some rest and we'll talk about it later."

"Okay. Thank you for keeping mom safe."

"I'd do anything for you and your mother, Trey. Disturbing times are ahead. You just do as Lyza says and we'll all be okay. Okay?"

"Yes Ma'am."

"Sleep well Trey. I'll see you this weekend. Go Pirates!"

"Thanks Aunt Kathy," he said after a big hug.

Dream

Trey Roberts settled in his room after showering off the day. He sat in a chair and stared at the sword he acquired from a flying cat-man.

This has to be a dream, he thought. There's no way I did all these things: fought a bunch of scary undead goblins with a mysterious woman named Lyza, befriended an electric furball, was captured and escaped from Centaurs, defeated a multi-sized bug in a riddle contest, teleported to Egypt, China and the Highlands.

Trey shivered as he thought about the Etherios where he had an ominous conversation with his Grandpa's spirit then finished off befriending a dragon.

This is completely unreal, as he continued with his thoughts, *I mean look, the house looks as if nothing happened there are no rogglets or enormous snakes. Teleportation doesn't exist. I'll wake soon and be freaked out at how real this dream was.*

Dream

He gathered the disk artefact he pulled from the snake demon, the Discolursor Annular that revealed Seth's true form, the bag holding the key to the Etherios spirit realm, an odd shaped gold coin and a small case containing a fireproof, an energy and a cloaking potion. He then placed them all into the chair next to the sword. He removed the picture of him and his father from a drawer and displayed it on his nightstand. After a few minutes he fell asleep from exhaustion.

Trey stood yards away from the edge of a desolate cliff which rose above an ancient bustling city a distance below. It was surrounded by desert. Sitting together, a woman and infant sang a pleasant song amid sand colored structures. A thin lonely cloud drifted in the distance. A small grey bird stared keenly.

Trey asked, "What is it bird? What do you say?"

A whispered thought of foreboding. An image of a man, no something much worse, a red demon with flaming sword in hand.

"Shriek! Shriek! Shriek!" screamed the bird hopping up and down.

Instant fire and destruction ravaged the city. Screams of women and crying babies filled Trey's heart. The long dark face of the demon turned. Blood red creases painted stony cheeks. Black hole eyes, as if no light could escape, transitioned to yellow with crimson pupils. Proud of his deed, the scarlet demon raised the sword toward the cliff of which Trey helplessly stood. A blinding bolt of plasma blasted Trey into consciousness.

"Treeeeey! Treeeeeey, it's tiiiime to wake uuuuuup!" he heard his mom sing from down the hall on a peaceful Friday morning. He opened his eyes slowly and shivered off the surreal dream. Rubbing them clear he focused on the sword leaning against the chair where he left it the night before. He tossed his head back and said, "It can't be real! There's no way! Arggg!"

Until Next Week

Trey's adventure continues in…

The Ancestor's Wish

Nick's Secret

Trey Roberts settled in his room after showering off the day. He sat in a chair and stared at the sword he acquired from a flying cat-man.

This has to be a dream, he thought. There's no way I did all these things: fought a bunch of scary undead goblins with a mysterious woman named Lyza, befriended an electric furball, was captured and escaped from Centaurs, defeated a multi-sized bug in a riddle contest, teleported to Egypt, China and the Highlands.

Trey shivered as he thought about the Etherios where he had an ominous conversation with his Grandpa's spirit then finished off befriending a dragon.

This is completely unreal, as he continued with his thoughts, *I mean look, the house looks as if nothing happened there are no rogglets or enormous snakes. Teleportation doesn't exist. I'll wake soon and be freaked out at how real this dream was.*

He gathered the disk artifact he pulled from the

snake demon, the Discolursor Annular that revealed Seth's true form, the bag holding the key to the Etherios spirit realm, an odd shaped gold coin and a small case containing a fireproof, an energy and a cloaking potion. He then placed them all into the chair next to the sword. He removed the picture of him and his father from a drawer and displayed it on his nightstand. After a few minutes he fell asleep from exhaustion.

Trey stood yards away from the edge of a desolate cliff which rose above an ancient bustling city a distance below. It was surrounded by desert. Sitting together, a woman and infant sang a pleasant song amid sand colored structures. A thin lonely cloud drifted in the distance. A small grey bird stared keenly.

Trey asked, "What is it bird? What do you say?"

A whispered thought of foreboding. An image of a man, no something much worse, a red demon with flaming sword in hand.

"Shriek! Shriek! Shriek!" screamed the bird hopping up and down.

Instant fire and destruction ravaged the city. Screams of women and crying babies filled Trey's heart. The long dark face of the demon turned. Blood red creases painted stony cheeks. Black hole eyes, as if no light could escape, transitioned to yellow with crimson pupils. Proud of his deed, the scarlet demon raised the sword toward the cliff of which Trey helplessly stood. A blinding bolt of plasma blasted Trey into consciousness.

"Treeeeey! Treeeeeey, it's tiiiime to wake uuuuuup!" he heard his mom sing from down the hall on a peaceful Friday morning. He opened his eyes slowly and shivered off the surreal dream. Rubbing them clear he focused on the sword leaning against the chair where he left it the night before. He tossed his head back and said, "It can't be real! There's no way! Arggg!"

"Trey? Did you say something?"

"No Mom!"

"Hurry up, breakfast is getting cold!"

The small house overflowed with aromas of sage and biscuits. Trey's stomach roared.

"Ok! Be there in a minute!"

He looked back at the pile of items in the chair and became startled when he noticed something was missing. "Olerand's Disk! Where is it!"

He looked on and around the chair. Nothing.

"Where'd it go?"

Trey ran down the hall, "Mom! Have you seen -" He brushed the pocket of his red and black checkered flannel lounge pants. "What's this?"

He pulled out the disk.

"Did I put that there?" he said confused. "I thought I left it on the chair."

"What was that, Trey? Do you need something?" him mom asked from the kitchen.

"Uh, no mom. Sorry."

He put the disk back in his pocket, then joined his mom for a breakfast of scrambled eggs, biscuits and smoked sausage.

"Thanks, mom. Breakfast is great," he said stuffing a piece of sausage into his mouth like he hadn't eaten in three days – which was mostly accurate.

She stepped from the sink, set her hands on her hips and said with contempt, "Did you leave your manners back at Marcus'? Use a fork, please."

He mumbled with a mouth full of food, "Sorry, Mom. I just forgot how hungry I was. Why the big breakfast anyway?"

"No reason. I've barely seen you these past few days. I missed you and just wanted to do something nice."

"It's nice. Thanks," he said smiling then forked in another piece of sausage.

Trey set his fork down while he struggled with a strong thought. He then asked, "Mom?"

She sat next to him and said, "What's bothering you, Sweet T?"

He temporarily felt abashed with the nickname. It usually didn't bother him (he normally welcomed it) but somehow, today, he felt a little too grown up for the childish name. He brushed his feelings aside and asked, "Did you know Mr. Smith? Don Smith?"

She studied her son, "No. I never met him. I've only met Clara once. She was very nice at the time and never mentioned her husband."

Trey thought she seemed to be holding back details.

"You know? The rumors aren't true." He continued with his breakfast.

She seemed ashamed but may have been more surprised that Trey knew what she was thinking.

"Rumors? What do you mean?" she said as if she didn't already know.

"Mom," Trey said frustrated. "I know everyone thinks he left her for another woman. It's not true."

"And how do you know that?" she asked like she didn't expect an answer.

"He came home yesterday."

"Oh-my-god," she said slowly. Her eyes were

buggy. "After all this time?" She looked off in the distance. She returned her attention to her thirteen-year-old son. "How do you know that?"

"I, uh, found him – I mean, I found out, uh…" He struggled for the words. He hadn't expected to be questioned today about how he rescued Don from a dragon in another world with the help of his dead Grandpa. "I, uh, Nick! I mean, Mr. H told me on the way home last night." He breathed a sigh of relief.

"Mr. Hampton? Really?"

"Yeah. He, uh, said he found him while travelling in Egypt."

"Egypt? What was Don doing there? What was Mr. Hampton doing there?"

"He, didn't say," Trey replied with evasive eyes.

"Huh." She said. "Imagine that. You never know what to expect from day to day do you?"

Trey couldn't hold in an uncomfortable chuckle, "You sure are right about that, Mom."

"So, why all this talk about Mr. Smith? What does he have to do with you?"

Trey shifted in the seat. He chopped his eggs slowly. His next words were difficult to say – as were all the times before since his dad left them. "Did you know that Dad and Don knew each other?"

She looked at him like only a mother could when her child was hurting. She placed her hand on his and said, "No, baby. I didn't know. Your father never mentioned him."

Trey, a little more anxious replied, "Did you notice he and Mr. Smith left about the same time?" He shuffled again and continued, "You say you hardly talk to Dad anymore and he hasn't come to see me in over three years. Do you think that maybe he's in trouble too? Like Mr. Smith was?" He couldn't help, just like any other thirteen-year-old, hide a hopeful expression.

"Honey," she said in a soft voice. She touched his face. He looked down. "I don't know what your father's doing. All I know is that whatever he's into is more important that you or I." She then grasped his hand firmly, "I know it's great that Mr. Smith is home."

Her closed-eyed grimace held back all but one tear. She wiped that one away then continued firmly, "Your father is different. You can't remain hopeful that he will dramatically return home one day."

It was just like she slapped him. The truth, as painful as it was, is what Trey expected.

Trey thought to himself, *I know it's improbable that Dad will ever come back to us. Even if he were in trouble like Mr. Smith, what are the chances I could actually help?*

"I know." Trey replied. He thought he was stupid for believing just because Mr. Smith knew his father that maybe he could bring his own father home too.

He held his head for a second then a thought crossed his mind, *that's right! Mr. Smith knows my dad!* He brightened up and said, "Thanks for the talk, Mom! I love you!" He then tossed his plate in the sink and rushed back to his room where he wrapped the disk in a sock and placed it along with the Etherios key and potions into a drawer. He picked up the sword, jabbed and sliced at the air a few times then hid it between his mattress and box spring. He gathered his backpack, then left for school.

His mind stirred endlessly on the way to school. Where was his father? Does Mr. Smith know? Does Lyza know? Would he be able to save him if he needed saving? He walked the sidewalk anxious and full of hope.

~ ~

"Kid! Where've you been?" Marcus said. He had too much gel in his hair. It was slick and shiny – distracting Trey from the conversation. "What's the deal? You don't answer texts anymore? Are you breaking up with me?" said Marcus jokingly to Trey in a school hallway.

"No, dork. I'm not breaking up with you. I was, uh, sick the past couple days. Sorry I didn't call."

Trey easily recalled nearly dying several times at the hands of ghoulish creatures in his house, Egypt and China; battling a zombie dog in a magical realm in the Libyan desert; literally dying when he defeated a demon in a fairy kingdom; and outrunning unwavering henchmen in a tiny oasis town. He believed his "sick" excuse was unsatisfactory at describing the past couple days to his best friend. He wanted to tell him. He wanted to share these experiences with him. He felt he needed to warn him of what might happen – no – what will happen (according to Grandpa and the Keeper).

But this information is too much for Marcus now. He thought. *Marcus won't understand. Plus, Lyza said we'd be safe for some time so there's no urgency in bringing him in...just yet.*

Trey had a terrible feeling Marcus would be involved. In every movie he had seen, the bad guy always goes after the protagonist's family and best friend. It's already been necessary to protect mom. It's only a matter of time that they discover Marcus.

I have to keep him safe.

Marcus looked at Trey. Disbelieving eyes revealed he knew there was more to the story, but decided to wait it out and said excitedly, "You've missed a lot. Jenny Jacobson broke up with Tom. Do you think she'd go out with me?"

Trey pulled his attention away from the past days and Marcus' hair gel, "Jenny Jacobson is one of the smartest girls in school."

"Don't forget she was also homecoming queen last year."

"Exactly. Unless you pick up your grades or become a handsome jock, I think your chances are slim. But what do I know. I've never had a girlfriend."

"I think she'll dig my quirky comedian personality."

"No doubt. I think, however, you'll find more interesting news this week besides who dumped who."

"Like what? You have good dirt on someone? Wait. I'm talking to the strait-laced Trey Roberts. If it's not dirt, then what could be more important than Jenny Jacobson? Oh, crap. Don't look, it's Donald."

Marcus turned toward the lockers, trying to become smaller so he wouldn't be seen. Trey stepped out to greet his new friend.

"What's up, Trey?" Donald said happily.

They high fived after which, Donald gave Trey a quick manly one-armed hug.

"Nothing much," Trey responded with a playful smile.

"You have time to hang out before your game Saturday?" Donald asked.

"Yeah! Absolutely!" Trey wanted to talk to Don

personally about his dad. Maybe he could make that happen Saturday with Donald. "Want to meet around 11 at the park then grab some lunch?"

"That'd be great. See you then!" He hugged Trey again just a little longer than before – he closed his eyes to feel it more. He then said with a whisper so only Trey could hear, "Thanks again. Dad told me what you did to rescue him. You don't have any idea how much you mean to me and my mom."

"It was my pleasure. I'm happy it all worked out."

Donald pulled away. His eyes were watery and a little red but no tears. "See you at eleven. What's up Marcus!" he said before walking off. Marcus stood bug-eyed as if he witnessed the most unbelievable occurrence of his life. His gaping mouth could hardly form the words, "What ... the heck ... just happened?"

"I told you something more interesting than Jenny Jacobson happened."

"No. Seriously. What just happened."

Trey smiled.

"Did Donald Smith; the guy that chased us through the playground earlier this week, the guy that I've been avoiding all week, the same guy that tormented you for years, just hug you?"

"Yeah."

"What the heck. What happened? What'd you do to make him not pound you?"

"We made up."

"Really? That's all you have?" he said with low cut eyes.

"I helped him out with something."

"Like algebra? Don't tell me you're doing his homework."

"No. Nothing like that. I can't really tell you right now. Maybe later."

"You have to tell me. I can't wait for later," Marcus pleaded.

Trey smiled and turned. Marcus chased him down the hall.

"You mean like later next period later or after school later?"

"Just later."

"Dude! You're killing me! I have to know. Please?"

Trey stopped. "Look. There's Jenny Jacobson."

"Yeah." Marcus said. He looked at the girl and said to Trey, "You suck you know."

"I know. You gonna to talk to her?"

"No. I'm gonna go make her laugh," he said with a level of confidence only Marcus Bouer could possess.

Marcus straightened his tucked in shirt then crossed the hall targeting a tall girl wearing a tight-fitting knee length skirt, blue top and long brown hair braided to one side. She smiled when Marcus casually approached with a quirky strut. Trey made out "Hey Marcus" from her lightly painted lips. She was easily half a foot taller than Trey's enthusiastic friend. He said something to her at which she giggled, then returned a comment Trey couldn't make out. Marcus waved bye, then returned to Trey.

"So, how'd it go?"

"She thought I was funny, just like I said."

"Good for you Marcus. That's the power of intention at work. Now all you have to do is ask her to the Homecoming Dance."

"Holy crows I forgot about the dance! You think

she'd go with me?"

"I don't know buddy. You're on your own with that one."

"What about you? Who are you taking?"

"I'm not going. I've got too much on my mind lately."

"Yeah? Anything I can help with? But none of that boring sciency stuff you're into."

"No. Just some personal things that I have to work out on my own."

"Well to add to that, I'm still mad you didn't text me."

"I know. I didn't mean to hurt you."

"I'll get over it when you buy me ice cream after the movie this Sunday."

"Sure thing," Trey said.

"Uh Oh. You have one other thing to add to your personal list," Marcus said looking up the hall.

"What do you mean? What is it?" Trey asked curiously – convinced Marcus couldn't know of anything that would stand up against his issues with Commerand – but he was wrong.

"There's someone else that would've liked a heads up," Marcus said urging Trey to look ahead at Sarah waltzing down the hall toward them.

She wore a flower print sundress that waved as she swayed gracefully. The alluring article rose into two broad straps that barely draped each shoulder. Her rolling blonde hair fell to one side exposing a luscious neck on the other. She flaunted a smile that would suck the wind from the largest sail.

"Oh no! I told her I'd walk her to school Wednesday. Ahhggg!" he said putting his face in his hands.

"Yeah, she asked where you were. I told her I didn't know. She didn't seem mad or anything. More concerned. I'll let you take it from here," he said as Sarah took his place in the conversation. She settled on one hip, closer to Trey than Marcus but not so close they could accidently touch.

"Hey Marcus."

"Hey Girl!" he replied giving her a high five. "I have to get. I'll see you two later."

He shot Trey a knowing glance as he walked off. Trey eyed him several seconds silently screaming for help.

Trey turned a forced smile to Sarah then said slumped in a disappointed posture. "Hey Sarah,"

"Hey Trey. Are you ok?" she asked with a scrunched brow. She held a couple books in one hand. Her voice was friendly and compassionate. "I figured you weren't feeling well. It's not like you to miss school two days in a row."

She notices when I'm not here?

"Yeah. I was pretty messed up. I'm sorry I couldn't meet you Wednesday morning. I would've enjoyed the walk."

She shifted hips. "It's ok. I waited a while for you. I thought you stood me up."

"No!" Trey said with too much emphasis. "I mean," he tried to correct his tone, "No, I didn't do it on purpose."

"I know. It's ok. Kenny Parker picked me up and took me to school."

Trey replied startled, "Kenny Parker? I didn't know he could drive."

"He got his driver's license a few weeks ago. His parents bought him a new car last week. A convertible.

It's really nice, especially this time of year. Wednesday afternoon was a great day for a cruise."

Anxiousness and fear crept into his voice. "So, he took you home too?"

"Yeah. We also stopped at Danucci's for ice cream."

"That's cool," Trey said dismayed. He felt his heart sinking. His stomach churned.

"He's friends with Rhonda's brother. I've known him for years. He's a nice guy."

Trey replied in the friendliest manner he could muster, "He plays on the varsity soccer team, but I don't really know him." He hoped she wouldn't recognize his anguish.

"Yeah, he does. I went to his practice yesterday. They're pretty good."

"So, I hear. You went to his practice too?" He looked away then back to her and said, "That's cool. So, you two are a," he shuffled, "a couple?"

Trey felt embarrassed after the comment. He wished he could take it back. He didn't want to know the answer – unless it was definitely no.

"No," she said quickly. "Well, I don't – I, uh – he's just – we like talking to each other and it's kinda neat hanging out with the high schoolers," she finally finished.

She didn't say 'yes' but Trey knew 'yes' was her answer. He looked at his aged shoes then said, "It's really none of my business. I shouldn't have asked."

"No. Really, Trey. It's ok."

Trey thought she seemed genuinely concerned and awkwardly ashamed for answering like she did.

"I, uh, have to get to class now. I'll see you later Trey. I'm glad you're feeling better," she said uncomfortably before strolling away.

Dang! I really messed up. That stupid disk! Why me? Why did all this happen to me! Kenny Parker of all people. Arggg! How do I compete with a high schooler with a car?

He hung his head, then pressed it against his locker. When he pushed away something clanged against the metal door. He reached in his pocket to find the disk.

"Wha – How'd this get here? The spell Aunt Kathy told me about when she gave me the disk. The spell must force the disk to always stay with me. Kathy didn't intentionally keep it in her purse. That's just where it stayed. I guess I'm stuck toting this thing around with me forever. The weirdness just doesn't end," he said to himself as he turned toward science class.

He greeted his science teacher as he strolled into class, "Hey Mr. H. Nice to see you again."

"Yeah Trey. Long time no see." He moved closer lowering his voice, then said, "That was a crazy few days huh? Are you ok?"

"Yeah, I guess. I messed up with Sarah and woke up this morning realizing the past two days weren't a dream. I'm having a really hard day."

"Sarah huh? Is there already trouble in wonderland?"

Trey gave a discontented expression.

"Sorry," Nick offered. "That was inappropriate. Seriously though, I think we've gotten ourselves into a big mess. Come by the lab after school today. I need to show you something."

"Sure."

Trey took his seat while Nick began discussing simple machines.

After science class Coach Rafiq caught up with Trey in the hall.

"Trey!" Coach Rafiq said urgently with a slow intentional Spanish accent.

"Hey Coach."

"Where have you been? Tomorrow's game day and you haven't been at practice."

"I know. I wasn't feeling well."

"You could have said something you know. You gonna be well enough to play tomorrow?"

"Yeah! I'll be there for sure."

"We are doing well with the 4231 with Davis at striker."

"Davis? Argg! This day!"

"I know you are disappointed. I'm starting him in the position tomorrow. You'll take his place at right midfield," he smiled then continued with a soft chuckle, "assuming you remember how to play the position."

He looked away from Rafiq and replied in a disappointed voice, "Yes sir. I understand. I'll be fine at midfield."

"You'll be at practice today right?"

"Yes sir," he said continuing his disappointed low voice.

"Great. See you then. Remember Trey, communication is the key to fútbol as well as life. Don't leave your friends and family out of the loop again. Ok?"

"Ok Coach. Thanks."

He turned to find a girl resting against the adjacent locker.

"That's tough about your position," she said wearing only a concerned smile for makeup. She held a book with both hands over her belly. Long auburn hair dangled in a ponytail as she leaned her head to the side. She looked up to make eye contact.

"Oh. Hey, Leslie. You heard my conversation with Coach?"

"Most of it. I'm sorry."

He felt embarrassed she knew considering he hasn't yet had time to process the news.

"It's ok. I'd probably do the same thing if I were him. I'm lucky to be in the game this weekend."

"If it matters, you played a great game last weekend."

"Thanks," he said smiling. "You came to my match – again?"

"I haven't missed one yet this year. You're fun to watch," she said in a pinchy voice then straightened her posture. She briefly looked toward her athletic shoes before regaining eye contact, "You move the ball so well, like the other guys are standing still. That last goal for a hat trick was unbelievable."

Trey looked over her head down the hall at two boys shoving each other. When the brief scuffle was over, he brought his attention back to the sparkling emerald eyes of the girl who pleasantly invaded his space – he failed to realize he didn't mind her closeness. He lost his concentration in her gaze – like peering upon a lush green meadow after a spring rain. He could almost smell budding flowers and hear bees gathering their spoils. He forced himself back to the conversation, "Thanks. But many of them are standing still," he said dismissively. "It's just middle school soccer," he said shrugging a shoulder. "Some of the other schools don't have the pool of talent we have."

She shifted her eyes toward the lockers then back to his. Her face brightened. "I joined the girl's team last week!" she said gently bouncing on her toes and with a slight squeal as she completed the remark. "I don't start," she said lowering her voice. "But I'm fast," she continued in her previously chipper tone. "Coach says I could be a great winger," she said with a faultless smile.

"That's fantastic," he said casually – aware of his heart beating a touch stronger. "Let me know when coach plays you and I'll come to a game."

"Really? You promise?" she said with wide hopeful eyes. A light splash of freckles danced high upon her cheeks and nose when she smiled.

"Yeah, uh, sure. I'll be there."

"I hope so! See you later Trey!" she said then skipped off down the hall.

Trey watched her ponytail bop side to side as she flittered away like a butterfly bouncing against invisible objects along an undetermined flight path.

On his way to meet Nick in the science lab, a short stocky kid strutted toward Trey. He wore a smug grin.

"Davis," Trey said in a condescending tone.

"Trey! Nice to have you back," he said significantly overdoing the sarcasm. "See you at practice today," he said staring coldly at Trey then roughly bumped his shoulder as he passed.

Trey shook his head then moved on to the lab

Nick met Trey at the door of the science lab. "Come see this."

Nick took him to an object inconspicuously located in the corner by the far window.

"That's the rock you were testing for conductivity, right?"

"Yeah. It is. But I'm not testing it for connectivity. I wasn't really sure what it was I built until Lyza brought us back home."

He uncovered the object revealing a dark igneous stone encased in a copper housing. A flat four-inch by four-inch panel remained accessible. The copper housing attached to thick shielded copper cables connected to long grounding rods buried just outside the window.

"I forgot about this after that morning. The stone looks just like..."

"A portal stone" Nick finished.

"Lyza was right."

"Right about what?"

"That Khaitu or someone related to him wanted you to build this and get the Eye of Kartho. We did just what they wanted us to do. But it's useless without a key to power the portals and Lyza has that and the Eye is missing."

Nick held up the opened ceramic box displaying a copper colored key he recovered from the bird spider cave in Asia over the summer.

"You have a key too! We're in it deep. Who else knows?"

"No one. Just you, me and I guess Lyza. But she doesn't know I have a key."

"And the creeper that led you to do it."

"Yeah. I suppose that's true. But why go through all that effort? Why not just send others loyal to Khaitu, or Commerand himself?"

"I don't know. It looks almost the same as Don's." Trey ran a finger across the cold surface of the portal. "Maybe when his didn't work out, they tried you. But if Commerand knew you had a key, he'd be here. Without the Eye, there's no other way for him to get to the other dimensions."

"At least none that Lyza has mentioned," Nick countered. "Remember, Don said he thought Commerand could open the portal. Maybe he has a key."

"Oh yeah. I forgot about that part. How many keys do you think are out there?"

"I have no idea. I didn't even know I had one until yesterday. You know," he said to Trey sincerely, "we talk about her a lot like she's this great guardian doing us favors. What do we really know about her? I mean, I'm not positive, but I feel quite certain she was responsible for Seth and I getting jumped at the Cairo airport."

"Really? That's what happened? Her and a guy named the Phoenix were talking about that. Said you gave 'em hell! That's awesome!" Trey responded excitedly.

"We nearly died."

"Oh yeah. That would've been bad," Trey said tempering his excitement.

"All I'm saying is that I'm not sure we can trust her. Think of the mess she's gotten you into."

"I've been having the same thoughts. She did conveniently show up at my house right before the rogglets attacked us and she did haul me off to nearly get killed in the desert. And I just followed the plan and won the Eye for her. I'm so stupid!"

"No, Trey. You just did what you thought was right at the time. But just in case you see her again, don't tell her about this portal or that I have a key. By the way, do you know how it works?"

"Yeah, she said you have to know the shape engraved on the stone to where you want to go and then think about where you want to go. Then as you saw, touch it to the stone. I wouldn't try it though. If you get it wrong, bad stuff happens."

"What do you mean bad stuff?"

"She tried to describe it to me but all I could imagine is falling forever until you die of old age which shouldn't be too much longer for you, huh?" Trey said jabbing Nick in the arm.

"Very funny, funny guy! It's about time for soccer practice, right?"

"Yeah, I need to get going."

"Did I hear right that Rafiq moved you to midfielder?"

"Yeah. Said I missed too many practices this week. It makes sense since I don't know how the team utilizes the new formation. It'll be ok. Davis will be a good striker."

"And you're wicked fast. You'll do fine," Nick said proudly.

About the Author

Lee Magnus is an American author who began creating the stories he wrote with his children in a storytelling game he called "Let's Build a Story" where each participant would, in turn, orally create a few lines at a time until there was an eventual conclusion. The Trey Robert's series and several of the characters came directly from this wonderful activity.

Born in a small South Georgia town, Lee Magnus was raised by an English teacher who encouraged reading at a young age. He is a proud UGA alumnus, plays various musical instruments but is particular to the piano, and has boys with wide imaginations. He currently lives with his family in Florida. Visit him at www.leemagnus.com